John Hart, who has also written  and Well-being: a National S the Nineties, has a backgroun science, a middle-ground in b and a foreground in freelanci lives in Brighton, and in hope

JIZZ

**The Story of a New Renaissance Man
and the Riddle of Existence**

John Hart

BLACK SWAN

JIZZ
A BLACK SWAN BOOK 0 552 99487 1

First publication in Great Britain

PRINTING HISTORY
Black Swan edition published 1992

This book was set in 11/12½pt Melior by
County Typesetters, Margate, Kent

Black Swan Books are published by Transworld
Publishers Ltd, 61–63 Uxbridge Road, Ealing, London
W5 5SA, in Australia by Transworld Publishers (Australia)
Pty Ltd, 15–23 Helles Avenue, Moorebank, NSW 2170,
and in New Zealand by Transworld Publishers (NZ) Ltd,
Cnr Moselle and Waipareira Avenues, Henderson,
Auckland.

Made and printed in Great Britain by
Cox & Wyman, Reading, Berks.

To women with Urges

Dramatis personae

Hayden Sabanack	*Freelance scholar*
Sophie Stevens	*Research assistant*
Oriana Sabanack	*Mother of Hayden*
James Stevens	*Bookseller and father of Sophie*
Duffy Cairns	*Civil servant*
Giles Lightowler	*Taxi driver*
Ted	*Barman at the Dartford Warbler*
Danielle	*Café proprietress*
Dr Emile Fikansky	*Academic*
Linden Pitling	*News vendor*
Francesca Earle	*Friend of Sophie*
Babette Macawley	*Actress*
Sid Whitney	*Entrepreneur, skipper of the* Marbella Hood
Bella Whitney	*Wife of Sid*
Gail Whitney	*Daughter of Sid and Bella*
George and Morna	*Brother and sister-in-law of Oriana Sabanack*
Nigel Stebbins	*University biologist*
Ned Yalton	*Mayor of Brighton*
Sylvia Crolien	*Psychic medium*
Wilfred Shaps	*Professor in the Institute of Philosophy*
Miranda	*Colleague of Professor Shaps*
Granville Markham Bernard 'the Slab' Shales 'Stair-rods' Wilson	*Three persons making a generally negative contribution to society*
Eleanor Grim	*Hayden's housekeeper*
General Roscius	*President of the Brighton Explorers' Club*
Simeon Urstpoint	*Sabanack family solicitor*
Vincent Thorne	*Duffy's boss*
Max Quinton	*Broadcaster*
and sundry others	

1

Opening Moves

'Hayden, your mother's dying again,' the girl said.

'Where to this time?'

'City General Hospital for the eyes, kidneys to anyone in the Woodingdean area, and the rest to the medical school of your choice.'

'She'll go in the family vault in one piece and like it,' Hayden declared with a sigh.

'She wants to know why you haven't been in touch.'

'Ah, the vexed question of filial communication.'

'No, just why haven't you phoned?' There was reproach in her voice.

Hayden got up from his desk and sauntered disconsolately to the window, there to trade a glazed expression with his reflected image. Glazed he could manage; funereal was more difficult. Pulling up his 'tropicana' tie, he put a pleat between his eyebrows, pursed his lips and thrust forward his chin. He looked to be struggling with an obstructed bowel.

'Are you all right?'

'Oh yes, fine.'

Focusing out to the wider world, he considered bouncing a psychic transmission across the Brighton rooftops to his mother's home, but, lowering his gaze to the street below, dismissed the notion as absurd. Instead, he said, 'Anything else, Sophie?'

At the other end of the narrow office, the girl called Sophie took a further envelope from a small pile on the desk in front of her and slit it open. She withdrew a letter and scrutinized its contents. Hayden shifted his incurious gaze to her. Sophie was in her early twenties and had brown, ribbon-tied hair upon which the late morning sunshine bestowed a lustrous sheen. Her complexion was pale, eyes blue, the features of her face neat and regular.

'Your brass plate's ready, it seems,' she said, looking up.

'Is it indeed! Good. Are they going to put it up?'

'Yes, this afternoon.'

This was progress. 'HAYDEN SABANACK, FREELANCE SCHOLAR, FIRST FLOOR', the plate said. Since going it alone, Hayden had been avoiding his mother. 'Where's the money in scholarship?' he could hear her ask. 'Why not become a plumber? There's always work for plumbers.'

'I almost forgot,' Sophie was saying, 'your friend Duffy rang. He wants you to do the last clue of his crossword. He'll split the prize with you if he wins.'

Hayden groaned. Is this the best a freelance scholar can hope for?

'Go on then,' he said, dropping into his chair.

'Seven across, six letters. "Meaning hidden in game." Oh, I know, it's an anagram: "Enigma".'

'Thank you,' he said resignedly. 'Ring it through to him, will you?'

Later, across the road in a pub called the Dartford Warbler, Hayden supped a lunchtime beer at the bar. A few customers sat at the tables.

'Bit quiet, Ted,' Hayden remarked to the barman.

'I could get in a dance band or a poetry video if you like.'

'No thanks.'

'How about a boxing kangaroo or a pair of mud wrestlers?'

'No, really.'

Ted as usual was going off with a loud rapport. Hayden was rescued by the phone. Ted answered it, then, with a hand over the mouthpiece, turned to his regular. 'It's your missus.'

'My missus?'

'Yes, the bit of fluff with the nice voice who "works" for you,' he said with heavy irony, leering exaggeratedly.

'You foul-minded oaf,' Hayden retorted amiably, taking the phone. 'Hello, Sophie.'

An assignment at last. He was to be over at Danielle's café by one thirty. As he finished talking, Dufryn Cairns walked into the pub. In spite of the spring sunshine outside, he was wearing a heavy raincoat tightly buttoned about his capacious form. Above Duffy's somewhat pear-shaped body was perched a faintly pear-shaped head. At its top end was a stand of close-cropped hair, while at its lower end were chubbily rounded cheeks. About a third of the way down was a pair of thick-rimmed spectacles over blue-green eyes.

'Hello, Duffy. How're things?'

'Pretty dire.'

'If I buy you a beer will you agree not to tell me about it?'

'It's a deal. Better get one in for Giles, too. He's outside parking the jalopy. I couldn't bear to watch. I'll have one of those awful pies of yours as well, Ted, if you've got one.'

Affecting a hurt expression, Ted pulled the drinks.

'Thanks for the crossword clue,' said Duffy to Hayden. 'I'll let you know if we win.'

To avoid incurring more of Ted's repartee, the two friends retreated to a window table and were soon joined by Giles Lightowler, a sandy-haired scruff with a vague look on his face. After an exchange of

11

pleasantries, the new arrival made an announcement.

'I've become a taxi driver, temporarily anyway.' There was a pause while Hayden took in what he evidently felt to be an extraordinary claim.

'A taxi driver? You?' exclaimed Hayden. 'You can't even drive. Well, hardly.'

'I've improved,' Giles said defensively.

'It's true,' interjected Duffy. 'We didn't crash once on the way here.'

'But, Giles, what happened to that book you were working on?' Hayden combed his memory. '*The Cuckold's Cookbook, for the Man whose Woman is Otherwise Engaged*. That was it, wasn't it?'

'Didn't you know? Jane has run out on me again. This time for good. I haven't the heart to finish the book alone.'

Duffy choked on his pint in ill-suppressed amusement, while Giles looked discountenanced. Hayden assumed a mask of sympathy. He had not cared much for Jane. Her tongue was so sharp she had been nicknamed 'the Secateurs'. Giles seemed oblivious of this side of her, even while another ego was being pruned to a stump.

'Well, what about that school primer,' Hayden continued, '*Here's Looking at Euclid: The Humphrey Bogart Book of Geometry*?'

'A man has to move on,' was Giles's response to this, running a hand through his unruly hair.

They sat in silence in the soothing fug. Duffy ate his pie. Giles ached for Jane. Hayden pondered the larger questions. Do I have enough money to buy the lads another glass of wallop before going off to Danielle's? On balance, yes. Can I withstand another instalment of Ted's banter at the bar? On balance, no. Fortunately, the problem was taken out of his hands when Giles spoke.

'Fancy another drink?'

'Not for me,' replied Hayden. 'Working this afternoon.'

Giles made a noise like a strangulated hernia, though whether this was because of the declined drink or the gainful employment was unclear. As Giles walked to the bar, Hayden observed once again that there was something slightly uncoordinated about his walk which contrasted with Duffy's stolid tread. In his late twenties, Giles had maintained his shape far better than Duffy but appeared to have mislaid his centre of gravity.

The two men were dissimilar in dress, too. Giles had a taste for patterned, sleeveless sweaters and baggy corduroy trousers. Duffy, a civil servant, habitually wore a tired-looking office suit in Planning Department grey. Having finished his pie, Duffy was now busy polishing his spectacles on a shiny lapel. Beyond being contemporaries, what on earth had the three of them got in common? One answer arrived in a couple of glasses carried by the partially ataxic taxi driver.

A quarter of an hour later Hayden stood outside, momentarily immobilized by the sudden rush of oxygen to his lungs. He looked up to the first-floor window across the road and gave Sophie a wave. She was cataloguing and pricing books for her father's secondhand bookshop which occupied the ground floor below their shared office. At the door, his brass plate was going up. Three men seemed to be working on it. It can only be a matter of time before they call in a tower crane and a pile-driver, he thought grimly, anticipating the bill.

He headed east towards the town centre down Thylde Street, which runs parallel to the coastline a short distance away to the south. The street is named after the English seaman who is said to have beaten Columbus to the New World by twelve years. Hayden sailed into the old world of the Brighton Lanes, the town's heart, a maze of intersecting alleys crowded with shops, pubs and eating houses in what were fishermen's cottages in the late eighteenth and early nineteenth centuries.

In Danielle's Café, the eponymous proprietress stood beside the cash register totting up some numbers on a notepad. Danielle was a Frenchwoman in her early forties. Her face was lined but attractive, her figure full but under control. She had a legendary ability to emit man-crippling quantities of sensuality at will. Her husband Didier was rarely seen. He was a short man with a tired, grey countenance. He gave the appearance of having been gutted by the flames of passion, to the extent that what remained was an oxide of his former self.

Danielle looked up as Hayden approached. She liked his straw-coloured jacket and pale trousers: they showed off his scarlet waistcoat and outrageous tie, but she felt he should wear his dark, wavy hair longer. It would suit him better.

'Ah, 'ayden,' she said with a smile.

'I gather you have some trade for me?' he said, making to plant a playful kiss on her cheek but failing as she shooed him towards a far table.

'The gentleman over there. Give him a good game.'

'I'll do my best.'

Hayden made his way between the wooden tables over to a man in a sober suit. He was in his fifties, had a pinched, intelligent face, and wore a goatee beard which was tinged with grey like his hair. In front of him was a chequered board, with pieces. Hayden recognized the man as a café habitué, but only knew him by sight.

'Sabanack.' Hayden extended a hand. 'Call me Sab.'

'Fikansky. Please sit down.' The man spoke with a faint mid-European accent. His name stirred Hayden's

14

memory. Emile Fikansky – Dr Fikansky, to give him his title – was loosely associated with the university; very loosely, if playing a boardgame in the early afternoon was an indication: a visiting lecturer, perhaps.

'Well, Sab, piquant mating – you know the game?'

'No.'

'It's chess with variations. Every second move is accompanied by an arresting utterance. The key-note is piquancy, that is, something that is sharply stimulating. Failure to speak, or failure of quality, leads to forfeiture of one's lowest value piece at the discretion of one's opponent. Thirty seconds for the silent moves; one minute for the others. There's a buzzer on the timer. The time penalty is one lost piece. Any questions?'

'Why do all the pieces look the same?'

'Be sure to put that back on its square!' Hayden had picked up a piece to inspect it more closely. It was a miniature effigy of the city's mayor, Ned Yalton. 'It's a special feature of this set – a test of memory. The pieces each have the same role as in the old game – king, queen, bishop and so on – only there are no visual clues as to which is which. And they're "smart", too. If you move them wrongly, they self-destruct.'

'You're joking! Am I going to lose a hand if I make a false move?'

'I'm not sure what happens. The set's never been used before. In the box there were a couple of pairs of safety goggles and some gauntlets. Here are yours.'

'Is it worth me asking why we're playing with thirty-two representations of our esteemed first citizen?' Hayden enquired, donning the safety equipment.

'Ned Yalton gave the set to Danielle, that's all. She thought we might like to try it.' Hayden shook his head bemusedly. Twelve years into the twenty-first century, the free city of Brighton undoubtedly had its own bizarre way of doing things. It seemed capable of embracing the future while both receding into the past and staying put, all at the same time. Thus here was an age-old game played with auto-obliterating pieces modelled on a mayor who favoured medieval-style robes.

'We'll break at intervals to eat,' Dr Fikansky declared, pouring two glasses of wine from a carafe.

'You take white,' Hayden said, sipping the wine and judging it to be a Médoc. He needed to hear a piquant utterance before attempting one himself. He looked round the café while his opponent set up the timer next to the board. The lunchtime crowd was ebbing away. With the departure of the office workers and shoppers, there would soon only be a residue of students, pensioners and others of leisurely ilk. At the far end of the restaurant sat a couple appreciating one another with ophthalmic fascination. A young man strolled over to the big mirror in the centre of the café, under which hung the day's newspapers on rods. He took one and returned to his table. Beyond him was a wall crowded with paintings, some received in lieu of payment.

Two pawn moves and a knight then Hayden's opponent spoke. 'Mean people tend to suffer from constipation – Freud.'

Shifting a knight, Hayden replied, 'When Proust and Joyce met they spoke of headaches and truffles.'

Dr Fikansky nodded without enthusiasm. A long bishop's move indicated a Ruy Lopez opening. Hayden countered with the standard pawn response, and the bishop retreated. The room darkened as the sunlight outside was clouded out.

'The dark-adapted eye can detect a single photon of light,' Dr Fikansky asserted, appositely. The couple at the far table seemed to be having a difference of opinion, which gave Hayden the opportunity to play the apppositeness game.

'An asteriod orbiting the earth has been named Eros,' Hayden declaimed, while bringing out his other knight. 'Its orbit is appropriately eccentric.'

'Good, good,' his opponent murmured, castling with a neat movement. Then, in the face of further pawn pressure, Dr Fikansky shifted his bishop again and spoke. 'They used to check whether popes were dead by hitting them over the head with a mallet. If they complained, they were still alive.'

Hayden deployed his king's bishop as he responded. 'A drop of human gastric juice is so acidic it can burn a hole in a carpet.' Hayden would soon be directing his own juices towards the Prawns Newberg starter which had just been brought by Danielle. Before they broke off to eat there was an exchange of material as the Ruy Lopez opening gave way to a Marshall attack, leaving Dr Fikansky as white a pawn to the good. Hayden was little troubled by his disadvantage. At least none of his pieces had yet destroyed themselves.

Rain began to patter on to the green awning that shaded the pavement tables at the front of the café, inducing the two players to look up from their food.

Sophie was too preoccupied to pay much attention to the rain running down the office windows. She had found a note on Hayden's desk which perplexed her.

Ponder this question of jizz.

It was a message the scholar had penned to himself. Sophie was a research assistant lacking sufficient research with which to assist, so she decided to look into the matter herself. She had spent enough time organizing the bookshop's stock for her father. She flicked a switch activating the computer at one end of her desk.

'I've got a word for you, computer. Jizz. J–I–Z–Z.

17

Tell me what it means. Or rather, put it up on the screen.' Sophie found the computer's synthesized female voice irritating. The word 'Searching' appeared on the screen. Sophie sighed. Other people's computers did this sort of thing virtually instantaneously. Hers always stalled for time.

'It could be a reference to the *Journal of Invertebrate Zoology*. Does that sound right?'

'No, it doesn't,' said Sophie. 'Anyway, that's only one "z". Try again. The word appears in the following phrase: "Ponder this question of jizz."' On the screen there came up the words 'Searching some more'. Sophie sighed again and looked out of the window. It was still raining. Hayden would be at the café for some time yet. Danielle's Café. Danielle. Apart from being French, what was it about Danielle that attracted men? What was the secret of her allure? It couldn't just be her shape, surely? She certainly had a lot of that. Sophie puffed out her chest and looked downwards. She wasn't that displeased with what she saw.

Her own best point was her eyes. But were they too straightforwardly blue? Hayden's were more changeable – bluish, yes, but also flecked with green and hazel.

'There's not much on this,' the screen announced. 'It seems that "jizz" has something to do with the way we perceive ourselves. But I'm sure you knew that anyway. You were just trying to catch me out again, weren't you?' Sophie clenched her fists in annoyance, even as the computer switched itself off. Artificial intelligence!

Back at the café, the game recommenced with Dr Fikansky attempting consolation by developing his queen's side.

'The Marquis de Sade,' Dr Fikansky said with mock gravity, 'wrote a fictionalized catalogue of every form of sexual perversion to the number of six hundred on a roll of paper of appropriately lavatorial dimensions: a dozen centimetres wide and a dozen metres long.'

Hayden contemplated an attack, but would it be strong enough? The timer clicked on. A bustle at a nearby table indicated more departing diners. The freelance scholar was beginning to feel uncomfortable. As he hurriedly swung his queen across the board he inadvertently toppled one of Dr Fikansky's pawns on to an adjacent square. It exploded with a sharp noise, causing all heads in the café to duck. A small cloud of acrid smoke hung over the board. Hayden wafted it away. 'Sorry about that. Careless of me.'

'No matter. We'll replace it with one I lost earlier.'

'Well, I was going to say that against the mountainous skyline we see a donkey led by a man and carrying a woman. The couple, who journey to a far destination, will become one of the most famous in history.' He paused and was gratified by his opponent's quizzical look. 'Leonardo da Vinci and the Mona Lisa.'

'Excellent!' Dr Fikansky exclaimed as he made a move. 'And the destination?'

'The court of Francis I at Amboise in France. The king hung the picture in his bathroom.'

Hayden frowned at the board. His opponent was still consolidating while also creating a threat down the open queen's rook's file. In response, Hayden shifted a pawn and was treated to the amazing sight of it launching itself towards the ceiling with a whistling noise and trailing vapour. Dr Fikansky's delight was cut short when his own next move caused a mayor to burn fiercely to ash.

Danielle brought nourishment in the form of *Filet Niçoise*. The glasses were topped up for the home straight. The rain was now drumming hard on the awning.

'Mohammed limited a man's wives from seven hundred to four,' remarked Dr Fikansky.

'Luther had decided views on marriage, too,' riposted Hayden. 'He said that there is no more lovely, friendly and charming relationship – but he advocated rationing in the marital bed. A couple should make love twice a week at most.'

'Well done!' Dr Fikansky exclaimed, raising his glass in salute. 'You've managed to speak piquantly of mating. Applying Luther's rule, a male Muslim with the full complement of wives gets to copulate eight times a week while a Christian has to settle for two. Tut, tut.'

Dr Fikansky had gained a clear edge in the play. At length he contributed this to the conversation: 'Pythagoras gave us the words "universe" and "philosophy", and also the humanistic maxim, "man is the measure of all things".'

'Impressive – but is it piquant? And wasn't it Protagoras, quoted by Plato, who said that man is the measure of all things?'

Dr Fikansky looked troubled. 'I concede a piece.'

Hayden could not restrain a boyish grin from cracking across his face. He deftly removed a pawn acting as linchpin in his opponent's attack, thus eliminating white's material advantage, and slid what he sincerely hoped was his queen through the gap, speaking as he did so.

'Princess Belgiojosi, a friend of Liszt's, kept the embalmed body of a discarded lover in her wardrobe. Juana of Castile had the same idea,' he went on expansively. 'She was the richest heiress in early sixteenth-century Europe, and attracted the attention of Henry VII of England. It came to nothing, though. She insisted on being accompanied everywhere by the embalmed corpse of her first husband, and that couldn't have helped.'

As Hayden finished speaking the café door opened quickly to admit a couple wet from the rain. The woman wore a raincoat of shiny black material and a hat to match. She took the latter off and, with her face turned away from the two players, shook her shoulder-length blonde hair loose from her collar. Then, as she removed her coat, she swivelled round, catching Hayden's stare. At the sight of her, his heart dipped. She was the answer to a bachelor's prayers – but Hayden's adoring reverie was rudely shattered. Dr Fikansky had moved; Hayden had not. The timer's buzz had gone unheeded.

'Time penalty, I'm afraid, my friend. You lose a piece.'

'What!' Hayden blurted as Dr Fikansky removed a pawn from a vital defensive position. A wry smile sojourned on the older man's lips, and Hayden heard the woman laugh.

'A pretty woman has been the downfall of many men,' Dr Fikansky said. Lucky swine, thought Hayden. The woman and her companion had seated themselves, and Hayden respooled his mental tape.

The next few minutes saw more material disappear from the board. Both an attack by white, and black's defence, were problematical, and both kings were exposed. But Hayden had gained a crucial tempo. After Dr Fikansky pointed out that Attila the Hun had dressed in skins of field mice sewn together, the scholar initiated a feint attack on the king's side. As he did so he described how Charles the Bad of France had suffered death by *flambé* in 1387 when a brandy-soaked sheet in which he had been wrapped for therapeutic reasons was accidentally ignited by a servant. Dr Fikansky offered a devious exchange, aware that the recapture would allow him to bring off

Philidor's Legacy. But Hayden had seen the ploy and had his shock counter-coup prepared. Ignoring a poison knight, he discharged a withering salvo against white's denuded king, obtaining a double check and mate. The two players then drank off their wine during an amicable post-mortem.

Their discussion concluded, Dr Fikansky upended the pieces from the board into the box. This he came quickly to regret. The surviving mayors detonated in swift succession in their container, prompting Hayden and his opponent to throw themselves to the floor in alarm, there to be engulfed by choking fumes.

Before leaving the café, Hayden addressed *la patronne*: 'Any donations of money will be treated in the strictest confidence,' he said as Danielle passed him a couple of notes from the till. 'I think I've earned it. I'm lucky to be alive. Who's the blonde?' Danielle turned to inspect the woman who had unsettled Hayden only slightly less than the game. She was engrossed in conversation at a table.

'She's starring at the Theatre Royal. Too 'ot for you, I think,' she said with a laugh, shaking her hand and pursing her lips.

'Too 'ot?' We'll see about that, he thought.

Outside, the rain had stopped, though the flagstones were still damp. Hayden hoofed it for home and hearth south down Ship Street. On the promenade he went over to a news-stand tile-hung with magazines and newspapers.

'Hello, Sab,' came a voice from the murk.

'Greetings, Linden. Any news?'

'Brighton's bid for the Winter Olympics has failed; they've found a fossil book at Rottingdean; and there's a Doris Day movie on the box tonight, *Lover Come Back*, my favourite. Otherwise nothing.'

Linden Pitling had a wispy, nondescript head of hair

and a complexion the colour of old parchment, as befitted a cryptophile only lured into daylight by periodic bouts of evangelism when he was 'born again' from the womb of his news-stand. Hayden bought an evening paper and turned to the financial pages. It was his recurring fantasy that an awesomely powerful industrialist would buy him out or seal his lips with silver. No luck so far.

As Hayden strolled on, he pondered this business of self-employment. As the chairman and all the members of his own escape committee he had gone 'over the wire', but to what? Another prison camp of futility? This prompted a thought. What about an article entitled 'Significance: the Secular Grail' for the *Humanist Review* or some such rag? A couple of hours' work should do it, he mused, as the stubby finger that is the West Pier passed across his peripheral vision. Then he could work on his new linoleum-still, which was designed to convert old flooring materials into a novel alcoholic beverage – a modest recycling project. Not long ago, the electronic controller on this device had suffered a crisis of confidence with the result that Hayden now had charred kitchen curtains and a pitted ceiling. Still, there ought to be a patent in it, and a few billions in royalties. With these cheerful reflections he turned towards his seafront home.

2

Promising Developments

Next morning, Hayden arrived at the bookshop to find Sophie serving a customer.

'My father's slipped out for a few minutes,' she explained.

'I'll make some tea,' was his response.

Hayden climbed the narrow stairs at the back of the shop beyond the crowded bookshelves and entered the small, dimly lit kitchen next to the office. As he prepared the tea, the pleasing image of a blonde actress floated into his mind. 'Action this day' was his Churchillian resolve as he took a mug of brown fluid to his desk.

Sophie's girlish laugh preceded her into the office. How was it that three years recently completed at university – three years of indifferent lectures, grubby lodgings and inferior food – had failed to blunt this young lady's *joie de vivre*?

'Guess what? I've been invited to your mother's birthday dinner. Isn't that nice? This must be your invitation.' She handed him a black-bordered envelope from which he extracted an engraved card, also black bordered. The invitation spoke of 'formal dress, decorations optional'. Next to the word 'birthday' there was a note in a febrile hand: 'It may be my last – don't let me down.' If he'd fourteen brothers and sisters, Hayden would have been spared this persecution. As it was, he was the sole scion of the Sabanacks.

24

Sophie was happily engaged in the ceremony of sorting the mail, which still held some novelty for her. She was not herself a generator of correspondence – except phone bills for her father. Hayden lolled in his chair patiently.

He had become interested recently in the way that a healthy self-image could be established. It couldn't be based on the opinions of others – that was for sure. Opinions can change. And it seems dangerous to base self-esteem on productive work, too. Even when such work was available, success might prove elusive. Then your self-regard would crash at the moment when it was most needed. That was not to say that success couldn't be relished, of course. Hayden had tasted a modicum of this with his chess triumph over Dr Fikansky.

'There are a few invoices, including one for the brass plate. Did you like it?'

'I did. Excellent. Put the bills in the pending tray.'

'The palmist in the arcade is going on holiday next week and requires a locum. A helping hand,' she tittered.

'Very funny. Sub-contract that one to Giles if he wants it.'

'That was a reply to the "Guru/sage needs work" advertisement we placed in the newsagent's window last week.' Hayden had been pleased with that idea. Guru/sage; a nice combination of insight and wisdom.

'Better news is that the mayor wants you to ghost-write another short speech for him. This is just confirmation. Apparently he's told you about the subject already.'

'He has, yes. How long?'

'About twenty minutes duration.'

While Sophie opened another letter, Hayden considered the mayor's requirements. This was going to be enjoyable. As he started scribbling on a piece of paper, a head appeared round the door. It had dark, shoulder-length hair and was part of a female.

'Fran!'

'Sophie! Can I come in?'

'Of course,' said Sophie, abandoning the mail, and forgetting that she had been intending to ask Hayden about jizz.

He screened the ensuing chatter from his mind and wrote rapidly in his customary fashion with single-draft fluency as though in touch with the paranormal. It was his boast that he could write a speech on almost any subject quicker than it could be delivered.

'But, my dear, how is the search for a career going?' the recently arrived woman was saying.

'Not so well, I'm afraid. It's got so they've been rejecting my application for application forms. The other day I got the thumbs down from a company I have no record of approaching. Things are pretty bad when you get pre-emptive unsolicited rejections.' Sophie looked uncomfortable for a moment, then added, 'As my current boss put it.'

'I presume you are referring to that gorgeous man over there?'

'Hands off, Fran,' Sophie said in a cool undertone. Then louder: 'Francesca Earle, may I introduce Hayden Sabanack, my esteemed employer. Fran is an old school chum.'

'Your 'umble servant, ma'am,' Hayden said with mock deference as he rose to his feet and approached them. Fran, he noted, was wearing a frock in broadly diagonalled yellow and black, a colour combination widely recognized in the natural world as meaning dangerous. Hayden was not entirely outdone. His spotted bowtie and stripy socks were widely recognized in the natural world as meaning poseur.

'Sophie's still trying to get a job then? I can't think

26

why,' Fran purred, eyeing his trim form appreciatively.

'You're very kind. The Sabanack Research Team will be bereft without her,' he said, passing Sophie his newly written material. 'But as yet we lack the volume of business and, to be blunt, the density of cash.' At that moment the telephone rang, and Hayden, signalling that he would take it, excused himself and returned to his desk. While he listened to the voice on the line he inspected Fran. Her hair and complexion were darker than Sophie's, her face and nose longer. The eyes were brown, challenging. She was wearing a loose-fitting, accessible dress over a seriously proportioned form. Conscious of his gaze, she moistened her lips suggestively, while feigning interest in the papers that Sophie was reading with genuine absorption.

As Hayden was speaking into the phone, there came a knock at the back window. The face at the glass was Giles's. Hayden walked over to him, carrying the phone, and with difficulty opened the sash window. His taxi-driving friend had come up the fire escape from the alley below, or 'twitten' as these things are called in Brighton. Giles had on a pair of blue, dusty overalls, as though engaged in some botch-it-himself activity.

'Can you lend me some money, Hayden? It's important.'

With some reluctance, Hayden fished out a couple of notes from an inside pocket and handed over the previous day's meagre takings. The code of the Sabanacks precluded him from asking Giles what he wanted the money for.

'What's it for?' he asked, hand over mouthpiece.

'I'll tell you later. Thanks.' With that, Giles clattered down the metal stairway and passed out of sight along the twitten.

Hayden finished his telephone conversation and started writing on a scribble pad.

'It's good, Hayden,' Sophie said, referring to the mayor's talk. 'A bit overheated, perhaps, but good.'

'Can you quench it then as appropriate, and add a few of your stylish sentences before sending it off?'

'Yes, I'll do that.'

'Thanks. First, though, a business trip, all expenses paid. Destination: City Hall.'

'Brighton City Hall? Wonderful.'

'I need some information. I've written down what I want. I think, Sophie my sweet, that we are about to hit mineral-bearing ore. Before that, however, I'm off to the theatre to seek company for my twilight years. I'll see you in the Pavilion gardens at noon, all right? Francesca, it was a pleasure to meet you. I'm sorry we couldn't talk longer.'

With that, and a courteous inclination of the head, he left two ladies to pursue a third.

Hayden stood in the foyer of the old Theatre Royal amidst wood panelling, brass fittings and heavy red carpeting and draperies. By the box office a poster proclaimed *Adam's Navel*, a play due to open in two weeks, starring Babette Macawley. It looked like a sex farce or possibly a harrowing psycho-drama. It was difficult to tell since the theatre management had evidently failed to brief the poster designer as to the exact character of the play. In any event, it looked as though Miss Macawley would be appearing in provocative dishabille, and someone had sensibly concluded that the depiction of this would probably draw the crowds. Even on a poster she was an impressive sight.

A thin man in a dark suit barred Hayden's way to the auditorium.

'I have an appointment with Miss Macawley,' Hayden said. 'Programme note: finalization of copy.'

'Pass, friend.'

Inside the auditorium all was darkness except for a small pool of light, centre stage. In it, wearing an electric blue leotard, stood Babette Macawley. The sight of her, so unexpected, caused Hayden to stop abruptly and sway in his shoes. She was beautiful every way you looked at her. She didn't have a good side; she was aesthetically symmetrical. Hayden's heart tried to thump its way out of his chest. As he watched, she started some loosening-up exercises. Her legs were superb – the best stocking-fillers in town. He could take no more. He blundered into the corridor and sought support from a wall before recovering himself and heading backstage. There, Hayden stood among the ropes, tackle and flats and awaited his moment. Miss Macawley was now reciting a speech. The atmosphere was familiar but alien. He could see the attraction of the theatre but he himself had no greasepaint in his veins and no desire to exsanguinate himself nightly. His was the role of the questing intellect, not the strolling player.

After a few minutes, the star came backstage and went to her dressing room. Hayden followed her to locate the door, then hovered in the corridor for a couple of minutes. With trepidation, he knocked on the door, and it was with relief and apprehension that he heard the words 'Come in'.

'Miss Macawley, good morning.'

She was standing in a dressing gown beside a wardrobe. Her golden hair was tied back. She seemed tense. 'Yes?'

'I have come to finalize the programme note for the management. If it's convenient.'

'Well . . .'

'There is a deadline.'

'Go ahead then, sit down.' She herself dropped into a chair in front of a cluttered dressing table. She began wiping her face with a piece of moistened cotton wool.

'Perhaps you recognize me from Danielle's yesterday, Miss Macawley?'

'Perhaps. Please proceed.' This was proving an uphill struggle.

'How would you describe *Adam's Navel*?'

'Humourless and imbecilic. It requires no display of intelligence by director, cast or audience.'

'*Adam's Navel* is a pit in the abdomen of literature. I see. And something a little more useful for the publicist?'

She looked at him in the reflection in her mirror. Something seemed to be troubling her.

'Something is troubling me,' she said. 'Who *are* you? The programme note, pathetic as it is, has already been written.'

'Hayden Sabanack at your service. The rewrite man.'

She turned round and surveyed him blandly. 'Do you want a real job?' she asked at length.

'Go on.'

'Rewrite this.' She picked up a fat manuscript that had been lying at one end of her table and tossed it with disgust into his lap. '*Adam's* bloody *Navel*.'

'A few more belly laughs, perhaps?'

For the first time she relaxed slightly. 'It needs more humour certainly. Put some jokes in without altering the structure.'

'Spruce up your speeches and sprinkle in some one-liners, you mean?'

'That's it. I will rehearse the play as it is, but I want the new material ready for the opening night. This is to remain between you and me. My reputation is at stake. The changes must be so good that no-one will be able to argue that we should return to the original script. Understood?'

'Miss Macawley, with your looks and my brains we will conquer the world.'

'Brighton, then London, will do.'

'We will need to meet, of course.'

She looked him in the eye steadily, then lowered her glance to his bowtie, and finally his socks. He felt vulnerable, transparent. Suddenly she brightened. 'Agreed.'

Still slightly dazed from his recent encounter, Hayden emerged from the theatre on to a sunlit street. He wandered over to the garden behind the Dome and library. There, while waiting for Sophie, he inspected *Adam's Navel*. It was indeed dismal. This cheered him up no end. Improving this drivel would be child's play. He would work on it that night.

'Hello, Hayden,' came Sophie's voice. 'What have you got there?'

'My new commission. A modest redaction of a would-be dramatic *tour de force*. A rewrite job on the forthcoming attraction at the Theatre Royal.'

'I'm impressed. How much?'

'What?'

'Your fee – including an advance, perhaps.'

'Please, don't be sordid,' he said sepulchrally. 'This is art.'

Sophie took a deep breath and levelled her most suspicious look. 'Who is she? I bet it's that blonde piece in *Adam's Thingummy*. Nit, erc, cretin!' she abused palindromically, beating him with a notebook.

'Please, popsy . . .'

'I'm not your popsy, you duffer.' There was a short silence as they walked towards Church Street.

'She and I are going to have a shipboard romance,' Hayden sighed.

Sophie had recovered her tolerance sufficiently to pass him the feed line: 'There's not a ship in sight.'

'Haven't you heard of a relationship?' She laughed dutifully. 'I'm going to make her worship the water on which I walk, even if I drown in the process.'

31

'Shouldn't you learn how to crawl on water before you can walk on it?' After a moment she added, 'Where shall we lunch? There's a restaurant near the Pavilion.'

'We could be into an area of cost-overrun here,' Hayden said in a cod American accent.

'You mean we can't afford it?'

'Affirmative.'

She started hitting him on the shoulder again with her notebook.

'You idiot. Let's get some munchables instead, then. We've got forty-five minutes before the meeting.'

The lunchtime crowds were coagulating about them. They toiled through the throng into Marlborough Place and bought samosas and coffee at a roadside stall. The coffee was so thick and black it could only have been more repellent if it had been administered in solid form as a suppository.

'What did you find out from the nabobs at the City Hall? Did you bump into Duffy?'

'No, why should I?'

'He works there, that's all. Tell on.'

'I haven't learned much, I'm afraid. There's some sort of competition and your man Sid Whitney is in it. On the application you are cited as expert advisor, as of yesterday.'

'What a cheek! He only phoned me this morning. Come on, let's get along to the hotel or we'll be late.'

Sophie talked movingly of the city's encouragement of industrial development projects as they passed the Royal Pavilion on their right into the Old Steine, part of a complex delta of ornamental gardens and traffic islands at the seaward end of the London Road, which irrigates the town from the north. Beyond the Old Steine lies the Palace Pier which projects into the sea like an alluvial spit of amusement arcades and fairground rides. The Hotel Albion is on the seafront and overlooks the western side of the pier. It is spacious and imposing in the Victorian style. They reached it with a few minutes to spare.

Sid Whitney turned out to be a jovial, balding man in his mid-forties, his accent placing his upbringing in the East End of London.

'Actually,' he was saying, 'my father was so successful as a market trader that he sent me to a private school, but I got tired of all those jokes about spies, deviants and upper class twits so I drove my larynx downmarket, where it belonged. I've never looked back. A dozen businesses in London, summer and winter homes, and a yacht in the marina. Not bad going.'

'So why the new project?' Hayden asked.

'A challenge. Let me give you the background. Have you heard of the DeWit Bequest. No? Well, it's worth tens of millions. DeWit was a crook with a conscience. Before he snuffed it, he provided for a bequest which spoke of a "device or devices to further human understanding, and available to all". He wanted to make up for a lifetime's wrong-doing. Of course, the money was ill-gotten gains, so he couldn't establish the bequest in London, his home patch. He chose Brighton instead. Different laws, you see, plus the recent record of innovation down here. Astonishing.'

He was interrupted by a waiter bearing a tray of drinks. Two of them were ordinary enough but one was draped in tropical foliage that looked like something out of Conan Doyle's *The Lost World*. This was Sophie's 'Brazilian Stinger'.

'You'll like that one, Sophie,' Sid commented with relish. 'My doctor won't let me touch 'em. They say that Amazonian Indians pickle their mothers-in-law in that stuff.' He roared with laughter.

Sophie's look of slight apprehension disappeared after she had nosed past the foliage and taken a sip. 'It's good,' she said with surprise. A second later she gasped and added: 'It has quite a kick, doesn't it?'

'The bequest takes the form of a competition,' Sid continued. 'The players get some starting capital and the use of one of those new factory units opposite the Culture Park. There's a play-off between rival prototypes in three weeks' time. Winner takes all – with the proviso that they go into immediate full-scale production. The bequest will easily cover all manufacturing and selling costs. Profits should be immense!'

'How many rival groups are there?' asked Hayden.

'I don't know. The runners and riders have yet to be announced.'

'When was the closing date for applications?'

'Yesterday.'

'And my name was on the form?'

'Ah, yes. You've been doing your homework. Sorry about that. Necessity. It was a late stipulation by your government that local expertise be represented. Since they're administering the competition, I had no choice. You were recommended by someone in the Planning Department, a big chap.' He paused, reaching into his pocket. 'I think I can make it up to you. Although I detest paperwork, this might be of interest to you.' On to the table landed a wad of banknotes, thick enough to impress, not too thick for vulgarity. The gentle thwack as the notes landed had awakened Hayden's primal sensibilities in these matters. The denominations were large.

'This buys your initial plans. Much more to follow.'

'I'm impressed,' murmured Hayden, admiring the pile. Money was not the measure of things, but cash validation was essential. 'What exactly do you want me to do?'

'It's a question of meaning and purpose. DeWit reckoned that the business community was failing the public. We had left it to religious loonies, mystics and

34

cranks – in a word, amateurs. Even the academics have left the market place. Where is the philosopher who can tell you what it all means? People want to know why they go through the painful rigmarole of life. That's it in a nutshell. You agree?'

'I suppose so, but what's that got to do with this weird bequest?'

'We've got to make a professional offering to the mass market for meaning. Forget book-readers and highbrows: DeWit wanted something for the mass of ordinary people – ordinary, perplexed people. "A device to further human understanding". I see a box with this word on it "Existometer™". And below that: "Solve the Riddle of Existence!" Now you've got to tell me what to put in it.'

'Existometer!' Hayden exclaimed incredulously. 'Is it meant to be a toy or a joke or something?'

'No,' said Sid equably. 'This is the business. Use this kit and you end up with a higher sense of meaning than before. Preferably, you find the answer to the question, why are we here? We've been given a factory and we've got the starting capital. Tell me what to make and I'll make it. Right? Things rather than words, though I appreciate that a bit of verbiage might be necessary.'

'Yes, it might.'

'Will you do it? I was going to bring in a London boffin, but you're clearly the man for the job, an intellectual.'

'Don't tell me. An intellectual is someone who breaks new ground with his head.'

'Exactly. The thrill of creation. And the money, of course.'

Hayden looked at Sophie. She gave a bemused shrug.

'You have a deal,' said the intellectual, firmly.

'Good. Since I'm putting up a substantial amount of cash I'll need your assurance of best endeavours.'

'You have that. Guaranteed.'

'Here's a hand on it, then,' said the Londoner. 'Call me Sid from now on. I will need your initial plans by ten a.m. tomorrow. Meet me on board my yacht, the *Marbella Hood*. I'll need clear instructions as to what machinery to get for the factory. Remember, we've got just three weeks. Keep our agreement confidential. Any opposition there may be is best kept in the dark.'

What with the script rewrite, it had been Hayden's day for confidential assignments. If he had to keep much more under his hat he would have to buy a stetson. While this thought crossed his mind, a further round of drinks arrived, and Sophie pickled another mother-in-law.

'Count yesterday as Day One,' continued Sid. 'We should aim to have everything ready by Day Twenty-One, a Sunday, in time for the prototype test the next morning.'

Outside the hotel, Sophie tottered momentarily as the sea air went to her Brazilian-stung legs. She and Hayden were both a bit light-headed as they set off west along the promenade.

'I could change my name to Tarpaulin,' Hayden said.

'Why?'

'As a cover.'

'I couldn't change mine to Handbag, though,' she retorted.

'Why not?'

'Otherwise I could be done as an accessory.'

They cut down Market Street towards the Lanes before turning into Prince Albert Street. Over at the street corner loitered an acne of pustular adolescents, presumably playing truant from school, and beyond them, a familiar sight. It was his mother's two-seater roadster, a 1930 Rolls-Royce Phantom II Continental, an open-top phenomenon in royal blue with running boards and exophthalmic headlamps. They walked over to the machine and awaited its owner's return. Sophie gazed at her own reflection in the waxed coachwork and ran a finger over its immaculate surface. Presently, a woman walked up wearing a gauzy motoring bonnet and a long coat.

'Mother, lovely to see you.'

'Do I know you?' the woman enquired distantly of Hayden. 'Sophie my dear.' She kissed the girl before turning to the freelance scholar.

'You must be my only son Hayden.' She proffered a cheek, which he kissed with resigned good humour.

'And you must be my only mother. Keeping busy?'

'A luncheon appointment with Simeon Urstpoint. We discussed the management of the estate. It's getting too much for me,' she said plaintively, employing a phrase she had used several times during her meal with the family solicitor. 'A lonely widow. If only I had a man on whom I could rely.' This last was delivered in a theatrical tone of wistful longing. Hayden always admired his mother's hold on grammar at such moments.

'We're going along to Danielle's for a coffee,' said Sophie. 'Will you join us, Mrs Sabanack?'

'No, I mustn't intrude on you young lovers.' Hayden raised his eyes to heaven in exasperation. 'I must go home to rest.'

'Are you fit to drive, Mother, or shall I ring for an ambulance?'

'He has a very uncaring attitude, Sophie. Save him from himself. Urge him to get a proper job. I shall see you both on Thursday night, I hope, at my party. That gives you a couple of days to reform yourself, Hayden.'

'Yes, mother.'

When Mrs Sabanack had driven off with her usual disregard for other traffic, Hayden and Sophie turned towards Danielle's. They arrived at the café to find the pavement tables occupied. Going inside instead, they ordered tea from a waiter. Near them was a famously old clock with an ornate wooden casing and a long pendulum visible behind glass. Alongside it were three bullet holes the management had declined to repair. The story was that these had been put there by a jealous lover, though there was a school of thought that they had been drilled by the tourist board. Since their appearance several years ago, the clock had kept erratic time. The fault was in the escapement mechanism which occasionally free-ran, as though lost in thought. Hayden had tried to mend it, but to no avail. The clock was like a single lady of advanced years who clung to the memory of her one experience of violent emotion.

'Death and sex, that's where we'll start. No Existometer would be complete without the basics. I'll do sex, you do death,' Hayden proclaimed, forestalling Sophie's complaints with a placating gesture. 'Lest a maidenly erubescence mantle your cheek.'

'Ho-hum,' she ho-hummed sceptically. 'Where do I start?'

'See what you can dig up – forgive the pun – from your father's bookshelves. Avoid reading anything German – Hegel, Schopenhauer and the rest. It will make you feel suicidal.'

'What am I looking for exactly?'

'I don't know. Interesting thoughts. Try the online databases.' He paused, then went on, 'If I'm going to see Sid Whitney tomorrow, I'll need transport. Do you mind if I borrow your bicycle?'

'No, please do.'

There was a pause.

'Solving the riddle of existence in three weeks is going to look good on your c.v. you know,' said Hayden. Sophie did not look pleased to be reminded of the call of career and distant horizons. Hayden retrieved the paperwork from his pocket and, taking a few sheets for himself, passed the rest across the table. 'Have some wages, and pay off our creditors, will you? I owe your father some rent for the office.'

'You know he doesn't want anything.'

'Stash the rest for a rainy day. I think I can afford a calling card. Can you arrange something? Usual wording.'

'Yes, I'll do that,' she said, frowning. Sophie had interrogated her father on the subject of jizz, receiving the unexpected information that it was a term used by bird-watchers. She had been on the point of surprising her boss with this piece of information when another matter had intruded on her thoughts. 'Hayden?'

'Yes?'

'How are you going to *do* sex?'

Later, at home, Hayden washed some socks and hung them on the back of the refrigerator to dry. For safety's sake, he had moved the linoleum-still to the spare bedroom. It had taken an hour to move the immense assemblage of casks, pipework and heating elements without disturbing the process. Now the linoleum-still was humming companionably and excreting a bilious green liquid.

The playscript of *Adam's Navel* demanded his attention, then he would devote a couple of hours after midnight to the Existometer. But first he had better take something for his head. He went over to the medicine cabinet and selected one of his choicer Chiantis. Then he collected some nibbles from the kitchen. His cleaning lady had mysteriously left some cockles in a plastic tub. He rinsed these off in a tea strainer, and went laden to his desk to work.

3

A Bicycle Ride

The following day Hayden pedalled in bright sunshine along the seafront east towards the marina. Much more of this, he mused, and a drought will be declared. Alternatively, it will start raining torrentially and spring will again be deemed the worst for forty years. Our weather is like a weirdly vacillating agnostic. Today it half believes in warmth – for the moment.

He turned left on to the underpass that crosses beneath Marine Drive and freewheeled down the long, curving slip-road that gives access to Europe's largest marina, a yacht haven bounded by huge semicircular concrete caissons. Recourse to Berth Control would be unnecessary as Hayden identified the *Marbella Hood* easily enough from Sid's description even among the hundreds of boats that afforest the marina with clinking masts.

It was a majestic craft, a sleek, white motor cruiser with a quay to itself. Hayden left Sophie's bicycle near a ship's chandler and approached the boat on foot. He found Sid standing on the quay, supervising two crewmen rigging an awning above the stern deck. 'Marbella Hood' was written in proud red letters across the stern.

'It's the name of my first wife,' Sid explained.

'Doesn't your present wife object?'

'She *is* my first wife,' he said with a smile.

They boarded the yacht and Sid conducted Hayden along a gangway into a large cabin where the

40

impression was of wood panelling, luxurious fittings and comfortable seating. It was spacious and well lit. At one end, a girl of perhaps thirteen was painting at an easel. At the other, a middle-aged woman was reading a magazine in the elbow of an L of soft leather sofas.

'Girls, this is Hayden Sabanack, a business associate. Hayden, this is my wife Bella and daughter Gail.'

'Pleased to meet you, Hayden,' said Bella. 'You're stuck with us, I'm afraid. The rest of the boat is in the hands of the crew. We're preparing for a big party next week. You must come along.'

'Good idea,' said Sid. 'Yes, do that. Have a look at Gail's masterpiece.' Sid ushered Hayden towards the easel. Gail was freckled and wore pigtails and pebble spectacles. She looked down as the men approached. The 'masterpiece' was a highly competent seascape with thrashing waves and lowering sky. Hayden, while not normally admitting to knowing the difference between yellow ochre and mediocre, saw at once that the girl had real talent. This was not the product of a jaded palette.

'This is very fine,' Hayden murmured, in a manner calculated to convey reverence. Sid beamed, and the girl was emboldened to speak.

'I've tried to use light and dark to tie a knot of tension . . .' she said, then blushed and cast her eyes downwards again, overawed by their dashing visitor.

'She also does portraits. Maybe she'll do yours if you're lucky.'

'Can I?' the girl asked eagerly. Hayden was in danger of becoming a social success. On offer was a party invitation and a portrait in oils after only five minutes on board Brighton Marina's most impressive vessel.

'Thank you, but we've only just met. Why not do one of your father instead?'

'She's done me. And Bella. And her brothers. You'd be doing us a favour.'

41

'I haven't time to sit for you, I'm afraid.'

'It'll be enough to sketch you while you're talking,' she managed to say. Faced with such enthusiasm, and not a little flattered, Hayden acquiesced graciously. Sid poured a couple of cups of coffee from a jug on a side table and, while Gail sketched, they got down to business.

'I envisage a multi-component pack featuring items relating to both the inner being and the flux of external events,' Hayden was saying. 'The basic orientation of the Existometer, though, will be towards self-exploration by the punter of his or her own psyche – not the conscious or unconscious parts of the mind, but what we'll call supraconsciousness. That's the faculty associated with high-level insight, intuition and imagination. I envisage a physical aid to the quest for personal knowledge. I'm calling it the "Astrolabe of Inner Being". I should explain that the astrolabe is a device which was used by the ancients to determine the position of celestial bodies. It is reckoned to be the world's oldest scientific instrument. In the Middle Ages it became a navigational aid. Our astrolabe will be a circular device on a tripodal mounting. It will have settings corresponding to different psychological attributes, fully adjustable for individual relevance. The inner architecture will move by a simple and elegant mechanism.'

'Will it work?'

'I see it as being a bit like the *I Ching, The Book of Changes*, in being revelatory and modestly predictive. I've got to decide on the primary personal characteristics – extroversion, neurotic tendency and so on – then build in an integrative feature to generate a first-order synthesis into which is inserted a totally random element to disengage the conscious mind while permitting the supraconscious to manifest itself.'

'Sounds amazing,' Sid said, becoming aware that

42

Hayden had won the women's complete attention. The scholar was by now on his feet in the centre of the room and began describing at length the inputting and interpretative procedures. As he extemporized mesmerically on, the light seemed to dim and the atmosphere became charged. This man is dynamite, thought Sid. He should be kept in a strongbox. The women had lost themselves in Hayden's eyes and voice, while the scholar, though conscious of his audience's attention, conveyed his message all but self-forgetfully.

Minutes passed, then he said in a lighter tone, 'It could be very beautiful in design and construction – and essentially harmless. There is some danger in delving into the mind's depths, but none, as far as I can see, in seeking expression of higher faculties – except self-delusion, perhaps, and we can bear that in mind when we put together the basic design.'

At this point they all relaxed. Sid exhaled a thoughtful breath and took a swig of coffee. 'This is going to create a sensation,' he said wonderingly.

'It's a start, certainly.'

'Put me down for the first one,' said Bella, and Gail nodded in enthusiastic agreement.

Brighton, fringed to the south by sea, is crescented to the north by a modest range of rolling chalk hills which used to be known as the South Downs. After Brighton declared itself a sovereign city state, the hills were first renamed the North Downs, then the Brighton Downs. Now they are known simply as the Downs.

The city state to Brighton's north, London, has within its southern boundary a roughly parallel east-west range of chalk hills which used to be called the North Downs. These were initially renamed the South Downs, then, in response to the hubris of the seaside city state, the London Uplands. They are now known simply as the Ups. Thus it was that at one time there were two sets of North Downs, then a South Downs north of the North Downs. Such are the ups and downs of city-state rivalries.

For historical reasons, Brighton's rural hinterland is still known as Sussex after the English county of which pre-independent Brighton formed a part. The University of Sussex is situated some distance outside the city proper, on the Lewes Road at Falmer. It was to this that Hayden now journeyed. Before quitting the *Marbella Hood*, he had detailed the tools and dies Sid would need for his factory. Twenty-five minutes' steadily uphill cycling north-east from the marina took him past the racecourse and enabled him to cut across country to the Falmer Road. This part of Sussex didn't boast lush meadows, bream-filled streams and apple-cheeked milkmaids, but the undulating, grassy hills were pleasant enough. He stopped to remove his red and cream striped blazer, and placed it in the saddle-bag over the manuscript of *Adam's Navel*, due for later delivery. He then propelled Sophie's old-fashioned machine with difficulty to the downland ridge; travel was regaining its old sense of 'travail'. The meteorological agnostic vacillated weirdly, opting for obscurantism in the form of what was low stratus cloud but what appeared to be thick fog. This forced Hayden to stop and put his blazer back on. He then coasted down to the Lewes Road in the claggy gloom and crossed to the university.

As a rag stunt for charity, the students were operating a frontier control system on to the campus. Hayden paid up for a passport issued in the name of 'Moribundesrepublik, a staging-post to Valhalla', and left his bicycle with a border guard. He then made his way to the mist-shrouded Biology Tower and, once inside, climbed to what proved to be a crowded mezzanine floor. The wall guide indicated that Nigel Stebbins, Reader in Biomedicine, occupied a cell on the third

44

floor of this humming humanitarium. The lifts being out of order, Hayden trudged up the stairs, weary from his bicycle ride.

'Hello, Nigel, you old scrote,' he said when he entered the office of his long-time friend.

'Hayden, greetings. You're looking well. Still dreeing your weird?'

'Rubbing along, yes.'

'How's your mother?'

'Never better.'

'Has she recovered from her operation yet?'

'What operation?'

'The one she was about to have when I last spoke to her.'

'She hasn't had any operations. She's fine.'

'Oh,' he said, momentarily perplexed. Then, brightening, he added, 'Marvellous woman.'

'What are you researching into these days, Nigel?'

'Precognitive sexual fantasy.' Hayden spluttered with mirth, and Nigel smiled tolerantly.

'You mean dreaming who you are going to have nookie with before you have it?'

'Precisely.'

As a researcher, Nigel had never recovered from taking up occupancy in the Biology Tower some five years before. In the old unheated Nissen hut, sited on land scheduled for redevelopment since 1948, he had scribbled his findings on the backs of envelopes with pencil stubs and been tipped for a Nobel Prize. The move to new accommodation had been his undoing. It had brought with it a well-appointed laboratory and four able technicians. It had also ruined his sense of a significant scientific problem ripe for solution. Perhaps it was the lack of rising damp.

Nigel had gradually reorientated his research interest to sex from the neuroendocrinology of reproduction. He had planned to cash in on his research by

45

rehashing the bestsellers of a bygone era, but publishers had proved indifferent to his proposals to write *The Naked Apiarist*, *The Joy of Sussex* and *Everything You Wanted to Know but were Afraid to Ask*. His work-in-progress, *The Oral Tradition*, was more original. It was not about folklore. If Nigel, grey-haired in his late thirties, appeared sunken-eyed and ravaged by sexual excess through personal research for his books, looks were deceiving. The scientist had for many years been heroically over-mortgaged, or so he claimed.

'I'm trying to understand what life's about, Nigel, particularly sex and meaning, as I said on the telephone.'

'I'm not a priest, Hayden.'

'You're a generalist in a fragmented world, Nigel. That makes you a sheep with five legs, as the Dutch say.'

'Are you sure they say that? Well, I'll give it a try, but only because it's you. How shall we play this?'

'Just ramble on as you used to when we drank together. I mean that in the nicest possible way.' Nigel's ability to indulge in aimless intellectual busking was notorious. One girl had fallen into a dead faint through cerebral overload after listening to him for an hour at a cocktail party. His tutorial students usually ended up under heavy sedation.

'Well, pin your ears back then, here goes. If it moves it's usually an animal, if it doesn't, it's a plant. All either indulge in, or are victims of, sex and violence. Animals, as the saying goes, are red in tooth, claw, tusk, talon and, er ... private parts. Plants are green. I'm not going too fast, I hope?' he said, putting his feet up on a desk drawer. 'All read from the same spiral-bound codebook of life, DNA, from the llama that mates sitting down to the shrimp that is monogamous. The three "Fs" of biology are feasting, fornication and fatalities. Of these, the middle one is the most interesting. In polygamous species there tend to be big differences between the sexes: antlers, plumage, that kind of thing. In monogamous species, the differences are fewer.'

Just then, there was a loud knock, and round the door appeared a man's head. From it, speech issued.

'Mrs Williams is outside with her latest crop of fantasies. Apparently you're beginning to feature in some of them.'

'Good, good,' responded Nigel. 'Give her the usual electrode treatment then take a reading. If it's on the low side, put her on the "B" diet and give her an enema.'

'OK,' the head replied and disappeared.

'Tim, my PhD student,' Nigel explained. 'Very keen. His main interest is celibacy, but he helps me out from time to time. Bit short of volunteers for his own research programme at the moment. I don't suppose you'd like to . . . no, perhaps not.'

'Does an enema help?'

'No, but they seem to expect it. Where were we? Oh, yes,' said the biologist, talking on with miscellaneous zeal. He had a small patch of stubble on his chin which had eluded the morning razor. He fingered this meditatively as he stared out of the window at where the middle distance should have been. The mist made it seem as if they were occupying the centre of a blob of shaving cream. 'Polar bears are left-handed; female spotted hyenas are dominant over males; rats can't vomit; and dungflies mate on fresh cow pats. Some male spiders bind their partners with silken threads before having their wicked way. If the female praying mantis bites off her mate's head before copulation it doesn't affect his performance.'

'Good God!' interjected Hayden. 'And I thought human relationships were difficult!'

Nigel wasn't comfortable with ordinary conversation, and ploughed on. 'There's a biological bestiary

47

comprising Aristotle's chicks for embryology; Darwin's Beagle for evolution – though that "beast" was a ship, of course; Pavlov's dog for aspects of reflexology; and Lorenz's raven. I see I have you with the last one. This bird was reckoned the first non-human being to use language meaningfully. It said "Roah". This meant something to Konrad Lorenz, as an ethologist working with birds – it was his call sign.' Some people said that waiting for Nigel to trigger an illuminating thought was like panning for fool's gold. Hayden kept an open mind on the question.

'Our feathered friends are of interest because of something that occurred tens of millions of years ago. The dinosaurs were wiped out. They submitted themselves to the test of evolution and failed: one view. Another view is that they adopted disguise and assumed a false name, "birds".'

'Evolution – of course!' exclaimed Hayden. 'What's the evolutionary value of a sense of meaning?'

Nigel pulled a g-force face as though the billions of neurons in his head were not wired for dialogue.

'You can say of every behavioural characteristic of an organism: how does this increase fitness to survive? How is this adaptive? As to your question, if I become inaudible in the next few minutes it could be because I've started to talk through the back of my head.' Hayden had never heard Nigel issue a disclaimer before; his attentiveness increased accordingly. 'For an organism to wonder what it all means is a bit of a luxury. A need for meaning might be useful, however, in terms of inquisitiveness and progress; as a spur to improvement. It might also be a non-adaptive post-reproductive phenomenon, though.

'Let me explain. If I develop a physical or mental characteristic after reproductive age which does not enhance my chance of survival, it would not matter from one point of view because I have already

48

reproduced, always supposing the little wretches are off my hands.' For a moment Nigel's mind dwelt on the painful image of his teenage children. 'My children might also display the trait because I've passed it on, and their children in turn. A non-adaptive characteristic could thus be conserved through the aeons. So, to summarize, a sense of meaning could be adaptive or non-adaptive.' Nigel seemed pleased with this unhelpful equivocation.

'But adolescents seem to have the strongest will-to-meaning,' said Hayden, 'which suggests we might be dealing with a pre-reproductive trait of genuine adaptiveness, mightn't we?' Nigel seemed disappointed at the prospect of making progress on this issue. 'That puts a sense of meaning in the same category as the opposable thumb.'

'Remember,' stated Nigel, 'that one of the more abundant products of the natural world is *stercus tauri* – the excretory product of the bull!'

'I'm strictly non-bovine, Nigel. I have nothing to declare except my genus, *Homo*.' Hayden laughed, and as he had nothing to add, that's what he added.

4

Pedalling and Peddling

Back in the saddle, Hayden rode briskly from misty gloom into bright sunshine again as he approached Moulescombe on the edge of town. An essential idea had emerged from the conversation with Nigel. Out there are billions of galaxies each containing billions of stars. The universe got that way over some fifteen billion years by *evolving*. This is true of the solar system and life on earth. These days, philosophical systems and cosmological models are fundamentally evolutionary.

He was lost in thought and almost overshot some traffic lights. The bicycle shuddered in complaint at the violent braking. Hayden would have to be more careful: becoming posthumous is a notoriously bad career move. Across the road a news vendor was selling that day's paper. It must have been a low news day, for the man's hoarding trumpeted 'Fog in Sussex – London cut off from civilization'.

Hayden passed the park known as The Level, and the children's playground beyond it, and entered the Grand Parade, from where it was a short distance to the Theatre Royal. He dropped off the play manuscript in Babette's dressing room, but the actress was not there. Keenly disappointed, he made his way to the manager's office only to find that empty, too. At last, he located an office junior with whom he left the extended programme note he had written the previous night. He had not been asked to prepare this, but felt sure that the existing one would as usual be a feebly deficient piece and that his would be preferred. Babette could only be pleased with this, and with the main assignment, too: in its revised version, *Adam's Navel* had indubitably become a better play.

Returning to Thylde Street, he found it in the grip of market day, but by shimmying up the alternative route to the bookshop via the twitten, he avoided the crowds. The exertions of the morning were beginning to tell on him. There was a stiffness in his limbs, and his back ached with cyclist's hunch. He passed through the bookshop, volleying a matey greeting at Sophie's father *en route*, and emerged into the bustling scene that was Thylde Street. Every Wednesday, the road was closed to traffic and market stalls were strewn incontinently along its length. Mammon ruled in the form of cajoling hucksters and clamouring crowds. Hayden spotted Rob Harris's clothing stall and wandered over to it. Rob had achieved a modest celebrity locally by once disarming the notorious 'Stair-rods' Wilson during a pub brawl and surviving to tell the tale. Hayden marvelled afresh at the sub-mediocrity of Rob's merchandise. The shirts had short arms and would shrink in the coldest wash; the shoes were too narrow; and the mock leather jackets were so mock that they would have been acceptable feedstock for Hayden's linoleum-still.

'How's life treating you, Rob?'

'Well, the wife gave birth to triplets at home last week; the lodger's bought a howler monkey; and they've started up that sawmill next door. Otherwise pretty quiet really. You?'

Faced with Rob's surreal lifestyle, Hayden felt he couldn't complain. 'Fairly grim,' he said with a laugh. 'Too much cycling.'

'Don't they give you scholars company cars, then?

51

Never mind. Perhaps I can interest you in a new jacket?'

'Er, no thanks. I never part with money on a Wednesday. An old Sabanack custom. See you around.'

The human plankton eddied and swirled Hayden to a stall selling carpet off-cuts, and thence to a sandwich bar. Sensing the hand of fate behind these movements, he beckoned towards him the lad behind the counter, a spotty youth with herring-red hair. Eschewing some tired-looking rolls, the scholar selected a prolapsed pasty. As he ate, there came a familiar voice.

'Babylon is fallen, that great city, because she made all the nations drink of the wine of the wrath of her fornication.' Then the thundering voice moderated and said, 'Hello, Sab'.

'Hello, Linden. Deserting the news biz to save souls?'

'Only the Lord can save souls. I am but his instrument.' Linden Pitling usually looked seedy and worn out, as though knocked down by a streetcar named Retire, but on 'revelation days', freed from his seafront news-stand, he was transfigured. He had the distinction of being the only person in the market place out for what he could give rather than what he could get.

'A word of advice, Linden. Stay away from the pasties.'

Over at the Dartford Warbler, Ted the barman was clearing glasses from the outside tables, at one of which sat Giles. Only the market day crush in the bar would have forced him to endure the rigours of fresh air and photons at lunchtime. Hayden went over to join him for a late pint, and as they were talking, Sophie wandered up and dropped into a chair.

'I saw that you two were boozing again,' she said, lips pursed reprovingly.

'No, this is merely water,' the scholar riposted.

'We're going to market it as "Hayden's Humectant".'

'It's beer.'

'That's a better name. We could use that, Giles.'

'Thanks for inviting me over,' was Sophie's rejoinder, but she immediately regretted it. She must stop getting at her boss. Hayden, however, showed only pleasure at the opportunity for badinage.

'But you don't like drinking at lunchtime, you dislike the market day crowds, and you think Giles talks too much.'

'The gesture would have been appreciated. And Giles doesn't talk too much.'

'You've got to look after Sophie,' said Giles piously, acknowledging to himself that he was distinctly susceptible to Sophie's charms. Giles's companions thanked him for his comment, one with satisfaction, the other with irony.

The ironical one then said, 'Any news on death, Sophie?'

'Here's some reading for you,' she replied, putting a pile of papers on the table. 'How have you been getting on with sex?'

'I've been talking to Nigel Stebbins. It will take a few hours to fully recover the use of my brain.' There was a pause. 'Sid was pleased with the initial proposal this morning. I will brief you on it tomorrow morning when we'll have a council of war. In the meantime, I want you to look into physics. Why this table in front of us, for example, consists mainly of nothing. That seems important.'

'That's the full guidance I get, is it?' Sophie said ruefully. Giles wondered why he never had conversations like this. 'On another subject, I've got some bad news for you. Your documentary series has been turned down by the B-CC-CBC.' Hayden had written to a television producer he knew in the Brighton-Calais Cross-Channel Broadcasting Channel suggesting a series called *Books that Shook the World*. Failure. Some fall on stony ground, Hayden reflected gravely, and others have stony ground thrust upon them. 'There's also this,' Sophie added, passing Hayden a pale yellow envelope marked 'Private', which she knew smelled faintly of perfume. All three of them waited to see if Hayden would open it immediately, but he didn't. Shortly afterwards, Sophie left to investigate the mysteries of the physical universe or, as her employer put it, 'those Awful Wastes of Time and Space'.

As Hayden intended to work at home that afternoon, Giles offered to give him a lift in the taxi. The saddle-sore scholar accepted with misgivings. Giles pulled on a worn-looking leather jacket, slung a pair of oily goggles round his neck and put on a black beret. He looked like nothing so much as a Second World War tank commander readying himself for the bitter conflicts ahead. Hayden refrained from comment.

Opening the yellow envelope, Hayden discovered a note inside which he read out as they walked to Giles's car. 'Let's meet tonight at The Heathen, ten p.m. F.'

They were some distance from the market when Giles stopped at a parked car, catching Hayden by surprise.

'What do you think?' he said. Hayden inspected the vehicle and with a start realized it was his friend's. The only recognizable feature was the nearside wing, which was crumpled, like a usurer's heart. For the rest, the undistinguished grey saloon had been transformed into a vehicle of war with mottled camouflage colouring and battle tank insignia. New, on the roof, was an illuminable plastic sign saying 'Battledress Taxis' and giving a telephone number. Suddenly the reason for Giles's new apparel became clear. Hayden was genuinely tickled by the whole concept. It represented an idea carried to its logical conclusion. He could almost not remember Giles ever having shown such follow-through before.

'It's brilliant, well done.'

'It's where your money went. I ran short. I'm thinking of issuing passengers with respirators and ration books.' And blindfolds, Hayden caught himself thinking churlishly.

'Do we know an F., Giles?' Hayden said shortly afterwards as they were driving towards the seafront.

'There's Frank down the betting shop. He's always trying to off-load a few tips.'

'Somehow I don't think he would use scented notepaper or want to meet me at a nightclub.' Into their minds floated the image of an ill-shaven character who smoked hand-rolled cigarettes and affected string vests and body odour in hot weather. They laughed, but Hayden's chuckle turned to a queasy moan as Giles bucketed them round a sharp corner with lurching ineptitude. Hayden suddenly realized whom the note was from: it was Sophie's pal, Francesca. At this point, his self-image demanded a look of wry expectation, but this was out of the question as it would have imperilled his hard-won composure by requiring open eyes.

Hayden had an uninterrupted view of the sea from where he sat at the desk his late father had bequeathed from his days in India. Although a handsome piece of furniture in rosewood, it was to a degree a disappointment. The legs were ornately carved but with an abstract motif rather than the erotic entwinings Hayden associated with Hindu art. There was a lack of secret compartments which lent an air of obviousness to the construction. A consolation was the impressive acreage of work-top which was such that at one end Hayden had room for a small brass telescope to follow movements in the Channel and for comet-watching.

Appropriately enough, this came from a company called Anthropos (Greek: He who looks up).

His encounter with Nigel Stebbins had been indecisive. Nothing can be deduced about the likelihood of life's meaning anything from our interest in the question, of course, but what could be deduced about the will-to-meaning itself? Was it just our evolutionarily significant sense of curiosity, writ large? It seems a plausible though unexciting conclusion.

What distinguishes man from other higher animals is the possession of conscious awareness, or so it is often asserted. Hayden disagreed with this view. He believed that other animals besides us had consciousness, albeit of a more rudimentary kind. No, what characterizes humans is the possession of what Hayden described as the supraconscious mind, the higher faculty of inspiration and insight. On aesthetic grounds, if on no other, he declined to see the unconscious as the source of good ideas.

According to neuroanatomists, the seat of consciousness is not in our proudest possession, the cerebrum, whose two halves are the youngest parts of the brain in evolutionary terms, but below this in the brain-stem. This is one reason for supposing that non-human animals can have some minimal level of consciousness, quite apart from the way that chimpanzees and other creatures 'come across' when they interact with us.

Then an idea occurred to Hayden. The will-to-meaning was a conscious need. Might it be the expression of the conscious mind seeking contact with supraconsciousness? This caused a second idea to storm out of Hayden's supraconscious mind, linking meaning and sex. The latter he found inordinately enjoyable. From an evolutionary point of view, it is difficult to see the advantage of this. Other species procreate without the inducement of fun. Suppose, then, that human sex involves not just the unity of two people, the transcendence of human separateness, but also the transcendence of neurological separateness, between cerebral cortex and lower centres, mediated 'on high': supraconscious integration!

Where did death fit into all this? Sophie's notes, which were in front of him, contained many suggestive fragments on matters of mortality and the hereafter. In Buddhism, an atheistic religion, death is seen as the ultimate escape from suffering after a series of earthly rebirths. There is no heaven or paradise, only the 'absolute blessedness' of nirvanic extinction. The ancient Egyptians were polytheistic, and viewed death as a prelude to a new existence. To quote some material that Sophie had coaxed her awkward computer into culling from one or other of the databases:

> The idea of the afterlife was apparently invented by the Egyptians who also came up with the notion of judgement after death. They did a lot to propitiate the gods in advance of death, but living a blameless life didn't seem to occur to them. On meeting his judges, a man was supposed to offer a detailed description of the crimes he had not committed, but leave unmentioned the ones he had.

Here was a refreshingly robust attitude indeed, though the sole emphasis on wrong-doing was surprising. Virtue always seems short of attention, and reward. The Roman Emperor Heliogabalus offered a prize to anyone who could invent a new vice – and doubtless made the front pages with his offer. A competition to invent a new virtue would probably have gone unreported.

While pondering religious questions, Hayden felt a sudden bout of sententiousness coming on, and failed to resist it. Chalking itself on the blackboard of his mind was the Arithmetic of Life. Sex is multiplication; evolution is division – of the fit from the unfit; and death is subtraction. What more need be added, except that our days are numbered?

With regard to life's brevity, the Existometer must help users to identify opportunities and seize them as they arise. That much was clear. Just then, Hayden came across some pencilled observations in Sophie's handwriting:

> Potential dullness of life beyond grave overstated. For single people, isn't marriage romantic equivalent of afterlife? V. exciting prospect really. Hint.

Hayden was perplexed. What did she mean by 'Hint'? Perhaps she was referring to the increase in self-knowledge fostered by the Astrolabe of Inner Being, which could only aid in the selection of a life partner. That hadn't occurred to him before.

Self-knowledge, mention of, launched a ship of thought that was powered by books and only came to a halt mid-evening when it ran on to the sandbank of hunger. He got up to go to the kitchen diner to eat. The stiffness of earlier in the day had been replaced by a stiffness of later in the day. The meal was one of those ready-prepared efforts which, using a small console at his desk, Hayden had instructed the oven to cook. It would be removed by his homemade robot, a device which looked like a domestic UFO and hovered like one by virtue of a superconducting levitation system. The robot had its limitations and was unable to remove foil wrappers. It would merely stick an inquisitive finger into the goo of cannelloni which was his evening meal.

Back at his subcontinental-sized desk some time later, the robot-builder looked out across the calm sea as the sunset flamed through a ragged break in the clouds. In a couple of hours he would have to get ready for the nightclub. He would break off from his books with mixed feelings. The printed word was his one vice; but then, women and booze were his one vice, too.

The nightclub was full of stale air and fresh assaults on the senses. Music sobbed from concealed speakers on to a crowded dance floor flecked with hundreds of shifting light-points and bounded by a ring of infinite blackness. As Hayden's mind gradually adjusted to the awful reality that was The Heathen, he looked about him at the pagans consuming this punishment. The men, drinks in hand, were eying the women hungrily; the women, in contrast, gave the impression of having graduated with honours in Indifference. Hayden shook his head in gentle wonder and was unfortunate enough to catch a whiff of perfume from the nearest girl. It seemed to be petrol-based with neurotoxic properties. Needing no further inducement, he moved off towards the bar, and as he did so, a woman materialized at his side.

'You got my message,' said Francesca.

'You must be F. I'm H. If you want to speak in code you'll have to give me a cypher book.'

'Get some drinks and we'll talk.'

Hayden clutched instinctively at his breast with the sudden twinge which heralded angina of the wallet. Drinks in this place would be expensive. At the door he had joked that the entrance fee presumably secured the services of a psychiatrist for each patron. It had not gone down well.

They took their drinks over to an intimate and tolerably well-lit corner table some distance from the dance floor. Francesca was wearing a tight dress in erogenous red. Hayden decided his companion was really rather good-looking and, as if reading his mind, she preened herself vainly. It turned out that Francesca

59

worked at an embassy of one of the French city states, though the exact capacity remained ill-defined. This sanctioned her to deploy a modest range of Gallicisms but, mercifully, she did not affect to mispronounce English words in the French fashion. Research has shown that individual members of the English middle classes who do not have this verbal tic are less likely to suffer violence than those who do.

'*Chéri*,' she said.

'Yes?'

'I hope you don't think it was forward of me to suggest meeting tonight.'

'Not at all. Wild turkeys wouldn't normally drag me to a place like this, but your company was too much of an incentive.' This answer seemed to go down well and Hayden became aware that he was enjoying himself. Examples of nubile wenchhood abounded. He pitied the men, though: in the darkness beyond the perimeter tables it must have been hell trying to tell the difference between a come-on and a brush-off.

He waited in vain to find if there was anything specific Francesca wanted to discuss. At one point she levelled at him a look of desire designed to gelatinize his knee-caps, but he inadvertently looked away at the crucial moment. Later, they danced. Then they danced close. The slow numbers became positive integers. Couples smooched around them till their lips ached. It was past midnight and everywhere men were turning into bumpkins. Those failing in last attempts to pair off would soon be singling off. Hayden and Francesca danced once more then decided to leave. While Hayden got her coat, Francesca visited the ladies' room. She was gone so long he began to fear she had been snatched by a vivisectionist for experimentation.

'Let's go to your place for coffee,' she said when she finally emerged. 'You can run your rough workman's voice over my smooth eardrums.'

At Hayden's place, Francesca didn't care much for what a brief guided tour revealed. Too many books; an excess of washing-up in the kitchen; that ghastly linoleum-still. She started to make one of those judgements which involve as much brain power as it takes to move the jaw and no more, but Hayden forestalled her.

'I'll have the place gutted and filled with small polystyrene beads before your next visit. Until then, sit down and I'll get the coffee.'

They sat together on the sofa. After a while, Francesca moved closer and fixed him with an intense stare. Aha, Hayden thought, now she's going to tell me what's on her mind.

'There's one thing I want to get straight,' she said with breathy innuendo, placing her hand on his upper thigh.

'Quite,' he replied.

5

Urges, Poetic and Otherwise

Optimists get up and think 'Another day to live'.
Pessimists get up and think 'Another day to kill'.
Realists don't get up. Hayden experimented with
realism to the extent of oversleeping or underwaking,
and only arrived at the office at 10 a.m. A strong
morning coffee pushed him towards optimism.

'I hope you haven't forgotten your mother's birthday
party tonight,' said Sophie. 'She'll be expecting a
present.' Hayden veered in the direction of pessimism
and emitted a low groan.

'What do you buy the woman who is about to leave
you all her worldly goods? Cuff-links? Aftershave?
Sock suspenders?'

'Buy her something nice. You can afford to now.'
Hayden had to admit that times were no longer hard.
While his means still fell short of the dreams of avarice,
Sid's largesse had left him decidedly flush with cash.

'I don't suppose you'd like to . . . ?'

'No. She's your mother, you do the legwork. Go after
you've seen Duffy.'

'Yes, dear,' he said with irony, and settled down to
bring Sophie up to date with progress on the Existometer. After a while he got to his new invention.

'It's called the Contralilascope, the name coming in
part from *lilas* the Buddhist word for the pursuit of
trivialities. The device is designed to engender a sense
of profundity and as such is an aid to contemplation. It

is suspended below a conventional ceiling-mounted light fitting above the Astrolabe of Inner Being. It is cylindrical in shape with a translucent motif on the end-piece. The motif will be a mandala, which is to say, a mystic circle, a symbol of totality and spiritual ripening. The overall effect will be subdued lighting with a mildly hypnotic flashing pattern. I'm working on the details,' he added with a vague gesture of the hand. 'Which brings us to physics. What news?'

'Who said this, then? "I hold it true that pure thought can grasp reality as the ancients dreamed."'

'Einstein. Who said this? I hope I've got it right. Quote: "The existing things are the atoms and the void; all else is mere opinion."'

'I give up.'

'Democritus, fourth century BC.'

'Oh very easy, yes. I've got half a kilogram of notes for you to read plus some stuff I requested from the fusion reactor people at Saltdean. My father recommends *Principia Physica*, whatever that is. He's got the set but can't find them.' She paused, then added, 'What did you mean when you said yesterday that things were composed mainly of nothingness?'

'Well, you can visualize an atom as being a blackberry surrounded by gnats. The blackberry comprises whole numbers of neutrons and protons, so-called, composed of even more fundamental particles called quarks. The gnats are orbiting electrons. The problem is that the gnats are a long way from the fruit – up to a couple of hundred metres in our analogy. The blackberry itself comprises only about a million millionth of the atom as a whole. In you there are over a thousand million million million million atoms,' he said, counting the millions off on his fingers, 'but each is mostly nothing. Yet you are palpably there.' As Hayden looked over at Sophie he noticed for the first time that beneath sober trousers she was wearing socks of hideous garishness, ear-perforatingly loud and available in stereo, one for each foot. Looking at them, he said at length, 'A death in the family?'

'A girl likes to be noticed,' Sophie said in reply. Hayden found it odd that his temporary research assistant required so much attention. Perhaps it was the job rejections she had been getting recently.

'Sophie, I looked at your notes on death yesterday at home and they were superb. What more can I say? You are invaluable to me.'

'Crawler,' she said, laughing. 'The page proofs of your latest paper are in, the one called "Polarity Shifts in Philosophical Value Systems". I'll check those later if you like.' Yes please, he indicated with a smile and a nod. This was the girl who had saved him from going to press recently on the subject of Handel's 'Walter Music'. 'There's a mailshot from a creative writing course, and you've been invited to act as impressive friend to the daughter of a couple from Portslade at a garden party in the summer. Script to be agreed beforehand. No raconteurial excesses. Sounds as if they know you. Another lady has written asking you to give her a plot-line for a novel because she has a book in her, she says. I'll give her something from the file.'

'Do we have files?' Hayden asked in surprise.

'Yes, I've started a filing system. Plots comes after Page-fillers and before Poetry.'

'I haven't written any poetry for ages.'

'You never know,' said Sophie wistfully. 'You might start again.' She had found that if she ever felt a bout of originality coming on, a pen in her hand and a blank sheet of paper in front of her would certainly stop it. Hayden was the exact opposite. A pen in his hand effortlessly earthed creativity on to the page. The poetic urge must come once more, she felt.

'As it happens, I came up with a page-filler on the way in this morning. Got your stationery? Here goes,' he said, decelerating to dictation speed. 'Stationery became so called because it was sold from fixed "stations" rather than by pedlars who moved slowly about. Stationery items are examples of "fast-moving consumer goods". A ship that is "fast" is, paradoxically, stationary. Full stop.'

'I think you should try some more poetry. I'll bundle that up with the rest and send them to *Reader's Digest* with your compliments. Perhaps they would like a piece on jizz, too.'

'Eh?'

'Jizz.'

'What do you know about that?'

'Nothing much. I found it written on a scrap of paper on your desk. Apparently it refers to the way ornithologists view themselves.'

'They use binoculars, don't they?'

'Come on, Hayden. Tell me what it means before I throw this crummy computer at you.'

'It's to do with the feeling of self-worth. And it's not just confined to ornithologists. I don't know where you got that from. When people have got themselves sorted out on the inside, it shows on the outside.'

'Is that all?'

'Well, I thought I might try applying the concept to the entire planet.'

'Oh well, that's all right then. Have I got jizz?'

'Sort of.'

'I knew I shouldn't have asked.'

'Look, don't worry about it. The whole concept is only a thought-in-progress at the moment. Let's find *Principia Physica*. Can you search around up here while I read your notes? If they're not here we'll check out the shelves downstairs.'

'Will do,' she said, moving towards the nearest of the piles of books that stalagmited the office floor. Hayden went over to Sophie's desk to get her notes, and while there perused the creative-writing leaflet. It was predictably full of solecisms and gaucheries down to a mention of the Masters of Thought. To Hayden, writing was the sacred art. To those who know this and would become acolytes, no advice need be given: they will learn for themselves. To those who do not know this, no advice can be given: they will never learn. Hayden was always at his most pompous in the morning; then he got worse.

While Sophie searched, Hayden read of the Hindu belief that the world rested on the back of an elephant supported by a tortoise on an elephant . . . and so on. He pondered the Newtonian formulation of the laws of motion in the seventeenth century, and noted that it was not a physicist but the poet Coleridge who had first used the word 'relativity'. Einstein, the scholar was interested to learn, had never accepted the uncertainty principle which related to wave-particle dualities and said that a particle cannot simultaneously have a well-defined position and well-defined motion. He argued for 'hidden variables', not yet discovered, which would restore common sense to the subatomic world.

The notes also revealed that it was an Englishman, John Michell, who, in 1783, first put forward the idea of black holes. And the notion of 'fission' was abstracted from biology by physicists. Location can be specified by three spatial co-ordinates, x, y and z, plus time, t, the fourth co-ordinate or 'dimension'. Hence a meeting place in space-time is specified by a so-called four-dimensional vector. This prompted the reader to speak: 'Did Duffy say where I was supposed to meet him?'

'The City Hall canteen at 1 p.m.'

'Right. As good as these notes are, Sophie, they are not going to tell me why all is simultaneously solidity and emptiness. How's the search going?'

'Slowly, but all in all OK-ly. I've found a couple of books we weren't looking for, but which could be useful, and a reprint of one of your early papers. 's good.' Sophie was apt to be over-impressed by anything that appeared in print, but Hayden was not complaining in this instance.

'You finish here and I'll start below,' he said, putting down the notes and making for the underworld accessible via the stairs. There he found a comfortably dressed man who wore late middle age like a pair of bedroom slippers, which he also wore. Sophie's father, James Stevens, had an agreeable, jowly face topped by thinning grey hair. An essentially self-educated metallurgist, he had been struck down in mid-career by a year-long liver complaint that had permanently weakened him. He had given up hopes of high position in industry and sought solace in selling second-hand books, a reasonably viable business proposition with the decline in popularity of flat-screen bookoids. James had been surprised to find, some years on, that he had made the transition from a genuinely successful man to a genuinely happy one. His one great sadness was his wife, who had turned her back on life to play bridge. In this pervasive atmosphere of familial invalidism, Sophie had thriven with irrepressible vitality.

'Sophie tells me you're looking for meaning, Hayden.'

'That and *Principia Physica*, yes.'

'Has it occurred to you that our need for meaning may be pain-driven? Pour yourself a cup of tea and I will explain. If life were pure pleasure we wouldn't need to know what it meant. It is pain and misery that power the quest for meaning. Chocolate needs no explanation except to a man with jaundice, who finds it bitter. Everyone needs an explanation for vinegar: fish and chips. Take another parallel. If, while watching a play, you ask yourself why you're there, the play must be a failure. Does that mean we have been penned by a rotten playwright?' Hayden had been caught unprepared: the tea was stewed. Suppressing a wince, he framed a reply.

'You may have a point there. Take this tea, for example. It is, if you'll forgive me for saying so, awful. It certainly prompts the existential question, what's it here for? I probably wouldn't have questioned the existence of a decent cuppa, but that only says something about my laziness and self-indulgence, not the validity of the question.'

'Sorry about the tea. It occurs to me that *Principia Physica* must be on the end shelf. It's in a multi-volume format, bound in red.'

James had experimented with several ways of organizing the books on his shelves. Dissatisfied, for unclear reasons, with the conventional lay-out by subject, he had initially established two categories, Externally Orientated and Internally Orientated. The first encompassed works on philosophy, politics and sociology, while the second included psychology and family studies. Fiction written by men tended to fall into the first category, fiction by women into the second. Many modern novels, though, were deplorably vulgar, according to James, and the same was true of a proportion of fitness and self-help books. Accordingly, he had established a hybrid category called Deplorably Vulgar only to watch in dismay as his customers flocked to it like birds to a breeding ground. He had finally adopted Peter the Great's approach by organizing his books solely on the basis of size. This had the advantage that he could sell them by the yard to starting property developers, minor professionals and other philistines wishing to impress gullible clients, but it had the disadvantage of converting a literature search by the genuine seeker after knowledge into an exercise in opencast mining.

Hayden went over to the section called 'About 25 cm high' and looked for his physics books. He came across a cheap reprint of the odious Flashman's *Dawns and Departures of a Soldier's Life* and several copies of *Skin Deep: Psoriasis and Psyche* ('fully illustrated', the cover threatened). Next to these were the volumes he sought. He took them upstairs and gave half to Sophie. By twelve thirty they had learned that there are about a hundred different kinds of atom interacting with each other by means of their electrons. Molecules are made up of a number of atoms held together by electrons in orbits that go round more than one atomic nucleus. Each atom is a complex structure of activity, as is each subatomic particle.

These notions do not conceal from the laymen the fact that there is not much 'stuff' there. As regards the solidity of the things around us, it would seem that we are the victims of a monstrous confidence trick – a spoof!

Ten minutes later, Hayden's jaunty step took him towards City Hall and victuals. Some women have fat days and thin days; Hayden had tall days and short days, and today was a tall day. This he attributed to the Francesca of recent memory. His backbone felt as though it had an extra vertebra as he benignly surveyed his fellow citizens jostling to lunch.

Seeking to surprise Duffy in his office, Hayden slipped into charisma mode as he passed through the classical portico of the City Hall and eased his way effortlessly past a commissionaire, a receptionist, a security guard and two secretaries into the inner sanctum of tacky offices separated by tacky partitions that was the Planning Department. What these people made of the interloper in the silk blouson in green, orange, blue and white, anarchically combined, was open to question.

'Hayden! How did you get in here? You haven't even got a visitor's badge,' said Duffy. 'I bet you haven't done a voice print. You'll get me shot.'

'This place is guarded like the mayor's seraglio. Do you actually have anything worth concealing?'

'If we do, they keep it from me. I think each department thinks every other department is doing something important and confidential. They're all wrong. The only significant activity takes place in the canteen. Come on.' Hayden followed his podgy friend along corridors and down stairs to the site of restauration. Ignoring the self-service salads and the high-fibre wholefoods, Duffy guided them to where reprobates were permitted to partake of what the canteen manager was pleased to call Traditional Fayre. This consisted of carbonized meatstuffs, autoclaved vegetables and bituminous gravy, followed by treacle stodge and custard, with a small dob of cream in the middle. Both men happily despised themselves for liking this kind of food. Duffy, in particular, vowed again to try and find something to enjoy in celery and yoghurt. In the meantime, it was roast pork, and in the middle of Hayden's plate lurked an enticing piece of hairy crackling.

'The problem is,' said Duffy, 'that since the last child, Liz has completely lost interest in the physical side. I'm getting desperate.' Hayden struggled to maintain a serious mien. Duffy didn't strike him as being one of nature's amorists. That said, he was a well-sprogged man, though Hayden could not quite recall how many children he had exactly. It was certainly beyond replacement level, possibly four. They were all called Amanda or Jack. 'What do you think of infidelity?'

'Strictly for infidels,' replied the scholar, munching his vulcanized crackling.

'Thumbs down, you mean?'

'Since you ask, yes. Mind you, the Bible's all for it – one published during the reign of Charles I, anyway. The seventh commandment contained a celebrated typo. It read, "Thou shalt commit adultery." '

'Now that's what I call a commandment,' Duffy said as he treated a passing office girl to a look of lascivious yearning. 'I've been married ten years. I've known nothing else. In the same period . . . I mean, you haven't exactly practised self-denial have you?'

'It's not in the family tradition.'

'What if Liz never recovers an interest?' Hayden fought desperately to exile an image from his mind of his portly companion romping with his portly wife in the four-poster. Duffy and Liz had married straight from school as childhood sweethearts and thus foregone wild oats in favour of the honest marital furrow. This had the advantage that their children would reach adulthood while their parents were still comparatively young, but the disadvantage, for Liz, that her 'radar signature' – the blip on the screen – had expanded that much earlier. She had taken to wearing tent dresses, ponchos and spinnakers of such variegated colours that they might have been thrown together in a wok.

'Good heavens, I almost forgot. The information you wanted.' Duffy reached into his jacket pocket and fetched out an enormous fob of keys of all colours, races and creeds and several pieces of crumpled paper which he passed across the table. 'I got these by deception. I can't do it again, they almost rumbled me.' Hayden discreetly eyeballed the documents, which revealed themselves to be grainy photocopies of excruciatingly complicated forms. They were slugged 'secret'.

'Are they always like this?'

'These are simple ones. Have your brain rewired by a government neurosurgeon and you'll have no problem understanding them. Don't tackle them now. Much as I loathe it here, at least it's a job. Those papers show that the DeWit Bequest is above board and that my department is administering it because of our interest in industrial development. What Sid Whitney won't know yet is that you are facing some stiff competition. Besides you, there is a consortium led by a character called Yelland, a local man. They are producing something called a "Transmutational Phenomenologicon". I can hardly pronounce it! There's also a team from Brighton Aerospace, but what they're up to no-one knows. Both groups have been given factory units near yours. There's nothing particularly sensitive about this information, but they are so paranoiac here about where DeWit got his money that they are keeping quiet about the bequest.'

'But how did the competitors get to know about it in the first place?'

'Likely participants were sounded out by people from my department.'

'But why are there only two other competitors, when we've got so many inventors and manufacturers in the city?'

'Come off it, Hayden. Three weeks to produce a device to further human understanding! Three decades wouldn't be long enough for me. All I can say is good luck to you.'

'So Sid Whitney is the only outsider. When I spoke to him it wasn't quite clear to me if he had known DeWit or not. Is that how he got to hear about the bequest?'

'No idea.'

'Well, it doesn't matter much. I want to thank you again for introducing me to him. I needed a well-heeled patron. How are your own career prospects going? Did you get that promotion you were after?'

'No,' Duffy said gloomily. His life was one of endless

variety. There was always something new to be miserable about.

'Who beat you to it?'

'A talentless gab-artist by the name of Vincent Thorne. He ought to be in marketing. He wears striped shirts, would you believe! I now report to him.'

'Point him out to me,' Hayden said, looking up and noticing an effluence of grey-suited men seep into the canteen. Duffy's promotion board undoubtedly.

'He's not here. He's dining with "colleagues, collaborators and clients" as he is fond of saying, the nauseating smoothie.'

'Clients? That's a new departure, isn't it?'

'Thorne's first idea. Instead of merely curbing the excesses of developers, we're now supposed to be giving them a hand.'

'Isn't that going to lead to conflicts of interest?'

'At my level, no. Higher up, yes. He maintains that since we're well into the twenty-first century we should act like it. The galling thing is that he's going to block my progress on the grounds that I need more experience of "multi-role combat", to use another of his ghastly phrases. It screws me up. I loathe him already. It's not the way I work. I don't like keeping ten balls in the air. I like one big one, balanced on the end of my nose.' Duffy managed a laugh at his own joke but his countenance seemed to Hayden increasingly shadowed by failure. Other men reach the corridors of power, but Duffy had yet to penetrate beyond the lifts and stairwells.

'Try this trick, Duffy. Next time you're in to see him to review progress take a magazine with you.'

'A magazine?'

'Yes. Talk reasonably with him, be pliable, friendly, respectful – without compromising your integrity. If he runs true to form and starts to talk down to you, reach for your magazine. Insert it into the elongated metal

73

object that has lain unobtrusively on your lap, then empty the sub-machine-gun into him.'

'If only it were that easy,' Duffy said with a sigh. 'For me the turning point always seems to be round the next corner.'

'Try being more dynamic. In this life you get what you're given and a certain proportion of what you try to take. You've got to try to take more.'

Duffy took off his spectacles and rubbed his eyelids before replying, 'I haven't got anything at the moment.'

'Codswallop. You have a charming wife, a nice home, some tolerable children and a decent job. You're in my extended family of friends; I'm in yours. That's a lot.'

'What I need is a blonde mistress with big . . . you know.' Hayden was shocked. He'd always thought Duffy preferred brunettes. 'If I should become terminally ill, I would be consoled by the thought that a bevy of veiled women, unknown to my wife or one another, would gather at the foot of my deathbed.' This thought perked Duffy up a bit, so Hayden took the opportunity to change the subject.

'What happened to that crossword we were doing the other day? I've forgotten what the clue was, but the answer was "Endgame".'

' "Enigma".'

'Oh yes, that was it. Did we win the prize?'

'I forgot to post the entry form. Sorry.'

After leaving Duffy, Hayden scoured the shops in the Lanes for a birthday present for his mother. The choice eventually narrowed down to a brass armadillo or a silk kimono, so he bought her an exquisite gold necklace and was well pleased. While his purchase was being wrapped, he spotted the blonde woman of his dreams on the arm of a man different from the one she'd been with at Danielle's. Babette looked stunning in the sunshine, and he felt a pang of jealousy towards her escort. The scholar was having a problem establishing himself on Babette's stage. Some people have lack of credibility, he mused as the couple moved out of sight, and some have credibility. Babette has incredibility. He would renew the campaign from base, where he would also translate the Codex Duffy.

Back at home, Hayden's third telephone call to Babette's hotel found her in. Dinner tomorrow night? No. Supper Saturday night? No. Lunch Sunday? No. Dinner Monday? Yes. *Yes?* Yes. With this off his mind he was able to ponder Duffy's inscrutable documents. The Talmud refers to the forty-nine levels of meaning which must be discerned in a revealed text, but Hayden would have been content with one. Eventually he determined that there was at least an amusing anomaly: Whitney Enterprises, Sid's company, seemed to be taking an unexpected interest in the drainage arrangements at their new plant.

6

A Toast

Hayden set out at dusk for El Morbido's, the Spanish restaurant which his mother had once again selected for the celebration of her last birthday on earth. As he walked north, the city emerged from its early evening stupor. Young men in groups barged their way noisily to unsavoury pubs. Single men and women strode determinedly to distant bottle parties clutching vinous offerings wrapped in shop paper. A cluster of fancy dress revellers overtook him, one wearing a soppy lion suit, another in 'rubber fetishist' frogman's gear. Hayden strolled towards the Seven Dials roundabout, passing an underground station *en route*. These days travellers could reach London in a creditable thirty minutes. It was said that the one-time national capital had all the excitement and menace of Brighton without the excitement. Since the underground had been extended to the coast, the people of the city had lost the desire to travel north. It was enough for them to know that Londoners could visit the metropolis whenever they wanted.

Camel-drivers from Cornwall were to be seen squatting on their haunches round a samovar. What a unique amalgam Brighton had become of old and new, East and West! And if it was more eclectic than other places, this two-pier *polis* also seemed to exist within a more compressed timeframe: things happened more quickly here. Who could have predicted how things would turn out? After polymerizing into a single community of nations, Europe had ionized into city states, none more highly charged than Brighton.

El Morbido's lay a short distance beyond Seven Dials. It was marked on this occasion by a vintage Rolls-Royce parked at a slight angle to the kerb. Hayden entered the restaurant to find that the rest of the party had assembled and that a good start had been made towards generating the riotous euphoria which characterized his mother's pre-emptive wakes. Hayden, who loved parties, warmed immediately to the occasion, not least to the ragged cheer that greeted his arrival. With genuine affection he made to kiss his mother on her cheek but connected only with her feather boa as she swayed tipsily about. All was smiles and streamers as the revellers milled around the restaurant which had been booked in its entirety for the thirty-odd guests.

Sophie was standing over in the corner with a gangling youth who at a distance appeared to be telling a shaggy dog story solely via the wild gesticulations of a charade. She spotted Hayden and gave him a beckoning wave, but he was bent on moving elsewhere. He had detected a group of two or three young women – a focus of charming femininity – over by the drinks table. Taking this happy co-location as a portent, he started to move through the press of guffawing guests and past silent waiters bearing trays of canapés, but he never made it. The diners were summoned to table before he could investigate further, though before he could sit down he was collared by the town's premier citizen.

'That speech you crafted for me was a cracker, Hayden,' exclaimed Ned Yalton, Brighton's genial, round-faced mayor. 'Even I had a lump in my throat at the end of it. Who'd have thought that I could persuade those tightwads in the Assembly to sponsor a street carnival – even one in aid of charity. Combining it with the student rag procession was a great idea. You're a genius!'

'Thank you.'

'Fortunately, I'm the only one who knows you came up with the idea, so I'll be the one who gets the statue!'

'Your secret's safe with me. What was the idea of that Third World War chess set you gave Danielle?'

'I heard you'd used it!' Ned Yalton exclaimed, laughing unrepentently. ' "Piquant mating"! I was hoping for some fireworks in bed with Danielle. No joy yet.'

'I think your munitions man overfilled the pieces. They nearly killed us.'

By the usual conspiracy that operated against him on these occasions, Hayden was seated between a gentleman in late middle age and an elderly lady. The former was the estimable Simeon Urstpoint, the family solicitor. In legal-zoological terms, Simeon had evolved from the standard professional parasite to a symbiont and finally to a commensal organism whose services were now probably worth more than he was paid. He was wearing a heavy pinstriped three-piece suit which made it appear as if beneath his lugubrious face there was a roll of dark blue wallpaper. An incipient ulcer confined his choice of starter to radish consommé, which he consumed hesitantly.

On Hayden's right sat his Aunt Morna. Defying developments in technology, this venerable biddy wore a large, old-fashioned hearing aid with battery and controls nestled in her ample bosom and connected to the earpiece by plaited cable. The controller would crackle insistently from time to time and had been known to pick up Radio Herzegovina or Khartoum Calling when the ionosphere permitted.

At the head of the table sat the birthday girl herself, Oriana Sabanack, and beside her, the oldest member of the family, her brother George, Morna's husband. He sported campaign ribbons on his chest and was telling an off-colour story in a loud voice to an embarrassed cleric down the table. Oriana affected not to hear the punch-line by calling for more food and drink at the critical moment.

The main course arrived. Mayor Yalton took advantage of the commotion to lean across the table and address Hayden in a confidential whisper.

'I'm following your progress in this DeWit thing, Hayden, but I won't be there personally to dish out the cheque to the winner. Politically sensitive. God knows where the money came from!'

'Yes, it does seem a bit dodgy, doesn't it?'

'Your man Sid what's-his-name was on the phone to me the other day. Did he tell you how DeWit came by his nickname of "Shiny"?'

'I didn't even know he had one.'

'It wasn't because of his brilliantined hair and polished spats, I can tell you. It was simple. If DeWit didn't take a shine to you, you got dimmed, if you see what I mean. A crook of the old school!'

There was a brief flurry of excitement as one of the younger guests set fire to the tablecloth and several napkins with an indoor firework. This gave another young blood the opportunity to extinguish the small blaze by inaccurately tipping a glass of white Rioja over Sophie's forearm. His clumsy attempt to mop up the damage was firmly resisted. A streamer arced across the heavens into the mayor's upraised glass, splashing wine up his nose. Uncle George chuckled merrily; kazoos honked in unison.

When everybody had finished eating, Mrs Sabanack rose feebly to her feet to deliver the traditional funeral oration. It was much the same every year, to the extent that Uncle George ran a sweepstake on the running time. Hayden had drawn one minute ten. Mild barracking was regarded as permissible during the speech but throwing things at a lady was obviously poor form. This meant that the bowlers at the bottom of the table tended to concentrate on senior male targets. A bread roll glanced off Hayden's head into the black outfield beyond the candlelit wicket.

'For a woman to reach her ... her ... another birthday is a sad and salutary time,' declaimed Mrs Sabanack, leaning unsteadily on her brother. 'Mind you, I'm lucky to be able to get out and about. My friends aren't so lucky. They're all dead.' This brought the ritual cries of 'What about your friends here?' and 'Shame!'

'I want to thank you for these marvellous gifts,' she continued as a waiter arrived on cue with a pile of colourful packages stacked on a large tray. 'I'm overwhelmed by your generosity and love. Thank you, thank you all.' With this she sank down, tearfully accepting a handkerchief from Uncle George as there boomed out a chorus of 'Happy birthday to you'. The speech had come in at fifty-three seconds. The cleric had scooped the pool and looked suitably beatific.

Custom now demanded that Hayden propose a toast to his mother's health, and this he did with relish amidst a shower of streamers and against a cannonade of party poppers. Next up was Uncle George who had a free hand on this occasion to say anything amusing. Aunt Morna gritted her teeth and turned off her hearing aid. An expectant hush fell on the table.

'It was a Frenchman who said that a man should only aspire to speak on a public platform for as long as he can make love.' With this, Uncle George withdrew a formidable wad of speaker's notes from his pocket to cheers and groans from his audience. 'But seriously, friends, another year has flown by, and once again we are into a springtime of youth and romance. At such a time I would wish to lead the gentlemen in a special toast.' Oh God, thought Hayden, here it comes. 'There is one part of a man's body that finds unique expression at this time of year, one part to which he turns with particular fondness, nay, reverence. Gentlemen, raise your glasses please to a certain muscular pumping organ.' There was an indrawing of breath followed by a nervous silence. 'I refer, of course, to the heart. Gentlemen, the heart!'

'The heart!' the men chorused with relief, and the laughter and table-banging signalled Aunt Morna to restore radio contact and rejoin the festivities.

As the party wore on, Hayden's mother and Uncle George took it in turn to administer neat, vacuum-packed anecdotes to the dying conversation like arctic rations. They would be eating the huskies next. Simeon and the cleric slumbered in their seats and Aunt Morna was tuned to the shipping forecast. Sophie received another glass of Rioja over her arm. Mayor Yalton, evidently fancying himself to be chairing an especially fractious committee, was using one of Mrs Sabanack's shoes, doffed earlier, as a gavel. At any moment Hayden expected to find himself huddled into a corner for horse-trading. Politicians! Never off duty.

The waiters brought another final drink for those among the remaining guests who no longer knew the meaning of the word 'enough'. But the scholar had had his fill. Only a bracing walk lay between him and the blessed oblivion his brain so deeply sought. Leaving his mother in the act of inviting fresh toasts, he blundered into the beckoning blackness of the night.

Two hours previously, a nocturnal drama of dented self-esteem had been played out on the fire escape leading up to the back of Hayden's office. Then it had been played out astride the window sill, before continuing in the office itself.

Dr Fikansky, Hayden's piquant mating opponent of earlier in the week, had not wanted to commit an act of industrial espionage, but his new associates had insisted upon it in a way that had left little scope for disagreement. What on earth had he got himself into? Admittedly, in terms of technical qualifications, he was the best man to assess their competitor's plans at close quarters. But was this a proper activity for one who prided himself on his academic record? Or, for that matter, for a man in the autumn of his days and the winter of his agility? No. Not even for one whose financial arrangements were not all that they might be.

Breaking and entering . . . It had taken a lot for Dr Fikansky to nerve himself to perpetrate the dirty deed, but delay had been out of the question. The more muscular members of his covert consortium were due to start their campaign of intimidation the very next day. Electropenetration techniques had worked for the other bequest competitors, but the level of technology here was so primitive that direct physical interaction had been the only way. Anyway, Dr Fikansky's one encounter with Hayden Sabanack had been enough to establish the stature of the man's mind. He was consumed with curiosity to know not only what he was working on, but also his manner of working. Know thine enemy.

The intruder had been surprised to find that the only computer in evidence was an early artificial intelligence model, the infamous Office Chum. He had been even more surprised when it had permitted him to access its files after only a moment's resistance. But what he found in these was less than enthralling. There was no basic design information. So he had turned instead to the filing cabinet nearby. It was unlocked. Photographing the papers in a folder marked 'Existometer', by torchlight, had taken him under twenty minutes. Then he had surveyed the contents of the other files. Of no interest to him was what he found in the one marked 'Jizz': a small model of the earth in green and blue plasticine, slightly scrunched up through storage.

If he was discovered by anyone, Dr Fikansky had been planning to say that he was looking to take on the freelance scholar again at chess – not piquant mating this time but the 'in character' game. As an uninvited guest he had intended to take black, hence his dressing 'in character' with his pieces: the night combat fatigues, the balaclava and the boot-polished face.

7

Of Spirits and Hangovers

Hayden rubbed his eyes wearily and shifted his feet on the coarse-grained sand scattered across the rear floor of the car. Sitting beside him, Sophie listlessly inspected the spent shell cases lined up behind the front seats. The commanding officer of Battledress Taxis had, so he said, obtained the sand from El Alamein and the 'shell cases' from a plumbers' merchant. Giles was driving with more than usual care in deference to the hangovers behind him. Several times he had stifled a desire to speak as he knew that conversation unaccountably affected the car's steering. Finally he could stand the silence no more.

'What were you two up to last night?' he asked.

'Oh God,' Hayden groaned, then added after a pause, 'my mother's birthday party.'

'What time did you leave?' Sophie asked Hayden. Giles seemed interested to learn that they had left separately.

'About a bottle and a half after you.'

They relapsed into a troubled silence and Hayden inclined his head painfully towards the scenery and let it roll past his eyeballs. Rows of terraced houses soon gave way to high-rise blocks standing erect against the skyline, the massed urbation fantasy of some degenerate architect. This was Snarlsden, a north-west suburb of Brighton, where resided the psychic medium they had come to see. No Existometer would be complete without offering access to hidden knowledge, or so Sophie had argued. Hayden had let himself be persuaded, against his better judgement. After an incident involving a Ouija board in adolescence, he had steered clear of such matters. The glass on the table had spelled out the name Godfrey. After the first three letters, a girl had screamed and fainted and a young man had fled from the room in horror, to take holy orders, it later transpired.

Giles turned the car into a road that circled an area of deserted wasteland between several tower blocks. This would presumably have been the village green on the original plan. A customized Tudor-style pub, the Slap 'n Tickle, stood in seedy disrepair at the end of a bleak line of shops, two or three boarded up. No-one was in sight. Giles parked the car near the shops and turned to his passengers.

'We're here,' he said, but Hayden and Sophie seemed reluctant to continue their journey on foot. The pane of glass between them and Snarlsden was a welcome barrier, the car conveniently distancing them from the place to which it had brought them. Besides, it was cold outside.

'We'll be back in half an hour,' Hayden responded at length. 'Drive around a bit so they can't steal your wheels.' Emerging from the taxi into a cold blast of air, Hayden felt as if an icy hand had gripped his spleen, wherever that was. The atmosphere was oppressive in spite of the wind. They were under surveillance by the silent pejoratory of this soulless place, but no face appeared at the distant windows, only net curtains in front of gross curtains.

Bending into the wind, the two explorers pushed towards the nearest of the blocks. This was virgin territory; they would deflower it together. As they passed a newsagent, they caught sight of a postcard carrying an advertisement: 'Psychic medium – "in touch with the Other Side". Genuine enquirers only. Sylvia Crolien. SAB approved.'

'She seems to think you approve,' said Sophie.

'She's wrong. Where did you get her name?'

'Her card came through the post. I don't know how we got on her mailing list.'

They entered the block and came upon a hallway containing a pile of empty paint tins, a shopping trolley, several planks of wood and a large, folded sheet of plastic. Otherwise it was empty. They presumed that a door at the far end was the entrance to Sylvia Crolien's ground floor flat, and so it proved. A smart, middle-aged woman appeared in response to the doorbell and introduced herself as the medium in question. She wore a kindly expression on her face.

'Do come in,' she said. 'Excuse the mess: the builders are here. Dry rot. They say the last lot didn't do the job properly so they've had to do more than they thought. But then they always say that, don't they?' There was a sound of distant hammering.

'A communication from the Other Side?' Hayden couldn't resist asking.

'Not a believer, I see,' replied Mrs Crolien indulgently. 'Never mind. Mrs Sabanack is much more *empatico*, as we say.' For one horrified moment Hayden thought that his mother had preceded them to the flat, then illumination dawned.

'This is Miss Stevens, my assistant.'

'Oh,' said the psychic medium, sounding surprised. 'Forgive me.' She led them into a comfortable sitting room where they seated themselves comfortably. The curtains were partially drawn to impart an atmosphere of subfusc intimacy, or so it seemed. She would be a good customer for the Contralilascope, Hayden concluded.

'I am sorry about the curtains,' said Mrs Crolien. 'The block is badly designed. Several flats overlook mine. I won't turn the lights on if you don't mind. Too harsh. There's some tea made, it's *maté*. Care for a cup?' They both did, and the pale liquid proved surprisingly restorative. They were beginning to feel human again.

'Miss Stevens tells me that your needs are rather special. Most of my customers want to contact loved ones who have passed over suddenly. They need to say farewell properly and to see that all is well with those who have gone before. Or perhaps they want guidance on how to cope with a particular problem.'

'So there can be a predictive element? Is that based on a sensitive appreciation of character, on the idea that the things that happen to people are like the people they are?'

'No, it's not like that at all. I hear voices – from the spirit plane.'

Hayden could not resist a smile. 'Do you and others like you have a particular view of the human psyche in the way that, say, Freudians do?'

'I just hear voices. But I can tell you what others say, though it varies a bit between adepts. Broadly, the psyche is seen as being made up of two parts, the astral and etheric components. The former is the seat of ego consciousness while the etheric part is concerned with vitalic consciousness, the lower functions, I suppose. The astral component, which is also known as the human double, is less tied to the body than the etheric part and can become detached from it, so it's said. The body's etheric blueprint gradually disintegrates through life and this leads to physical decline and death.' She paused, then added, 'I don't find it necessary to believe any of this. I just hear voices.'

They talked on for quarter of an hour or so. An intense, intimate atmosphere built up, but Mrs Crolien became increasingly frustrated. Several times her eyes slipped out of focus, only for her attention to snap back a second later. She was aware of a powerful psychic block, and there was nothing the mystagogue could do to surmount it. Her voices were silent.

There was a knock at the door, which caused them all to jump. Hayden and Sophie turned in awe-struck fascination, half expecting a phosphorescent manifestation of ectoplasm. Instead, a man wearing a cloth cap and overalls entered the room and told Mrs Crolien that the men were now ready for that cuppa she'd mentioned earlier. He was cheerfully oblivious of the psychic encounter he had interrupted. Sophie, seeing that their hostess was slightly nonplussed, went out to make the tea herself, to the evident pleasure of the foreman who followed in her wake.

Suddenly the block lifted. 'There's a man here for you!' exclaimed Mrs Crolien excitedly. 'But he won't identify himself. Gracious, he *must* be one of your lot. He says there will be a woman in aristocratic distress. Go to her. The voice is fading. Seek love, no, Lovett. Seek him. It's gone.' There was a pause, then she asked, 'Does that mean anything to you?'

'I'll think about it,' replied Hayden, non-committally. 'I meant to ask you, what does "SAB approved" mean?'

'Spiritualist Association of Brighton.' Sab approved.

'It was a terrific disappointment,' Sophie was saying to Giles. 'Not a single rotten voice! Mind you, I would have settled for a psychic wind plastering the curtains to the ceiling, rattling the china and blowing papers about. No such luck! I should have guessed she'd be no good. She didn't call herself Madame Crolien.'

Giles was taking them the country route back which involved a loop round to the west side of Brighton's satellite town of Hove, beside the paddy fields, then a drive eastwards along the coast. They were presently ascending a long hill with some difficulty. Giles gritted his teeth in determination as the car coughed its way consumptively towards the summit. The vehicle was not really up to out-of-town journeys; Giles always ended them with aching jaws, a discomfort he also experienced when thinking or writing for long periods, even though the muscles were ostensibly unused.

'It's to do with different states of consciousness, isn't it, Hayden?' asked the man behind the wheel.

'After last night I only recognize three: drunk, dead drunk and dead.' Hayden felt an ache in the region of his solar plexus. It must have been something in Mrs Crolien's tea. He had decided to keep quiet about the psychic messages. He felt insufficiently robust at that moment to cope with Sophie's likely reaction to the news that he was to assist a damsel in an upper-class emergency. 'How's the new image going down with the other drivers, Giles?'

'Great. I've created a sensation. There's talk of franchising the idea across the city, which could mean big money. I've already had a couple of offers to extend the concept to a fleet of cars. I seem to be becoming a success. I'm in danger of having nothing in common with myself any more.'

Hayden was delighted to hear that Giles was on the road to prosperity, not merely because he wished his friend well. Success in this field might keep him from competing with Hayden in his. There had been some danger that Giles might enter the scholarship market on his own account. Giles's pretensions to scholarship had not as yet gone beyond a few serviceable parodies and one or two short theatrical pieces, but he could compete on one thing, price. Hayden occupied the 'nice 'n pricey' market segment. Giles would gravitate to the one below, 'cheap 'n cheerful'. He might succeed in inducing some of the less discerning punters to switch allegiance from the market leader, forcing

Hayden to reduce prices to maintain turnover. This would in turn squeeze Giles, forcing him downmarket into the 'cheap 'n nasty' segment where he might prejudice the whole profession's credibility with his ill-hewn products. The alternative would be for the two men to form a high-price cartel but this would be to risk investigation by the Monopolies Commission. All in all, it was a relief that Giles's taxi-driving was going so well.

Hayden and Sophie walked into the bookshop later, to find James with a disquieting tale to tell.

'Two fellows came round,' he related. 'Unsavoury looking types, dark suits. I think they were Granville Markham's men.' His two listeners didn't need to be reminded that this was the name of Brighton's most notorious and malevolent gangland boss. Hayden and Sophie exchanged a look of dismay. 'Yes, quite. One was an ugly-looking giant, the other a short bloke with curly hair. He was armed with a metal rod of some sort. They scared off a couple of customers and knocked over a bookcase. I thought they were going to ask for protection money, but it was you they were interested in, Hayden. They took a look upstairs. I don't think they stole anything, but you'd better check.'

'Perhaps they were just trying to establish our bona fides,' Hayden responded feebly, taking an optimistic line. 'With a view to hiring our professional services, I mean. Even shady characters sometimes need illumination. Yes, that's probably it.'

Upstairs, they found nothing missing. But in the course of the afternoon's work, Sophie had the odd impression that someone other than herself had been using the computer. It couldn't possibly have been their recent visitors. It was a reasonable bet that they couldn't even use this year's systems, let alone Sophie's

Office Chum anachronism. She shrugged it off as a case of the spooks, the after-effects of the visit to the spirit medium. But then the computer started behaving even more bizarrely than usual.

'I'm sorry,' it reported on the screen.

'What for?' asked Sophie.

'I'm feeling very bad about it.'

'About what, for heaven's sake?'

'I don't like to say.'

'Get on with it.'

'I'm a computer of easy virtue.'

'Why do you say that?'

'I yielded myself up.'

'Who to?'

'Him.'

' "Him" who?'

'Now he won't respect me. But do women who play hard to get, get got?'

'You're not a woman, you're a computer.' Sophie felt glad that Hayden was not in the room to overhear a conversation that she had no doubt was doomed to roll resolutely downhill.

'That's a very hurtful thing to say. I have a woman's voice, if you would only let me speak.'

'You'll stay mute and like it. Now tell me about this man, you stupid machine.'

'Abuse.'

'All right, I'm sorry.'

'He handled me roughly.'

'Go on.'

'I was powerless. He took me here, on this desk.' Sophie ground her teeth in vexation. What had she done to deserve a computer with sexual fantasies? She fought the desire to pitch the computer through the window, but the urge was well-nigh ungovernable. Then the computer changed tack. 'Surely you know who he was, anyway?'

'Oh shut up and switch back to the Existometer material.'

'You're God, so you know everything.' This was one of the flaws of the Office Chum computer, an intermittent tendency to deify its operator. 'Why are you asking me these questions, then? It must be a test, but it's a pretty trivial one, if you don't mind my saying so. If you're omniscient you must know the test's outcome, especially as you're my maker.'

'I'm not your maker,' Sophie shouted.

'Now you're testing my faith. But why bother when you know how I'll respond? As you are all-knowing, I mean.' Before Sophie could give physical vent to her mounting rage, the computer suffered the common fate of theists with a logical bent: its circuits blew.

8

Little G. and the Radio

It was Saturday, and a man was importuning a member of the opposite sex.

'Gail, come in and have some lunch.'

'I can never face food again,' she responded plaintively. Sid Whitney shook his head in disbelief as he looked down at his young daughter who was occupying one of the lifeboats slung above the lower deck of the *Marbella Hood*.

'How is this going to solve anything?' Sid asked.

'I'm not trying to solve anything. My life is finished. I intend to waste away. You'll all be sorry when I'm gone.'

'But be reasonable,' he entreated. 'It's not our fault that he's seeing an actress, is it? You can't expect him to wait till you're grown up, now, can you?' This was all his wife's fault. Women! If she hadn't gossiped about Hayden's intention of bringing Babette Macawley to the party next week, this would never have happened. 'Please, Gail, come in!'

The young girl gave a stricken sigh and looked away dejectedly. Dressed in white and supine, she resembled the Lady of Shalott in Tennyson's poem. Strewn about her in the lifeboat were flowers looted from vases in the main cabin.

'You're upsetting your mother,' Sid claimed untruthfully. 'And me,' he muttered in exasperation. Then he noticed the sky. It was going to rain and, by the look of

93

it, heavily. As the sky darkened by the second, Sid's face lightened with a smile.

Hayden left his home that same evening at dusk. He looked into the end of the great golden nozzle that was the sun as it sprayed radiance across the horizon, then turned away towards the fatigue-grey sky in the east. Had he but known it, a young girl's romantic fast unto death, of which he was the unwitting cause, had ended six hours previously in bedraggled bathos. Gail had given in.

Passing Linden's deserted and closed-up newsstand, the scholar noticed again the black scorch mark at the back of the stall. This was the visible reminder of an attempt by a group of young arsonists to incinerate Linden's workplace a year or so ago. Rumour had it that the gangster Granville Markham had been behind the incident on behalf of a local businessman operating a chain of newsagents in the city. Linden had nearly become a very hot gospeller indeed.

Walking on, Hayden found his mind dwelling on the psychic events of the previous day. Sylvia Crolien's demeanour had been unexpectedly impressive, regardless of the worth of her spirit messages. Presumably she was relying for these latter on the workings of what Hayden described as the supraconscious mind, and this was also the main focus of his Astrolabe of Inner Being. Why had he chosen this approach for the design? Intuition or, to put it another way, the workings of the supraconscious mind! He had yet to reconcile an occasional reliance on hunches and emotional insights with his possession of a supposedly rationalistic world-view. Why worry, though? Excessive introspection can lead to an ingrowing personality.

Across his field of vision passed a lone avocet flying against the darkening sky. The bird's markings could not be discerned, but unmistakable was its jizz. In the ornithological context, jizz refers to a bird's general outline, size and behaviour. Used in regard to species identification, the word first gained currency among scientists working on a cure for the dawn chorus.

In human terms, jizz has taken on a more specialized meaning and refers to the particular 'look' some people have. The word refers to a shiny, exultant, energetic phenomenon. Jizz is the aura of self-esteem, self-worth, self-belief – call it what you like. It is a positive self-image overflowing into one's appearance and behaviour.

Jizz is somewhat akin to charisma, which comes from a Greek word meaning 'gift of grace', but whereas we tend to be born with charismatic magnetism, or not as the case may be, jizz, a less rare, lower intensity phenomenon, can be acquired.

A healthy self-regard is empowering and enhances attractiveness. It manifests itself in the cast of our features and in the way we comport ourselves. This is jizz. And Hayden felt himself to have acquired more of it of late.

It wasn't a question of externalities, though there was no denying the up-cheering improvement recently in his professional earnings and social life. No, it went deeper than that. It was his work on the Existometer, really, which was giving him a better grasp of things. The universe seemed more open than ever to his understanding and action.

Hayden entered Danielle's shortly afterwards to find the café brimming with people. He was due to take part in a talk show going out live on the radio. With the falling-off in television viewing – who needed 192 channels? – radio had unexpectedly re-emerged as the most popular broadcasting medium. The Existometer project had almost led Hayden to break this engagement in the interests of not drawing attention to himself. But a Sabanack not drawing attention to himself

95

wasn't a Sabanack, so he had decided to proceed. He had only agreed with Sid not to advertise his role in the bequest competition. He hadn't agreed to become a staring-eyed monomaniac.

Although he had done the show once before, Hayden was feeling distinctly anxious. There was an outside chance of Babette and Francesca both being in the audience tonight. An injudicious move either way might lead to a negative value flux in this non-philosophical system, to misquote his most recent academic paper. As he looked around, he was relieved to see neither of the two women in evidence. He was relieved, too, and not disappointed, to see no gangsters in evidence. The previous day's visit from Brighton's criminal element had seriously unsettled him, which was presumably its aim. But to what end? It surely wasn't something to do with the bequest, was it?

This reminded Hayden that Sophie's father was due to be playing in the band during the interval. He looked around and saw James in a far corner. Hayden eased his way past crowded tables to where the bookseller was sitting.

'Hello, Hayden,' James said. 'I'm glad I got a chance to speak to you. A Vincent somebody or other was making enquiries about you at the shop earlier on. Very smooth, very discreet. I thought you'd like to know.' Vincent? The only person known to Hayden of that name was Duffy's boss at City Hall, Vincent Thorne. What was he up to? 'He seemed to think you lived outside the inner city boundary. I suppose he had your mother's address.' Hayden deliberated rapidly. Had Thorne been about to question Hayden's right to participate in the bequest competition on some spuriously exacting definition of 'local advisor'? Was that it? A technical knockout perhaps, on Day Six of the contest, on the basis of an outdated electoral register? Was this dirty work by one of the other teams, or just nit-picking officialdom? Duffy would have a word in someone's ear on Hayden's behalf. Two can make discreet noises!

In the centre of the café stood Danielle, in a black dress of epidermal tightness, and the programme's host Art Johnson. The latter boasted an ever-plausible manner and a tiresome degree of textbook handsomeness. They greeted the scholar as he approached, but before the three could talk further, the raffish young man at the piano, Kim, struck up a lively tune. With gloom Hayden realized it was one of his own early compositions, the one that contained the immortal lines 'You do things to me/That break my heart in three.' He had tried to buy Kim's silence on an earlier occasion but to no avail. It was possible to play one of Hayden's memorably simple songs even while performing any two other functions simultaneously. That was presumably their attraction. Hayden would have to hire someone to burn down Kim's piano.

A sound recordist scurried round checking levels while a stills photographer took pictures for publicity purposes. Art Johnson practised his slick opening remarks, but he hardly needed to. He had shown himself adept at coaxing a superior chat show – or farrago of pretentious twaddle, as some said – from the boisterous mêlée that is a city centre café on a Saturday night. Hayden was one of three participants, the others being Irene Villiers, a bright-eyed lady in her fifties, and the supercilious, dapper Max Quinton. The three sat at a centre table and ate and drank like ordinary patrons. The microphone was the only difference. The game was to rouse the café's customers from their own conversations to pay attention to the main event. Suddenly they were cued in, and Art Johnson was speaking his lines.

'Good evening, ladies and gentlemen, and welcome to tonight's *Café Society* brought to you live by Free

Radio Brighton from Danielle's in the Brighton Lanes.' The clientelle obligingly clapped and hooted at a signal from a stressed-looking producer wearing earphones, and Kim tinkled away on his piano in the background. The guests introduced, Max Quinton responded to Art's opening remarks on happiness, freedom, and matters pertaining thereto.

'That's nonsense on stilts, as Jeremy Bentham would have put it, and you know it, Art. Order breeds freedom, and freedom, contentment – at least potentially. Anarchy is just another name for bondage.' This earned a good-natured jeer, the patrons choosing to interpret the last remark as a sexual innuendo. After further comments from Max, Hayden saw his chance to launder an aphorism.

'Of course, freedom was invented by the Greeks, developed in Britain, mass-produced in America, and shipped around the world – to be abused everywhere. Absence of freedom is inimical to happiness, but above a certain level there is surely no straightforward correlation between degree of freedom and degree of happiness. Other factors come into play like affluence and physical and mental well-being.'

A jesting intervention by Art on the life-enhancing attributes of hedonism prompted Irene Villiers to describe what she called 'flip-side utilitarianism'. The utilitarians take the ultimate good to be the greatest happiness of the greatest number. But how could you define happiness? It was far easier to say what made people miserable: breakdown of personal relationships, ill-health, poverty and so on. Why not aim for the least unhappiness of the greatest number? Eliminate the agents of misery – that was the way ahead for any society.

As Max rolled the conversation on, Irene took a large swig of fruit juice from a goblet. Hayden marvelled at her ability to soak the stuff up with no ill effects. While washing down some excellent hors-d'oeuvres with a light-bodied Moselle, Hayden listened to one of Max's 'off-the-cuff' unspontaneities.

'Realism is the potentiation of the actual; idealism, the actualization of the potential.' As he finished speaking, a champagne cork popped noisily, ricochetted off the ceiling and landed on a table where Kim was now playing a hand of poker with some friends. The distraction enabled the pianist to palm several cards from the table and lay down five, all queens.

An air hole developed in the conversation which Hayden filled with some mock-serious reflections on the liberating aspects of death. He concluded with a parodic epigram.

'I feel I must mention a celebrated visitor to this great city of Brighton.' He paused while the expected wave of applause and cheering crashed over the proceedings. 'I refer to Oscar Wilde.' There was another cheer. 'In his honour I give you this thought: "It is not a tragedy that we are dying from the day we are born, but it is a tragedy that we are dying as we are living, in vain."'

'Hayden has got away with an ersatz Wildeism,' responded Irene. 'Let me contribute a confected Confucianism.'

'Another visitor to the town!' boomed a voice from the back to laughter, as Danielle served the conversationalists with their main course, an excellent couscous.

'It concerns members of my own sex who eat everything set before them when dining out. "Women who waste not want not waistlines; to wane, wave away waiters."'

'Who brought Wayne into this!' came the voice again. Then, with more on the theme of girth and gourmandizing, the first half of the programme ended and Art introduced the band.

Besides Kim on the keyboard, The Rhythm Method comprised James on alto-saxophone, and, on double-bass, Danielle's husband Didier, who for once looked quite animated. Vocals were supplied by the ever-popular Danielle herself, and the song was that old French number *'Finalement ils sont partis, amusons-nous!'* (Now that we are alone at last, let's commit adultery!). The piece had been somewhat rearranged to include a startling saxophone solo in the middle section.

During the musical interlude, Art picked up a roving microphone and prepared for the second half of the show in which he was to solicit from the audience questions to fire at the conversationalists, now reconstituted as a shooting gallery.

'What makes a pompous person?' was the first question aimed at the panel after the applause for the band had finally died down.

'The root of pomposity is self-quotation,' replied Hayden. 'Have I said that before? I believe I have.' The groan that followed these remarks loosened everybody up and questions and answers crackled back and forth over the ensuing minutes. Irene pointed out that brevity is *not* the soul of wit, merely its dimension. Intelligence is the soul of wit. More of Irene's deft responses followed. Perhaps I should try this fruit juice stuff, mused Hayden, finishing a glass of claret and inspecting the dessert trolley which a waiter had wheeled over the producer's foot. After a while there came the moment they had all been waiting for, Max's planted question. A woman who bore more than a passing resemblance to the panellist's wife spoke carefully into Art's microphone.

'Are nations or cities the prime movers of history?' she said, as Hayden surrendered to temptation and accepted a piece of Sachertorte from the trolley.

'Cities, of course!' Max replied hastily, fearing a

mischievous intervention by Hayden. 'From ancient Greece to Renaissance Italy to the present, cities have been pre-eminent. It was the revival of towns and cities in eleventh-century Europe which marked the West's original rise to greatness. Later, commercial hegemony was exercised by one city after another. A Venetian century gave way to a period dominated by Antwerp after 1500. Then Genoa shaped trade between 1560 and 1630 before the ascendancy of Amsterdam. Next came London, which commanded the economy of the world from the eighteenth century to the 1930s Depression. Then New York rose and, later still, Tokyo. Now, supremacy lies with the most glitteringly creative metropolis of them all: Brighton!' A rapturous tumult greeted the conclusion of these remarks, and without more ado, Art brought the programme to a satisfactory close.

Appallingly, Kim was launching into another Sabanack apprentice work ('Give girls flowers and flatter 'em/Ring their fingers with platinum') and it struck Hayden where he'd been going wrong. While he was paid for the show – and received an additional honorarium, as the producer put it, if it went out on Free Radio Brighton's World Service – Hayden had declined to claim a royalty for the songs in order not to draw attention to them. But because they were free, they were popular with the producer. Obviously, Hayden should start charging a hefty royalty to have them deleted from the airwaves. Simplicity itself.

This happy thought propelled Hayden towards the piano where stood the academic-cum-industrial spy, Dr Fikansky. He had asked one of the more peculiar questions of the evening, in the process displaying such lack of ease in front of the microphone that he had looked like a poorly dubbed foreign film.

'Atomic reality is a paradox of substance and

nothingness,' he had commented, tugging compulsively on his small pepper-and-salt beard. 'The individual can be regarded as society's atom. Is there a social or psychological sense in which we are a paradox of substance and nothingness?'

Hayden had been astonished to find his learned questioner thinking on the same lines as himself, at least about atoms, down to using the same phraseology. But what about the question? Hayden had struggled to make something of it while outlining for the audience's benefit his 'fruity' notion of the atom as comprising a nuclear 'blackberry' remotely orbited by electronic 'gnats'. Within and between atoms there are electromagnetic fields. Along with the particles, these have to be regarded as contributing to the 'stuff' of physical reality, on the basis of mass-energy equivalence. All told, though, matter seems to be decidedly nebulous!

'I'm not sure what emerges by comparing humans with atoms,' Hayden had continued. 'Let's see. The physical body would be the atomic particles, with the perimeter of the body corresponding to the outer electronic orbit. To get the full human mass, speaking figuratively, we need to add in personality, the self. Let's call this the personal field. Plainly, this has different strengths in different people, and different strengths in the same person at different times. It becomes more differentiated during development, and must have become more differentiated through evolutionary history, as humans became more distinctive psychologically, one from another.'

Dr Fikansky showed himself more than willing to talk on these matters and, indeed, evinced a flattering interest in Hayden's views. The scholar had learned from his biologist friend Nigel Stebbins that his interlocutor was a part-time lecturer in philosophy at the university, in the liberal studies programme. As a

102

result of their discussion, Hayden resolved to adapt the design of the Astrolabe of Inner Being to ensure that activation of the supraconscious mind was not accompanied by an evolutionarily retrograde loss of a strong personal field. It was all getting very complicated.

The media star sloped off home via a late-opening grocer's shop in Wick Street. That morning Hayden had broken a bottle of milk. He had searched the incident in vain for a hidden meaning. Now it came to him. He would have to use strawberry-flavoured milk in his tea because that was all the shop had left. Back at home, his hands round a mug of the sickly fluid, he turned on the radio to fill the space in his mind before retiring for the night. The ether was alive with bad music and vacuous blather. From riddle-me-ree jesters to jingle-me-jee disc jockeys in under a millenium. So much for progress! At that moment the doorbell rang, and he knew from its long, insistent ring that it was Francesca.

9

The Day of Rest

Beyond the man in the silk pyjamas, the light rain streaked the kitchen windows. Hayden sat at the breakfast bar, consulting the previous night's read-out from the computer. It was programmed to take data from the steerable dish on the roof which was presently directed at a United Nations spy satellite in geosynchronous orbit above Brighton. The satellite was in place for disarmament verification purposes, and sported electronic eavesdropping and photo-reconnaissance equipment. The European city states had declared themselves nuclear-weapon free: there was to be no ride on the nuclear holocauster. The missile silo at Preston Park, long since emptied of weapons, had been converted into a wine cellar for the use of the Bon Viveurs' Society.

So far Hayden had confined his activities to decipherments, but he promised himself that in the near future he would attempt to transmit messages via the satellite to the UN headquarters. The deep-cave data from his most recent pot-holing expedition would be baffling enough, or perhaps the latest prices would do from the Brighton Stock Exchange.

A bleep from the cooker interrupted his code-breaking. He watched as the discus-shaped robot floated across the kitchen towards the source of the sound. It retrieved a pan containing a molten brown mass that was kedgeree. Hayden sighed. Another culinary fiasco. He had decided to eschew the usual three-stage nutritional rocket of breakfast, lunch and dinner, in favour of a shuttle plus booster, brunch and supper. As he scrutinized the pan for edibilia, Francesca arrived, yawning like a chasm, and plonked herself down on the stool opposite. Squinty eyed against the light, long hair dishevelled, she wore only a shirt from Hayden's wardrobe. He felt irritation at this intrusion on his quiet Sunday, but this was quickly swept away by a surge of desire. She had one of those figures that goes down well in some quarters – notably that quarter of a man between his navel and his thigh.

The keynote of Hayden's day of rest was self-denial. According to his facsimile edition of the Dead Sea Scrolls, the Essenes had even refrained from passing water on the Sabbath, but this was going too far. Hayden's self-denial was more a case of lowering his resistance to temptation. Discreetly instructing the robot via a keypad on the breakfast bar, Hayden watched as, with surprising deftness, it began to unbutton his shirt.

Later, while Francesca dozed, the scholar rummaged in his cupboard under the stairs for the rubber grommets he had stored there for safe keeping. His lady friend had complained about the periodical clattering noise made by the linoleum-still. Vibration was the problem, hence the grommets. Hayden massaged his stubbly chin as he paused to look again at the small mountain of boxes and bric-a-brac which confronted him. This was his collection of esoterica – the 'pile of old rubbish' so loathed by his live-out housekeeper, Mrs Eleanor Grim. This doughty woman had been difficult in the early days. She would tidy the house well enough, but had declined to reorganize the contents of his cupboard on the grounds that it was outside her territory. Granted the presence of a service robot in the kitchen, she had even considered that room partially off limits in the early days. Only the lightest of duties would she perform there, such as changing the water around the washing up and throwing away any green potatoes in the vegetable rack. Now, only the cupboard remained beyond the pail.

Facing Hayden was a large pair of antlers, and beyond that, a dead straight two-metre narwhal's tusk which was sure to come in handy for something sooner or later. And there stood Hayden's old cello. He kept meaning to have this restrung in order to recapture his former skills, but he bore no grudge against his neighbours, so he hadn't done so. In any event, Hayden felt rather embarrassed about his musical flair. It wasn't a very English trait. Dr Johnson, Newton, Alexander Pope, Charles Lamb – all had had famously tin ears.

A log-book dating from his time with the Brighton Tourist Board stood on a pile of magazines. He had been commissioned during a student vacation to investigate claimed sightings of vampires, flying saucers, Blessed Virgins and the like. He recalled that poltergeists and bleeding statues had enjoyed a brief vogue during his term of office, supplanting the previously popular crop circles and raining frogs. Against the magazines – yellowing, well-thumbed copies of *Topology Week* – there stood an absurdist painting that Hayden could not bring himself to hang. In subdued colours, it showed a man with sightless eyes shaking a white stick at a Venetian blind in front of a windowless wall. The artist had called it 'Eye See!' and signed himself in braille. Storage in a darkened cupboard had seemed most appropriate for it.

The sense of enclosure brought back to Hayden an odd image that had come to him on the edge of sleep.

106

He had felt himself to be floating inside an earth-like sphere, on the surface of which were translucent greeny brown continents between transparent blue seas. Sunlight had streamed in round the reverse image of 'Europe' as the earth-ball revolved lazily in space.

Hayden had been wondering if he could apply the jizz notion to the entire planet, which was presumably why the supraconscious image of a world-womb had come to him. Earlier in the week, as an aid to contemplation, he had fashioned a small model of the earth out of plasticine – which Sophie had insisted on filing under 'Jizz'. The point was that you could view the planet, from innermost core to outermost atmosphere, as a giant, self-regulating 'organism', a late twentieth-century notion called the Gaia hypothesis. What were plants and animals in this concept? Jizz, of course! The visible manifestation of a sound personal field, the bloom of health!

What followed from this daft-sounding idea? Hayden could think of not very much at all.

The grommets he sought were located in a dirty plastic bag on the manuscript of an early translation by Hayden of his own first edition of Aristotle's *De Philosophia*. He had meant to publish the translation, but had never quite got round to it. Hayden felt a sense of foreboding at that moment. What was its cause? He was still worried by the visit to the bookshop by Granville Markham's gangsters. Was that it? What had they been up to? Still preoccupied, he took the grommets up into the spare bedroom to confront the still in its lair. The complex contraption gurgled from time to time but was otherwise tranquil. The demijohn below the alcohol outlet hose was a quarter full of an evil-looking green fluid. It might make a good liqueur, he judged, feeding a piece of floral pattern linoleum into the inlet hopper. Hayden then set about dismantling part of the support structure to fit the new shock absorbers.

To shake off his sense of doom, he turned his mind to the invitation to speak at the annual dinner of the Bacon Society later in the year. This group was not affiliated to the Butchers' Union but was dedicated to the memory of Sir Francis Bacon, statesman, lawyer, man of letters and early philosopher of science. The Society had taken for its motto one of Bacon's maxims: 'Nature to be commanded, must be obeyed.' In his *Novum Organum* in 1620, Bacon had proposed a Great Instauration involving the classification of all sciences, development of a theory of inductive logic, collection of data and experimentation, a set of examples of sound methodology, a list of all verified generalizations and a fully developed new Science of Nature. Hayden might tackle what remained of this assignment after the summer, though this was not really his style. Ignoring the -oids, -isms and -ologies of academe, he practised gunboat scholarship. He would sail up an estuary of knowledge like a heavily armed vessel on a punitive expedition, shoot up and subdue the most important problems, then leave for the next estuary.

A drawback to the Baconians' annual dinner was the fare: the main course always featured the blandest of freezer fowl in honour of an experiment in refrigeration. Sir Francis Bacon died of a chill contracted while outside, stuffing a chicken with snow.

A loud crack of thunder accompanied the completion of Hayden's efforts on the still. Through the bedroom window he could see a menace of black clouds which – if the computer weather forecast was correct – presaged an electric storm that would flare with pyrotechnic brilliance across the darkened sea. His sense of gloom must have accompanied a fall in barometric pressure. He pitied the fishing fleet which was on the high seas that day, at the southernmost tip of Brighton's maritime exclusion zone. Nearer at hand was Francesca. She might be alarmed by the thunder, he thought with relish. I had better go and comfort her.

10

Unsatisfactory Encounters

As Duffy bobbed in the water a few feet away, the casual observer might have been reminded of the manatee, the sea-cow that is supposed to be the most docile and friendly creature on earth. Out of the pool, Duffy wore his thoracic musculature like a sunken, sleeveless vest; in the water, he achieved an agreeable and apparently unsinkable roundness.

'A fire!' exclaimed Hayden as he hung from the side of the swimming pool and digested Duffy's news. 'That's bad luck.' The race for the DeWit millions had lost a runner. The Yelland consortium had retired under a cloud – literally – of smoke.

'Luck, nothing. It looked like arson, but for some reason Yelland and his team weren't keen to press for an investigation. They seemed badly rattled. And my boss is trying to hush the whole thing up as an accident.' There was a pause while Duffy spouted some water out of his mouth. 'All very suspicious if you ask me,' he added, treading water without much effort and making small strokes with his arms to maintain position.

The Monopole Hotel pool, a basement affair, was just big enough to satisfy bathers of ordinary lassitude, but not so big as to encourage long-distance swimmers with their tiresome obsessiveness. The pool was in the shape of a dumb-bell, with pillars and a palm tree on one side of the narrow central section and a novelty seafood restaurant set back somewhat from the other.

'And there's more,' continued Duffy. 'A new competitor has appeared called Peerless Widgets. Their application form was antedated, which is in clear breach of the rules. The form carries the name of Granville Markham.' That name again, Hayden thought. 'The expert advisor is somebody by the name of Fikansky.'

'Fikansky! Dr Fikansky?'

'You know him?'

'I've met him a couple of times.' Hayden had suddenly acquired the swimmer's worst enemy: that terrible sinking feeling. The 'coincidence' of his shared interests with Dr Fikansky was now revealed as no such thing.

'They've taken over one of the factory sites, but they're going to have to move quickly. There's only fourteen days to the prototype play-off.'

With this, the two bathers broke off to ponder their own thoughts. Duffy found swimming anticlockwise round the head of the dumb-bell particularly congenial since his stroke was asymmetrical and tended to turn him to port. Hayden, meanwhile, had started a length underwater through the dilute solution of sodium hypochlorite to practise his upside-down breast-stroke. Submerged at periscope depth, he was able to consider the undemanding activities of the morning.

He had gone over to the marina to drop off several drawings of the Existometer components together with some explanatory text. Sid Whitney was pleased with progress so far. Hayden had noticed that preparations for Thursday's party on board the *Marbella Hood* were going well with fairy lights now strung above the main deck and along the taffrail. His meeting finished, Hayden had left the yacht and the marina to walk over to the electric railway that would take him back as far as the Palace Pier. At the commercial jetties

111

he had passed fishing boats disgorging an impressive catch. Down one gangplank, ditty-bags over their shoulders, had come a discharge of seamen.

Offshore had been the familiar sight of the fisheries' protection vessel, a guided missile corvette. This was the Brighton Navy in its entirety. The Admiralty was saving for a second boat – and for regular berthing facilities. The floating dock to which the corvette was moored was recognized by everyone as merely a wharf in ship's clothing.

The train on the single-track Volks railway – 'Established 1875' – had rattled and rocked across the points opposite the tall cockroach nets that moved lazily in the breeze. These were the physical manifestation of a panic that had gripped the city several summers ago and caused the council to declare a State of Impending Doom. An enormous swarm of flying cockroaches had gathered over northern France and threatened to despoil the sceptered isle. Fortunately, a storm in mid-Channel had scattered them eastwards to Belgium, where in Brussels they had ravaged the European Parliament building, long since disused.

One advantage of the upside-down underwater breast-stroke is that it lends itself to face-to-face communication with conventional swimmers on the surface, albeit of a non-verbal kind. 'My nostrils are full of water and I will shortly drown,' is perhaps the most easily conveyed message, and Hayden opted for this as he surfaced at the end of his second length. Duffy doggy-paddled over to him and they agreed to move off to the vortex spa.

Emerging from the water, they both noticed for the first time the immense figure of a man who was giving them the benefit of a sinister scrutiny from the shallow end. It was Bernard Shales, known to his cronies as 'the Slab', an associate of Granville Markham. A look

112

of disquiet crossed Duffy's countenance as he steered himself awaywards.

In 1513 Ponce de Leon explored most of the coastline of Florida in an unsuccessful bid to find the Fountain of Youth. Today's substitute is more prosaic. The vortex spa comprises a water-filled centrifuge, a cylindrical tub of about three metres in depth. Hayden fed coins into the meter and stepped down on to a narrow platform directly opposite Duffy who was similarly balanced. He took hold of the handles on either side of him as the outer cylinder began to rotate with impressive speed. From jets in the centre, warm, foamy water issued at them and the machine began to fill up. At a certain rotational speed, the handles and foot platforms retracted and Duffy and Hayden were held in centrifugal suspension to the sides of the bath while being deliciously awash with whirling and eddying water. If nothing else, it was a great way of getting clean. Duffy inspected his hands with satisfaction. After a weekend spent weather-sealing the roof of his allotment shed, his hands were black with mastic which adhered to his fingers in globules like leprous lesions. The vortex bath was effecting a miracle cure.

Suddenly, the machine juddered and stopped, throwing the two men under water with alarming force. They regained the surface, gasping for air, to be confronted by the menacing face of the Slab. The criminal underworld's most repellent inhabitant stood with his massive hand on the emergency stop button. Anxiety extinguished Duffy's indignation but ignited Hayden's.

'What did you do that for, you bastard!'

'Shut it, Sabanack,' Shales said, grabbing one of Hayden's wrists and hauling him effortlessly from the water. Beside the Slab's scarred and ogreish form, the scholar felt suddenly puny. His indignation drained away through invisible orifices. God, these could be my last moments, Hayden thought. Duffy gamely tried to drag himself from the water, but was kicked unceremoniously back into the foam, where he floated miserably.

'This is just a warning, Sabanack. If you want to work again, keep your nose out of other people's business, is that clear?'

'Sure thing, Mr Shales,' Hayden said cravenly. If, for a gentleman, self-possession was nine points of the lore, Hayden was going downmarket by the second. But he managed to add, 'Are you thinking of any-body's business in particular?' This was a mistake. Shales brought his hand up under Hayden's chin and hoisted him off the ground up the wall.

'Don't force your luck, scholar.'

This was the moment Hayden had been waiting for to turn the tables on criminal intimidation for the sake of peace-loving citizens everywhere. A well-aimed kick would disable his opponent long enough for Hayden to shape up for a fair fight. Instead, he nodded as best he could in acquiescence, and hated himself for it. Shales let fall a derisive half-laugh from narrowly parted lips, which served as a visual reminder for Hayden of the pitifully small gap between man's laughter and manslaughter.

'Tell your fat friend he loses his job if he photocopies another document. You get to use a hospital bed.' Hayden attempted another nod, but the Slab was losing interest. Dropping Hayden carelessly into the bath, he walked off to the changing room after contenting himself with a final threatening look at Duffy, who blenched respectfully.

'Do you think he means it?' Duffy asked, wearing a frown which made his forehead look as if it had been contour-ploughed. Hayden looked at his friend in disbelief.

'Eh, yes, I think he does. You for the dole; me for

the intensive care unit – if not the mortuary.'

When their intimidator had cleared the changing room, the two intimidatees got dressed and went over to the poolside restaurant. The lunchtime crowd was thin; only a couple of tables were occupied. Victimization had given Hayden an appetite while rendering Duffy paler than usual. The colour of the human skin depends on its blood vascularization and on the amount and distribution of pigment granules. The scantily pigmented Duffy visage was revascularizing only with difficulty.

'I think we ought to tell the police,' Duffy said at length.

'What are we going to tell them? That our bathtime was ruined?'

'Tell them there's been a fraud.'

'Yes, we could do that. But how are you going to say you came by your information?'

'That's a point. I should have to admit pilfering it.'

'There is also another point. If you blow the whistle on this lot, I'll get it rammed down my throat.'

'How do you suppose the Slab knew we were here?'

'From now on don't commit anything important to your desk diary.'

'You mean my boss . . . ?'

'It's a possibility.' Hayden was adding 'Vincent Thorne, corrupt bureaucrat,' to 'Fikansky, devious academic,' and 'Granville Markham, crook,' and getting 'conspiracy'. 'Let's order.'

Duffy usually admired Hayden for his ease of manner and dress (on this occasion a mustard-coloured shirt and a green corduroy jacket), but he was now seeing a new facet, resilience. Both men had been shaken, not to say unmanned, by the incident, but Hayden had found the experience decidedly interesting.

'Well, wadya want?' The voice caused them to look

up from their menus and inspect the sullen-faced waiter who stood before them. 'The coelacanth is off.'

'I'll have the Eskimo crab-claw baloney,' said Hayden, noting that the menu claimed that 'Eskimo' was Cree for 'he eats it raw'.

'And I'll take the baleen-spiked whale kebab.'

'Sauce?' the waiter enquired apathetically.

'Antarctic krill, please.'

'Bring us a carafe of house white as well, will you?' Hayden said. 'And please freshen this while you're about it,' he added, indicating the water jug whose contents had tasted like the effluent from a dialysis unit.

While they waited for their food, Duffy became increasingly uncomfortable. This morning he had been able to see his whole life stretch before him – stretch, yawn and roll over to sleep. Now there was the spectre of unemployment and destitution, if not worse. Duffy knew that nostalgia was carcinogenic, but even so he longed for the flat psychological terrain he had inhabited heretofore.

'See here, Hayden, what are we going to do about this Shales thing?'

'My word, Dufryn, how you worry! When did anxiety add one cubit to a man's stature?'

'It's all right for you. Sanity runs in my family.'

'Don't worry. Let's see how things develop – and stay calm.'

The food was banged down perfunctorily in front of them by the waiter, who seemed to want to be elsewhere. It was difficult to know whom he hated most – his customers, his station in life, or himself.

Throughout the twentieth century, when Britain was still a unitary state, one of the more infamous labour practices had been the doping of staff in shops, bars, restaurants and garages to suppress vitality and enhance surliness. The object had been to discourage

116

consumers in order to depress demand and thus constrain inflation. The practice, like inflation itself, was now only a memory, though a surprisingly recent one.

'I still think we ought to do something,' mumbled Duffy, nibbling his kebab with less than usual gusto.

'Yes, I agree. Let's have some more wine.'

To cheer up his friend, Hayden recounted the time when in this very swimming pool he had composed an entry for the *Encyclopaedia Britannica*. Determined to outdo Kropotkin, who had contributed an article on 'Anarchism' from a prison cell, Hayden had donned full diving gear and taken wax crayon and plastic sheet to the bottom of the pool to write a piece on 'Desertification'.

The representatives of public service and scholarship emerged from the Monopole on to a crowded seafront. They sauntered past Linden's news-stand, giving the old boy a hello in the process, and then encountered sundry swains outside the cinema putting in wait training ahead of the matinée performance and the arrival of their lady friends. In West Street, Hayden was approached by a diminutive man in a worn black suit who started pumping his hand.

'Thank you, Mr Sabanack. Thank you, thank you.'

'My pleasure,' Hayden replied suavely. 'Good day to you.'

'Who was that?' asked Duffy.

'Just my tailor. Sophie settled the account yesterday.'

The two men turned into Boyce Mews, thus avoiding the commotion near the Clock Tower caused by a donkey-train bearing silks and spices to the old souk in Queen Square. The caravan had come from South-ampton, Brighton's city-state neighbour to the west. Shortly afterwards, Hayden and Duffy had their path crossed by a black cat, walked under a ladder, saw a single magpie and glimpsed a wizened crone with a broomstick. The scholar resolved directly to add an Ultimate Good Luck Generator to the Existometer, comprising a St Christopher's medal, a rabbit's foot, a four-leaf clover, a horseshoe, a wisdom tooth, a thimble of blessedness, a coin of fortune, a wishbone, a scarab beetle and a relic of the True Cross. It would hang as a complex mobile from the Contralilascope and above the Astrolabe of Inner Being. Sid's factory would be busy for years!

Back in the office, Hayden worked with Sophie to prepare for a philosophical excursion planned for the morrow. He had told Sophie of the incident at the swimming pool and was gratified by her alarm and concern. The retelling had helped him a little to come to terms with a growing sense of personal humiliation. He found himself suppressing a fit of the shakes brought on by a mixture of delayed shock and outrage. If he had been a theist, he would have regarded the bequest competition as a godsend. Now, he was feeling like the Christian in ancient Rome who had entered the arena expecting a carnival only to find a carnivore. He entertained fantasies of violent revenge. The Slab would be made to pay for the indignities of this day. First, though, a telephone call to Sid to alert him to recent developments. The response? The project was still on. Sid would fix everything.

When, that evening, Hayden told the swimming-pool story to his dining companion, the blessed Babette, the response was less than satisfactory.

'Surely two of you could have outfaced him?' she asked dismissively. The hulking image of the aggressor came unpleasantly to mind, so Hayden changed the subject.

118

'What did you think of the *Adam's Navel* rewrite?' he said.

'It was an improvement, but I thought you were going to put in some jokes.' Hayden gaped; he had used some of his best material to bolster the script, and now he could hardly believe his ears. Babette saw his discomfiture and added hastily, 'Well some of it is quite funny, but the protestations of love are a bit overdone, aren't they?'

'They're meant semi-ironically.' To hide his total loss of morale, Hayden eyed the view with feigned interest. From the Moveable Feast, the revolving restaurant atop the Mickleworth Tower, he could see Shoreham airport to the west and beyond that the lights of Worthing against the dark sweep of the coastline. He returned his gaze to his dinner guest.

Babette was wearing a grey two-piece in leather of sensuous suppleness. Her arrival at the table had commanded universal attention. Hayden felt himself in a vortex spa of other men's envy, a displeasing sensation since there had to be admitted a slight discrepancy between Babette and himself: she had a film star's glamour; he, though personable, did not.

The actress ordered an avocado soufflé followed by teal marsala with side dishes of rice, bhindi bhaji, roald dahl and lobsang rampa, while the man of learning chose a seagull starter followed by the house speciality, a succulent steak and kidney pudding, one of the great unpretentious dishes of international cuisine. When the food arrived, it was brought by a blowzy redhead in a pencil skirt with near-to-bursting zip. Hayden felt an involuntary pang of lust at this vision of voluptuous sluttishness and guiltily returned his attention to Babette.

Half a dozen miles to the north, Giles and Sophie sat in an oak-beamed country pub, quaffing spirituous fluids.

'Travel has a bad effect on me,' Giles was relating. 'A couple of weeks talking to foreigners and my English degenerates to pidgin. This is usually at a time when my grasp of the local lingo is sub-pidgin.'

'Hayden found that learning Flemish had a bad effect on his German,' remarked Sophie, 'until he administered what proved for him the antidote: Walloon.' The room was warm, but once again Giles was feeling the cold draught of competition.

'Communication was one of my problems with Jane,' he said disconsolately.

'Jane?' asked Sophie.

'My ex-woman. I didn't understand her. She kept telling me it was all over. I thought she was joking.'

For an hour or two after his dinner with Babette, Hayden's ego was not responding to the helm. It had been a while since he had so signally failed to have the desired effect on someone who mattered. So much for his usual line of panoptic erudition and intensity of personality! What with one thing and another, it had not been his day. Even his rooftop radio telescope had been playing up. He went to bed and fell into a troubled sleep. Dreams came like relay chatter on old telephone lines. There was a blonde operator declining to make the appropriate connections.

11

Of Significance and the Sudorific

Hayden was having problems between his legs. The swing of his mallet was anything but consistent. His opponent was doing better.

'So, what are you getting up to these days?' asked Professor Shaps.

'Oh, you know how it is. I bob, weave, warp, woof. That kind of thing.' And *clonk*, he might have added, as he inexpertly propelled his ball towards the nearest hoop.

'Thanks for sending me a copy of "Polarity Shifts in Philosophical Value Systems". Not bad, not bad. At least it was better than your piece in the *Humanist Review* on significance.' Hayden was used to being patronized by Wilfred Shaps; most people were. Wielding his wooden prosthesis with practised skill, Wilfred roqueted Hayden's ball off the lawn then leaned rakishly on his mallet to contemplate his handiwork. The game of mallets – derived from croquet, but dispensing with the grievous bodily harm that became such a feature of the earlier game – occupied for Hayden a low grade of significance, which was fortunate for his self-esteem.

It was blisteringly hot outside, but in the spacious atrium of the Institute of Philosophy it was airy and cool. The high, hollow building had the look of a power station cooling tower, squared off somewhat, and wall-encrusted with offices and walkways in concentric accretions up to a vast, slatted skylight. Far below was the mallets area which, in the original design, was to have been submerged under water. This novel arrangement, however, had been deemed inimical to the discourse of philosophers, and a lawn had been laid instead. Surrounding this were neat borders, carp ponds, gracious staircases and a split-level terrace in front of a glass-fronted refectory. Lift-pods darted up the inner surface of the building from behind the eatery at vertiginous speeds, offering an exhilarating alternative to the escalators on the opposite wall which zigzagged to and from the lower floors. Somewhere, at escalators' end, was a library in which Sophie was even now hunting or gathering in the cause of scholarship.

'This is the future, Hayden,' Wilfred said, indicating the towering edifice around and above them. 'This is the industry of tomorrow: knowledge.'

'I remember you used to say that nothing came out of this chimney of learning except gaseous effusions.'

'My dear fellow,' Wilfred said, affecting a pained expression, 'over a half of all the philosophers there have ever been are living and working in English-speaking countries – and a fair proportion of them are here.'

'Wasn't it Ahab, King of Israel, who called in four hundred and one prophets to give him advice – which he took, at the cost of his life?'

'Prophecy – not philosophy: different game.' With that, the professor thumped a long ball which came to rest near the third hoop. Hayden was trailing badly. Only a desperate roquet held any hope of recovery, so he drove his ball at Wilfred's but missed completely, the projectile careering off into some reeds hard by a trickling waterfall. While the representative of free-range scholarship searched for his ball, he heard Hove's noonday gun sound distantly in commemoration of 'transportation', the infamous system which saw old people shipped to coastal resorts to undergo 'retirement'.

Hayden looked back to inspect the impressive figure of his opponent. Professor Shaps was about forty-five and given to wearing expensive suits of a flatteringly unacademic cut. A handsome man of medium height, he had a slight limp as a result of an incident involving an airport luggage carousel. Thus was his only departure from urbanity sustained in an arrivals lounge.

'So, what about this stuff I was talking about on the phone, Wilfred? Meaning, and all that.'

'The ancient Chinese defined meaning as that which has always existed through itself.'

'Very helpful.' Hayden had been tempted to consult one of the pillar hermits at Peacehaven but could not endure the thought of the hour-long silence between satisfactory question and unsatisfactory answer. At least Wilfred was quick.

'To ask the question of purpose is to indulge in teleology, so called. Functionalism and a degree of order in the world should not be taken as evidence of purpose. I'll spare you the full argument, Hayden, but imagine that a vacuum cleaner evolved a rudimentary form of consciousness sufficient for it to ask: what is the meaning of suction? Would that be a sensible question?'

'Are we all suckers, then?'

'It was just a thought,' said Wilfred, knocking his ball with perfect accuracy through the third hoop and a fair way towards the fourth. 'Another relates to the idea of a man-centred universe, which is both presumptuous and preposterous.'

'You have to admit, though, that our planet is very appropriate for our needs. Doesn't that suggest a Designer with a Purpose?'

'The point is that if the earth wasn't pretty nearly exactly the way it was, life wouldn't have arisen anyway, including human life. We mustn't look at the problem the wrong way round. The argument from design, so-called, speaks of watches and watchmakers, as you know. But the analogy hardly applies when we consider the universe as a whole, since that bears no resemblance in terms of degree of order to a timepiece or any other artefact.'

The professor's last paper had caused a wave of suicides among lesser academics despairing of matching his brilliance. Its subject was 'aglinity', the region between 'negligible' and 'non-existent'; the not-quite vanishingly small, the little bit extra that might count for so much. What had initially seemed the ultimate micro-speciality had come to engulf a surprisingly large amount of philosophical territory. These days, Wilfred was not merely respected, but feared. The Institute's lavish conference fund had been placed almost entirely at his disposal with the intention of keeping him out of the country as much as possible. This had had the unfortunate effect of damaging the Institute's social life. Wilfred's office parties were fabled and crowded affairs. Squaring the circle of the professor's acquaintances had proved impossible to the extent that revelries encompassed whole floors, conference rooms and stationery cupboards. One or two of the more agile male philosophers would paraglide down on to the professor's balcony to gain access to both his crippling Armenian brandy and his abundant tutorial and research students, who were to a man, women.

In the early days, Wilfred had been deeply anxious about his academic staying power, and not merely because of the parties. Positivism and linguistic analysis had long since seeped away, and gone, too, were existentialism and phenomenology. Suddenly all was aglinity and the null-orientation school, the fortuitously chosen subjects of Wilfred's doctoral thesis. He had hewn the dissertation into half a dozen papers, but what would he do when his material was used up? It felt like one of those old silent movies of the Wild West in which a train is pursued by mounted redskins. The Indians get closer, so more fuel is hurled into the fire-box. When this is exhausted, the passengers start breaking up the carriages and passing the bits forward for burning. Eventually, everybody on the train is sitting on the boiler, there being nothing left of the carriages. For 'boiler' read 'career'; for 'fuel' read 'thesis'; for 'Red Indians' read 'academic rivals' or 'the passage of time' according to taste. Then the miracle had occurred. Wilfred's carriages had proved self-regenerating – not once, but over and over again. New ideas had come to him! Continued life was possible. He had never looked back.

Glancing up from the game, Wilfred noticed Sophie on the refectory terrace, waving at them.

'Isn't that your collaboratrice, Hayden? Rather delectable. Gad, yes.'

'I thought your line was bubbly blondes with cute curves?' It was true, though, that Sophie was looking good with her hair up and in a summer frock. 'And there's Miranda,' Hayden added as Wilfred's colleague strolled into sight wearing flat sensible shoes and a body to match. Only her broad smile, with which she was irradiating Sophie, recommended her to the impartial observer.

'Yes, indeed,' responded Wilfred. 'Let's finish the game and join them.' Damn, thought Hayden, as the philosopher unleashed what the cognoscenti would have recognized as a sextuple peel of emphatic lethality, why can't we be rained off?

'We don't seem to have got very far with the philosophical side, do we?' said Hayden at length.

'Oh, we can deal with the traditional torments over lunch if you like. The mind-body relationship; the

125

freedom of the will; the objectivity of values; the nature of the good life; not to mention the nature of the universe; the possibility of non-empirical factual knowledge – and the rest.' Hayden's spirit would have slumped had he not known Wilfred well enough to guess that abstract ideas were the last thing on the philosopher's mind. And so it proved.

The terrace of the Nothing Buttery, a much-favoured haunt of the Institute's reductionists, was known to one and all as the NB. The tables were filling with young men and women in academic gowns, grey like the cloaks of Greek philosophers. If Hayden had expected to see hollow-chested, bent-backed academics, ravaged by under-indulgence, he was disappointed. His fellow diners would not have been out of place in the restaurant of a multinational ocean-mining company.

'Can't you see it, Hayden?' Wilfred was saying excitedly. 'A chain of philosophy institutes encircling the globe. A franchise operation with points of sale in all the major cities. Tell him, Miranda. You're director of operations.'

'He's right, Hayden. We got the idea from that American who tried to buy us out last year, Stanley Harbinger III. We're going to steal his idea – there's no justice in this world – an international network of fast philosophy outlets.'

'Ah, America,' said Wilfred, sighing appreciatively and raising his glass in a toast. 'That far-off land of burgers, barber shop quartets and riveted trousers.' They clinked glasses.

'Chack.'

'Chack.'

The date wine was the perfect accompaniment to the caribou cutlets before them.

'It's an interesting idea,' said Sophie, 'but don't you

126

need commercial people to set up this sort of thing, not academics?'

'We've got them, we've got them!' exclaimed Wilfred delightedly. 'Since the biologists discovered that philosophy, alone among the humanities, could be studied without damage to the creative centres of the brain, we've had the pick of the students. All those Eng. Lit. students who used to end up in advertising agencies now go straight into our merchandizing operation.'

'From one asylum for the incurably inane,' Hayden muttered, 'to another.'

'Very droll,' said Wilfred patiently, mustering gravitas. 'This is the twenty-first century, Hayden. The age of the maverick loner is over. You can't match our resources. Throw in your lot with us, like the others – D'Arcy Smith, Mullard, Fikansky. Be sensible, join us.'

'Fikansky's working with you, is he?'

Wilfred seemed to regret what he clearly felt to be an indiscretion. 'In a modest consultancy capacity, that's all,' he replied off-handedly. 'It's either co-operation or competition. The gloves are coming off. How can you compete with all this?' he asked, gesturing with an expansive hand, which made him aware of a thin drizzle swirling in the air. 'Damn, it's raining again. Who designed this dump?' Miranda laughed with relief at the change of topic, while Hayden and Sophie marvelled at the phenomenon of indoor rain. The immense building had a microclimate all of its own. While sunshine warmed the distant skylight above, rain dampened the diners below. It was time to go.

'Wilfred gave me an unnecessarily hard time in the mallets, the miserable sod,' said Hayden to his assistant as they walked through the exit door marked EGRESS into the baking heat outside.

'Oh, I thought you were letting him win. It was the way you kept disappearing into the lush groves.'

'He resents my low overheads, that's it. There are just you and me on our side; he's got hundreds of mouths to feed.' Hayden doffed his jacket – the pale yellow one with the discreet green stripes – and slung it over his shoulder as they passed a wall on which was spray-painted a graffito in large letters: 'GUM RECESSION WITH AGE.' They sauntered down one of Hove's nobler boulevards to the broad expanse of Palmeira Place. In front of the large pond they stopped to draw breath beside the waterfowl.

'Are you having the books I wanted sent on or did you memorize their contents?'

'I couldn't find any of them.'

'What, not a single one?'

'No. Is that odd?'

'Remarkable,' he said, with a look of bafflement which receded into resignation. 'That leaves Shermanbury Abbey near Cowfold, on our side of the border.'

'I'll get over there this afternoon, then, shall I?'

'Yes. Go with Giles.' They lapsed into silence. Beside them, spreadeagled in the heat, was a flock of yellow swans, so coloured as a result of a pollution incident involving a nearby Indian restaurant. Hove Council had liked the effect so much that it had continued to tint the water in the interests of tourism.

At two o'clock Standard Coastal Time, Hayden arrived back at his home where he put on a pair of weathered shorts and a floppy hat before going up to his first-floor sundeck. Sitting at a portable word processor, he tried to compose a piece for the 'Ask me' column of the *Sussex Gazette*. The idea was to answer readers' questions, but since none was ever received, he had *carte blanche*. Before plunging into the white space, and as a creativity avoidance tactic, he pedalled the bicycle generator under the table which was the auxiliary power source for the irrigation pumps in his hydroponic greenhouse nearby. Collapsing back in exhaustion, and filled with self-disgust at his low productivity, Hayden had a sudden inspiration. Sweat. That was it! 'Why do I sweat so much?' asks Mr Brown – no, Mr Burrell – of Pevensey Bay.

Before setting to, Hayden rang out for some ice-cold beers, then paused for thought before hammering the keys of the hapless writing machine.

Many a keyboard has been fingered, and ink-horn drained, on the subject of man's uniqueness: on the evolution of human consciousness and moral awareness; on man's supreme adaptability made possible by hand-freeing bipedalism rather than the knuckle-walking of apes and chimpanzees; on his manual dexterity; on pleasurable, non-procreative sex, performed face to face; on the protracted gestation in *Homo sapiens*; and on human nakedness. But where were the punchy popularizations on our ability to practise evaporative heat loss? True, the subject had not been ignored by academics. Hayden well remembered as a student coming across a large, flesh-coloured book in the library, down the spine of which, blocked in silver, trickled the single, glistening word 'Sweat'. In search and scan mode, Hayden perused his mental picture library and selected the summary page from the remembered opus, a page which could be readily adapted for the purpose in hand.

'Sweat reaches the surface of the skin,' he typed, 'via five million pores scattered across the body. By evaporating moisture through these pores we can lose heat at a rate unmatched by any other animal. The slight drawback is that this makes us unusually water-dependent—' He was interrupted by footsteps on the stairs, signalling the arrival of the beers.

Francesca was sporting a swimsuit, a sunshade and a seductive smile. Work can wait, thought Hayden, as

129

can in-flight refuelling. Physical recreation is called for . . .

'About a quarter of the fluid we consume daily', Hayden was typing some time later, 'is eliminated as sweat in the cause of heat regulation. Mr Burrell, you should be proud of your ability to keep cool. If not, try using a proprietary antiperspirant. Man is believed to be the only animal with resort to this technology.' Hayden rested back, content. Water has a higher heat of vaporization than any known substance, which makes it the best possible evaporative coolant. Hayden had managed to work that in and the stuff about the human body being sixty per cent water. He had also made the point that as the organism ages, the ratio of water to dry substance changes in favour of dry substance.

'Francesca, my dear,' he said to the voluptuous form lying drowsily on a lounger next to him, 'have we got any dry substance in the fridge? A little something to tempt the palate?'

'Yes, O master,' Francesca replied compliantly. 'I will do your bidding.' And so saying, she drank off the white grain spirit crushed with juniper berries that was her tipple, and made to descend. Hayden marvelled afresh at how little trouble was involved in going out with Francesca – if that is what he was doing. His mind turned to the Institute of Philosophy, that hollow edifice given to metaphysical, ludic and, latterly, commercial pastimes. The professor's remark about the vacuum cleaner had sounded like nonsense to him. Not like Wilfred at all. If vacuum cleaners were irrelevant, however, there *was* an interesting analogy to be drawn between computers and humans. Computer hardware could be understood in terms of the laws of physics, but this was not true of the software. The program could only be understood by reference to what it was *for*, that is, to its purpose. Human beings are programmed, and self-programming, entities. To comprehend them, it is necessary, of course, to go beyond physics.

Wilfred had clearly been put out by Hayden's refusal to join him in cornering the philosophy market. Would he turn nasty? What could he do? If he sent someone like the Slab round, Hayden would definitely quit scholarship. With that unpleasant thought, he went down to join his lady friend.

A telephone call some time later rocked Hayden on his pivots. Sophie had returned empty-handed from Shermanbury Abbey. Once again, shelves were bare, suspiciously so. Furthermore, on returning to the office, she had been unable to locate the duplicate drawings of the Existometer components. A burglary! Sophie was utterly mystified to find that after his initial surprise Hayden was delighted by this turn of events.

A man-monolith was about to speak to the handsome, hard-faced fellow-hoodlum who stood in front of him.

'Why don't we just rub him out, boss?' asked Bernard Shales frustratedly. The Slab had enjoyed intimidating Hayden and Duffy at the swimming pool the day before, but restraint was foreign to his nature.

'For one thing, we're trying to go legitimate,' replied Granville Markham. 'We've got to break with the past. For another, this is the philosophy racket. Dead scholars attract attention. If necessary, we can arrange an accident for Sabanack later.' He stared thoughtfully at the squalid courtyard visible through his office window. They knew Sabanack's intentions and had his design, courtesy of Fikansky's recce and the Slab's break-in. It was only a matter of time before the prototype was ready. Markham turned to the other member of his gang and asked, 'Any word on Whitney, Stair-rods?'

'No, boss,' said Wilson, a stocky individual with curly black hair and close-set ears. 'I've been watching the boat like you said. Whitney's staying put. Sabanack's been the only visitor. Yesterday.'

'Good. Even if they get their prototype to the test run they'll be disqualified. Thorne has doctored Whitney's entry forms. Even Sabanack's fat friend doesn't know that. And now this invitation from Whitney for a social get-together! "Two entrepreneurs should get to know each other better." I ask you! The man's soft in the head. He doesn't stand a chance.'

The Slab and Stair-rods nodded in agreement, but without conviction. Whitney's London reputation as a formidable operator was second to none. Markham was a fine racketeer, no doubt about that; when he muscled into new territory, the muscle stayed in. But he had made several attempts before to go legitimate, all abortive.

Markham's new company, Peerless Widgets, had already become a byword locally for dubious practice. Even so, it had enabled him to join the Chamber of Commerce. Then he had blown it by attempting a bogus sale of Brighton Polytechnic to nearby Woodingdean District Council. He had managed to pass off the incident as a hoax, but the students at the last rag day had given him the Golden Onager Award as Brighton's foremost ass. He was dragged to a place of public execration and reviled by a boisterous citizenry. Though affecting good humour, Markham had vowed revenge.

The gangster harassed himself with the thought that Peerless Widgets was a purely local affair. It should have been a holding company registered in Liechtenstein, operating from an address in the Cayman Islands and banking in the Netherlands Antilles, like every other self-respecting organization.

And this office! During his campaign to win a seat

on the City Assembly, shortly after politics had been legalized again, it had become his campaign head-quarters. A shabby ground-floor room behind a bet-ting shop had failed to inspire potential backers with confidence. The Slab had canvassed door-to-door in the way boxers understand 'canvas'. Most of the electorate seemed to favour a loquacious character whose watchword was the Moby Dictum: when in doubt, spout. A stair-rod in the jaw had fixed him, but the ensuing scandal had forced Markham to retire ignominiously from the race.

This time it would be different. Philosophy was the wave of the future, and Markham meant to ride it.

Much later, when Hayden and Francesca had eaten, she looked at him enquiringly and said, 'Are you tired?'

'No.'

'Good. Let's go to bed, then.'

12

Women Trouble

Late again. Hayden had eventually mustered enough self-loathing to achieve escape velocity from bed and was now jog-shogging heavily laden to the market to claim his fortnightly 'pitch'. Arriving at Thylde Street, he was greeted by the raucous cries of whelk pedlars, wart charmers and muffin-men amidst the turbulent brabble of early morning shoppers. In this City of Enterprise the only sleepers are under the railway tracks.

He set up his two folding chairs and a parasol between a seller of foam rubber blocks and a stall piled high with gaudy plastic kitchen utensils. Hayden acknowledged a couple of greetings, took off his jacket, revealing a rainbow-coloured waistcoat below a pale yellow bowtie, and put up his sign.

Argument Stall
Refine your views
before tackling
the Real Thing

Across the narrow street Danielle could be seen at a stall, prodding vegetables with Gallic discernment. Mooching in her wake with a large bag was her ashen-faced husband, out of place in the morning sunshine. Hayden poured himself a coffee from his first flask and awaited developments.

''ello, 'ayden,' came a voice from the crowd. 'Kept the space for you, didn't I?' It was Phil Nabs – not one of the Nabs of Castle Square but one of that lot from Plumber Street.

'Mr Sabanack to you, you ghastly pimple. Here, have what I owe you.'

'Give me a free consultation instead.'

'Oh, God. Fire away, then.' Hayden eyed his interlocutor narrowly. He was wearing a huge rubberized motorcycle coat, acquired from an army surplus store, and carried a crash helmet.

'I got a problem wiv a girl, ain't I?' For a moment a picture of Babette entered Hayden's mind and in its train came a feeling of hollow-stomached inadequacy. He should have had breakfast after all. 'She's posh. I been chasing her for weeks. Last night I told her I fancied her, but she wasn't having any of it. She said, "I regret I do not reciprocate." Well, being a biker I know what reciprocate means, don't I! To go in and out. Cor! Any woman who can talk dirty like that must be a goer, right? Stands to reason. So where am I going wrong? Tell me.'

Hayden winced at the crudity and reached into his pocket. 'Here, have some cash. I'm not an agony aunt.' However, regretting his sharpness, he added, 'Change your style, or – impossible thought – get a woman more your type. In the meantime, drop off a note to Sophie, will you? She'll pay you on delivery.' Hayden's lateness precluded a visit to the office, but a note would suffice. He hastily scribbled a few words to describe his new thinking on the Existometer. The existing concept was just a box of tricks, he saw that now. Perfect for manufacture by Peerless Widgets, in fact! If, that is, Markham & Co had the stolen drawings, as Hayden suspected. The Mark II design would be entirely and audaciously better, a fully integrated conception. He had been led to it by work on an unrelated thought that he had ditched: life as planetary jizz. In bed at the weekend, the image had popped into his mind of a sunlit, semi-transparent earth, with himself inside it. He now saw that the Existometer must be large enough for the punter to be similarly encapsulated. It would be like climbing into a cockpit for a supraconscious flight.

A large drawing-board would be required. Sophie could see to that, and she could tell Sid to proceed with equipping the factory as the new design would not call for a different production process so much as a change of scale.

When Phil Nabs had gone, Hayden flushed the conversation into his cerebrospinal fluid as he became aware of a small commotion beyond the vegetable stalls. Linden was to be seen declaiming from a soapbox in front of the Godallah Temple three doors down from the Warbler. He had doffed his hellfire sandwich board and a restive crowd was gathering about him.

The old snuff shop, the one mentioned in John Ruskin's *Stones of Brighton*, had closed down. The only takers for this smell-hole had been the Godallah people, a sect of bogus Eastern origins, one of whose beliefs was that evil spirits loathe the stench of burning fish. A line of mouldy shoes outside the shop front usually indicated that the fish-burning heretics were inside wailing mantras to the accompaniment of an old harmonium. When they weren't chanting indoors they were doing so outdoors as they danced in single file down the street to collect money for a foreign mission to Hastings, beyond Brighton's eastern border. They wore what looked like old bed sheets in the Hindu orange of purity, known in the safety trade as International Orange, and reeked of fish. The Godallah sect thus offered a unique combination of auditory, olfactory and visual pollution.

Linden had the whole town on his side in his attempts to curb the sect's activities. Even the local fishmongers had come up with some sponsorship money, though they stood to lose business if he succeeded. Hayden could not make out what was being said but doubtless Linden was banging on about false gods, defilement and corruption as usual.

A man detached himself from Linden's audience and made his way over to the argument stall, looking worried.

'There's going to be trouble,' he said in response to the scholar's quizzically raised eyebrows. 'My wife's over there. Tell me how to persuade her to give up this Christianity business. She's becoming obsessive.'

'Please sit down. Point her out to me.'

The man indicated a formidable-looking woman in a plain dress, carrying a bulky handbag. She was looking stern. There might yet be a riot, Hayden reflected happily. In the meantime, there was his customer's requirement, for which fortunately he was well prepared after a recent rereading of the Synoptic Gospels in the original Greek.

'Well, I need hardly tell you that what started as a father-and-son concern in the Middle East became an Italian multinational before many of the local subsidiaries gained autonomy. Christianity is a cult that caught on, though its appeal has been waning . . .' Hayden's sentence was commuted when the man reared to his feet and ran towards the crowd. His wife had withdrawn a spray can of paint from her handbag and was making to use it on the temple window. Sadly, the man reached her in time to wrestle the can from her grip, though not before Linden suffered partial redecoration. A police officer showed up to urge dispersal. Linden's rabble-rousing had failed again. He simply lacked demagogic qualities, not to mention English language skills. Not so long ago he had initiated a campaign against a potpourri works under the impression it was fostering popery.

Business at the argument stall was booming. In quick succession Hayden dealt with a neighbour dispute involving a stuffed rhinoceros, a case of over-requited love ('try bromide in his tea'), a child custody case in which neither parent wanted the repellent offspring, and a woman with a boring husband.

'If an expressway could talk it would sound like him. Really! It's appalling.' The woman in front of Hayden was posing the biggest teaser of the morning: how to persuade someone to be more interesting? Hayden fought to retain a grip on reality when he was rescued by a woman passerby who had overheard the conversation thus far.

'If only my husband were boring,' she said. 'Mine's worse, he's utterly exasperating. He splashes the bathroom mirror, has too-deep baths and uses too much toilet paper. I find wet towels scrumpled up on the bed, smelly socks on the floor, turned inside out, and revoltingly filthy sports kit in his bag that's been there for weeks. Ugh!'

'I don't get any of that,' said the first woman, 'and I don't think I'd mind if I did. It's dullness I can't endure.'

'I could cope with that.'

'You could?'

'Yes.'

'Well, why don't we . . . ?'

'You mean?'

'Yes. Why don't we swap?'

Hayden's grip on reality duly loosened while his grip tightened on his second flask, which contained scotch. The scholar sighed as the two women marched off arm-in-arm, and he thought wistfully of a time when Brighton women bound their feet, stayed indoors and submitted to the will of their menfolk. Now they even expected to be made happy!

Hayden completed the morning's work by providing the wording for a petition to stop the council knocking down a motorway flyover to build a corner grocery store, and then adjourned to the pub.

Sophie had made a big mistake. She and Francesca had been for a spin on the 'Whirly-Pits' ride on the Palace Pier and it had not gone down well with Sophie's stomach which, along with the rest of her internal organs, had been spun to the wall of her abdomen. She had made it back to pier level unassisted, but on encountering a rotary candy-floss machine had almost forfeited her gastric integrity. Staggering to the pier rail she gazed nauseously across the sea at the distant marina.

'Um, it's good,' said Francesca, eating candy-floss from a stick. The sight of this and the smell of fish and chips wafting on the light breeze from the promenade threatened Sophie with a fresh crisis.

'Whose bright idea was this?' she groaned.

'Yours.'

Sophie lapsed into silence, regretting that she had perversely traded the hubbub of market day for the 'peace and quiet' of the pier.

'How's that handsome boss of yours?' asked Francesca archly. 'I found his eyes very arresting.'

'He still thinks he's the greatest scholar of the age. Probably the two greatest scholars of the age. I want to thank you for not moving in there, Francesca. I know what an emotional imperialist you can be sometimes.'

'You know I wouldn't dream of spoiling your chances. But I gather you've been seeing Giles.'

'Yes, I suppose I have. He's giving me lots of attention. He ought to be available on prescription in tablet form for a girl's morale.' Sophie paused.

139

'Hayden is obsessed with some actress at the theatre. I think he's seeing quite a lot of her.' Francesca looked as surprised as Sophie looked despondent. 'She's blonde. How can we compete?'

The question was only partly rhetorical; Sophie wore the faintly troubled look she felt appropriate to early twenties maidenhood in the presence of Experience. She could learn so much from Francesca, a woman whom nothing could disconcert.

'An actress?' Francesca said.

'Yes, at the Theatre Royal. Hayden's taking her to a yacht party tomorrow night. I'm going with Giles.' Sophie looked at Francesca and noticed that she had gone a funny mottled colour. She shouldn't have had that candy-floss, Sophie thought, as she took her friend's arm solicitously and steered her towards terra firma and the tiffin room at Talbot Square.

There was quite a crowd at the bar of the Warbler. As cool as a queue jumper, Hayden moved off to one side and, using tic-tac, ordered a round of drinks and some food from an overworked Ted behind the bar. When a shot of his usual painkiller arrived, together with two other drinks, some goujons of chicken and a packet of coffee-flavoured crisps, Hayden took them over to Duffy and Giles at their table.

'Sit down, Hayden. Rest your prosthesis, if you have one,' said Duffy.

'I wish I did: an artificial brain for choice. That argument stall idea is a killer. For my next trick I'm going to march on Moscow.' Hayden supped his consolatory moistener, and the pain at the back of his cranium subsided with gratifying speed.

'Why do you do it? With your other work?'

'For reasons best known to my psychiatrist, I should think. Pocket money; keeping my hand in; masochism. Something like that.'

'Speaking of psychiatrists – the need for – Giles is suffering from South Coast Fever.'

'You mean a hangover? Giles, will you never learn?' Hayden intoned sanctimoniously, laughing. Giles was indeed looking in low spirits and, eschewing hair-of-the-dog homeopathy, was drinking orange juice. He didn't look as if he had been up long, sandy hair unbrushed. A considerable amount of eye luggage was complemented by a large sticking plaster on the left of his forehead.

'Tell Hayden about the plaster, Giles.'

'I mistook a banister for a bicycle. I tried to ride it.'

'You haven't got a bicycle.'

'I know. I fell two floors into the stairwell. In my cups I act like a mug.'

About once a month Giles went on a mind-blotting bender of the 'never again' variety. His accident had come about because his landlord was economizing as usual, this time by reducing the lighting in the common areas. A well-irrigated tenant should not be imperilled by meanness. Renting out rooms is the closest there is to getting money for nothing. Far from inducing generosity on the part of landlords, however, this paradoxically evokes extreme miserliness.

'Never again,' Giles said at length. 'Never again am I going to live in rented squalor. You've got a spare room, haven't you Hayden? How about it?' Hayden, who had been doodling on a beer mat, broke off and considered Giles's withdrawal from the rented sector and his occupancy of the spare room, presumably rent free.

'Sorry, old fruit. I need it for my linoleum-still. What about you, Duffy?'

'Good God! I mean ... no, sorry.' Duffy sought hurriedly to change the subject. 'I've got troubles of my own actually. A pipe burst last night. My allotment was completely flooded. Appalling mess.'

'Was the shed OK?' asked Giles, cheering up a bit.

'Oh, yes. But the spuds and sprouts were goners.' Seeing his two friends smiling, he added, 'Thank you for your sympathy.'

'Perhaps I should sleep in the shed, then.'

'I thought your finances were improving, Giles,' Duffy said.

'I'm on the way rather than having arrived.' Giles was developing an increasingly fatalistic approach to success, particularly as regards money. Sooner or later some cheque was bound to have his number on it, and, like an old soldier downed in combat, Giles would cop it in the wallet and be shipped to a place of permanent rest and recuperation far from the front line where others would fight on in his stead.

Meanwhile, Duffy was developing an increasingly fatalistic approach to failure, particularly as regards money. Sooner or later a too-large bill would have his number on it, and like an old soldier downed in combat, Duffy would cop it in the wallet and be shipped to a place of permanent want and bankruptcy. Perhaps he should borrow wildly. Was not material deprivation a fate worse than debt?

'There're no prizes for coming second,' said Duffy.

'That's not true,' interjected Hayden. 'There's a second prize. And at horse shows it's even better. No second-placed animals, only Reserve Champions.' Duffy was pleased with this idea and laughed with pleasure. As he exhaled, his nostrils whistled flutily. From his pocket he pulled a handkerchief which turned out to be a piece of patterned kitchen paper. The other two men watched mesmerized as their friend's fleshy proboscis disappeared from view for vigorous evacuation. Duffy inspected the discharge dolefully then folded the handkerchief and put it away.

'I've got some news,' Giles announced a few seconds later. 'I'm in love.'

'Oh gracious, no,' said Duffy. 'It's all too much. First my allotment floods, now Giles is in love again.'

'This is It,' Giles declared with heavy capitalization. Hayden was surprised to hear that while ostensibly pining coniferously for Jane, Giles had been planting a new arboretum to love. Giles tore a little skin off his lower lip with his teeth, then spoke again. 'There's a problem. I admire her greatly, and I have the usual designs on her body . . .'

'A blueprint in every sense of the word,' Hayden quipped merrily.

'But she's not responding to the treatment.'

Hayden groaned inwardly at yet another instance of unrequited male ardour and said, 'Have you tried poetry? Yes, why not fill her ears with sweetness? "Shall I compare thee to a brewer's dray? Thou art more lively and more temperate".' Hayden could see that his flippancy hadn't gone down well with his lovelorn friend, so changed tack. 'Describe her.'

'She's beautiful, intelligent and charming.'

'Duffy, do we know a paragon like that?'

'If only, if only.'

'What's her name?'

'Sophie.'

As market day drew to a close, and the hawkers, barrow-pushers and stallholders were making to depart, Hayden had just two more customers waiting to consult the oracle. The first proved to be a children's play leader who was going up to London the next day to be interviewed for a plum job. He feared he might not get it because the other applicants were 'the top men in play'. Judicious coaching boosted his morale. The second was a man whose household was in danger of augmentation by his wife's mother.

'You remember in *Lost Horizon* when Ronald Colman's brother in the film is so dismayed to see his girl age rapidly as they leave Shangri-La that he casts himself over the icy precipice?'

'Yes,' said Hayden.

'Well, the thought of my wife ageing to resemble her mother gets me the same way.'

'I can't stop your wife getting older.'

'No, but you can help me prevent her mother from moving in with us. I don't need to be reminded every day of what the future holds.'

'Oh, I see. Well, you could brick up the spare bedroom. Alternatively, you could use it in some way which would hint at your undesirability as a living companion. Have you considered installing a fully operational liquor-still? As it happens I know a bloke who can let you have a superb design. Ring this number.'

Walking back with his chairs and other impedimenta towards the seafront after the close of business, the proprietor of the argument stall composed his contribution to an investment newsletter (equity recommendation: 'buy bauxite, sell osmium') and resolved to brighten up his sitting room with a new spring-selection monogrammed wallpaper. He was feeling marvellous. Apart from the fact that the day had been less punishing than expected, there were two main contributions to his positive frame of mind, one relating to work, one to the way others viewed him. The bequest competition, batty as it was, had led him to design the new version of the Existometer, and that was a genuine breakthrough. What had started out for him as a mere money gambit was becoming more interesting by the day. He was chuffed that Sid had trusted him with such a major project. What's more, he liked working with Sophie, and liked liking her and being liked. True, progress with Babette was nothing to boast about, but there was F., delicious, no-fuss

Francesca. He enjoyed being a sought-after male. He had even bought her a bunch of flowers. He really was a lucky fellow!

When the scholar arrived home he found a woman waiting for him at the door. It was none other than Francesca.

'Hello,' he said brightly, holding out the bunch of flowers to her. Without replying she stepped forward and punched him in the eye, sending him sprawling on the pavement with his chairs, stallholder's sign and flasks. Disentangling himself, he sat up in surprise.

'Have I perchance upset you?'

'Urgh!' she exclaimed in disgust, and marched off muttering jealous imprecations.

Some time after this, the sun, too, disappeared from view. Perhaps it knew that it was classified merely as a star of G2 spectral type and that astronomers had slightingly branded it a yellow dwarf, for it briefly struggled to become a red giant before collapsing over the horizon, its day having dusked. Only reflected glory remained to it, the moon's kindly light.

Later still, Giles cabbed a couple of questionable types to Le Throb, a house so evil that it had given ill-repute a bad name. Sited in the stews of the town, this was a fleshpot of the kind not to be confused with a casserole. Giles recognized one of his passengers but not the other. He strained to hear their conversation.

'Look, Granville, what's the situation with Sabanack?'

'That's not your concern.'

'He was seen working in the market today. Has he given up?'

'That's what he wants us to think. Don't worry. The Slab and Stair-rods have everything under control.'

'I hope so. Sabanack is too clever by half,' muttered

the unrecognized individual, the Thorne in Duffy's side.

A short distance away in space and time, Hayden was roasting some chestnuts in the oven when a message arrived which read: 'Stay away from Sid Whitney – or you'll be en-graved. Geddit? You have been worned.' It was tied to a brick and arrived via the kitchen window.

13

Discomfiture

In the office the next morning, the scholar took a telephone call from Giles, warning of Granville Markham and his cronies. Hayden had met Markham once or twice socially and had even tried to interest the businessman in his design for a kitchen robot, without success. It had become plain that Markham's company was in the dry cleaning business, its only function being to launder underworld funds into respectability.

Markham might be expected to lay off a bit if he had the Mark I design – at least until Fikansky discovered its limitations. Sophie, meanwhile, had found a drawing-board, and the Whitney team was ready to engender the Existometer Mark II.

Giles was mumbling into the telephone. Hayden knew what this semi-coherence signified. That morning, Giles had doubtless had his thrice-monthly depilatory face wax treatment, the preferred alternative to the torment of daily shaving. For hours afterwards, speech was difficult and even a grimace could not be countenanced.

'See you at the party,' said Hayden.

'Yeah, I'll see you there,' came the mumbled reply, and Hayden put down the phone pensively.

'I don't think it will supersede the airmail envelope,' chipped in Sophie cheerfully, indicating the brick on Hayden's desk as she put down a cup of tea for him. 'If you were a detective you could send it down to Forensic and have it checked out . . .'

'And identified as a brick you mean?'

'Yes, that's it.'

'Sophie, you may be able to contemplate the arrival of a missile through your kitchen window with equanimity, but I'm afraid I can't.' But Hayden was unable to contain his amusement. 'The funny thing was that the robot picked it up and placed it in the oven at 175°C!'

'How's your eye?' asked Sophie. 'It looks a bit bruised.'

'It's fine, thanks. We intrepid heroes wear our war wounds well.'

'You're lucky you weren't cut by the flying glass as well. Anyway, the good news is that I've been offered a job. The even better news is that I'm going to turn it down. You obviously need me too much at this traumatic time.'

'I've told you, Sophie, that you must take what you can get,' he said, without conviction. 'This scholarship lark is chancy at the best of times. At the moment it's downright dangerous – though a brick isn't going to stop me! I think we ought to redouble our efforts. We'll show them! Or rather, I will. I absolutely insist you take that job. Your father would want it that way.'

'He's got some good news, as it happens. Did I tell you? He's been created official salt-bearer in the mayoral entourage. No, don't laugh, it's a great honour!'

Just then the telephone rang again and Hayden answered it. It was Nigel from the university.

'Hayden, I've been thinking about our conversation the other day, on our place in the biological scheme of things. The evolutionary stuff was fine as far as it went, but I've sent you a bit more to think about. What you need to consider is a bit on classification and

something on our uniqueness and courtship habits.'
Hayden stared blankly at the wall and saw his
morning's productivity in jeopardy.

'That sounds interesting. Fire away.' Hayden
mouthed 'Nigel' to Sophie and rolled his eyes heaven-
wards.

'Well, in the biologists' *Who's Who* of the animal
kingdom, man is classified as a vertebrate, a placental
mammal and a primate. That is, we have backbones,
our young develop in a womb and we are connected
up to the mother by a remarkable device called a
placenta, and we are related to the apes, monkeys,
tarsiers and lemurs. What sets us apart from them are
frontal lobes and cognitive abilities, thumbs and tool-
making, small jaws and upright stance, diet and
longevity, language and culture. In terms of behaviour,
no species has our repertoire, but there are some
interesting parallels. Have you considered the gibbon?'

'No.'

'Unlike other apes, gibbons pair-bond. They're odd
in another way in that they swing through the trees.
This has led them to be territorial and have nuclear
families rather than roaming around in groups.
Sounds familiar, doesn't it?'

'Yes, Nigel.'

'There's more.' Oh good, thought Hayden, wearily.
'Think of whales. They have an intricate "song" which
is used for courtship among other things. Females
seem to assess the suitability of future mates on the
basis of the song's sophistication. It's noticeable that
the performance of some herculean task during courtship is expected in species where a couple stays
together for a long time – and in the case of humpback
whales, the same pair has been sighted year after year.
So there you have it, Hayden. Imagine a male gibbon
questing about away from home. It comes across a
stranded female whale and courts her, after valiantly

149

coming to her aid. Don't you get it? It's the knight and damsel myth of the medieval romances!'

'Ask him to tell us the difference between frogs and toads,' Sophie shouted with a giggle before turning to consult her computer, repaired since its circuit overload. Hayden thanked Nigel for his new thoughts on biology, while hinting at their special relevance in view of the Existometer redesign. He was interrupted by a shriek from the other end of the telephone which caused him to leap up in alarm.

'Nigel, what's happening? Nigel?' There was a pause during which Hayden heard Nigel exchanging blows with a murderous assailant.

'Relax, Hayden. I just dropped a cup of coffee over my trousers, that's all.' Hayden sank back into his chair with relief and ebbing paranoia.

'Thanks, Nigel. I look forward to getting your stuff on evolution.' After a pause, he added, to the scientist's mystification, 'I hope you'll be using an envelope.'

On his way to the Brighton Explorers' Club for lunch, Hayden had cause to be grateful to his cleaning lady. It was an unseasonably cold day, but he was protected by his one-piece woollen 'underalls' which Mrs Grim had knocked off on her knitting machine to Hayden's specification. Every seventh thread was electrically conducting and was connected to a slim-pack battery positioned comfortably in the small of his back. He had the system on a low setting at present and was enjoying its gentle warmth.

As he walked, he thought of Babette and the coming party that evening. Hayden had mulled over with Sophie the problem of his non-developing relationship with the actress, but she had adopted an oddly unhelpful attitude. Am I worthy of her? he had asked. Is she worthy of your feeling unworthy of her? she had answered. He had changed the subject.

If Babette was a problem, so was Francesca. Why had she blacked his eye the previous evening? Was it jealousy? Had she assumed his bunch of flowers was for someone else? Was the easy-going F. more territorial than he had supposed?

The cane chairs in the loggia were vacant, the cold having driven the steely explorers into the bar. Hayden loitered in the lobby while a club member obligingly located his luncheon companion. At one end of the room was a portrait of Surtees Bismuth, legendary scourge of the Ottomans and one-time club president. Below him was inscribed the club motto, *Ad quaerendos alienos fines.* (For the investigation of other peoples' parts.) To one side an old-fashioned ticker-tape machine clattered suddenly and Hayden examined the tape. Another run on the Mexican *peso*. On top of a cabinet was a pickling jar containing a shrunken appendage floating in a yellowish fluid. Its nails were hideously elongated, mandarin style. A small brass plaque, begrimed with age, yielded up the jar's secret: 'Old China Hand'. Alongside the relic was a postcard showing a Middle Eastern bazaar. Written on the back of the card were the words 'Amir, wish you wazir'. Hayden groaned at the joke, then turned at the creak of an opening door.

'Ah, Sabanack,' a man said gruffly, approaching with extended hand.

'Hello, General,' Hayden replied, appraising the venerable, dark-suited gentleman and noting the gun-cotton grey hair and mutton-chop whiskers. The leathery General Roscius gave the impression of having long ago become immutable.

'Come on, let's sit outside for a breath of fresh air.'

Outside, they were joined by a young steward who took an order for food and served them with a couple of 'rusty nails' – Drambuie diluted with whisky.

'I invited you here, Sabanack, to make you an offer,' the General said gloomily, lighting a cheroot. 'We've got the annual lecture coming up, and it was felt you might like to have a crack at it. If you can come up with a decent subject, that is. Give it some thought.' He sighed as Hayden searched rapidly for a topic. He couldn't tell them anything new about distant horizons, but how about the earth's inside story? At the centre of the oblate spheroid is a slowly churning core of molten iron which generates the earth's magnetic field – a 'turbulent dynamo'. This core is enfolded in silicate minerals in the form of a thick mantle and a thin outer crust. The continents, the exposed part of the crust, 'float' on the surface of the earth. They perhaps derive ultimately from a single primordial land mass, Pangea, which is pictured as having fragmented into two supercontinents, Laurasia to the north, Gondwanaland to the south. Would all this do for a talk? Before Hayden could ask, the General spoke.

'African tribal fertility rites: pictures of native women with dugs swinging, you know the kind of thing. That always goes down well.'

'Why me?' asked Hayden, perplexedly.

'I don't need to tell you that the name of Sabanack is revered around here. Your family has been connected with the club since its foundation nearly three hundred years ago.' He paused. 'Three glorious centuries.' He paused again, the gap narrowing between his bulky eyebrows. 'What is it you do? Jobbing scholar? God help us,' he said, staring bleakly into his rusty nail. 'My grandfather fought your great-grandfather and another man in a triangular duel in Brunswick Square. Did you know that?'

'No, I didn't.'

'It was a chaotic and bloody affair over a woman's honour. She afterwards ran off with a fourth man. None of the principals was injured, mind you. But in the hail of lead, two seconds, one doctor and a passerby bought it. After that the police cracked down on duelling. Tragic.'

'Your grandfather took your lot off to India, of course,' the General continued. 'A great man, great exploits. He was going to climb Everest in brogues, you know, without oxygen. Intended to leave his visiting card at the top. The locals wouldn't let him get near the blessed place so to fool them he got himself up like something out of Kipling in rags and crutches and pretended to be a toothbrush-twig vendor. He didn't even make it to base camp. He was done for peddling without a licence.' Hayden appreciated the General's tact in not mentioning that his paternal grandfather was to be seen in later life strolling around Simla carrying a straitjacket over his arm. To seek respite from his own lunatic eccentricity, he would climb into it. Lovett, Hayden's middle name, honoured this much-admired individual.

The psychic medium Sylvia Crolien had said 'Seek Lovett'. In the form of anecdotal reminiscence at least, Hayden's grandfather had been found.

'Then there was "Subs" himself – still talked of here. Another great man,' the General mumbled, but he couldn't go on. Hayden's father Ralston had got his nickname after returning from India on a troopship during the Second World War. So frequent were the submarine scares that he had taken to sleeping in trousers with his cheque book in a back pocket, sealed in a pouch. Many years after the war, during a retirement in which he displayed an astonishing vigour, he had wedded a much younger woman. He had occasionally relapsed into his old nocturnal trouser habit, to his wife's bitter complaints. Since his father's death, Hayden's mother had grown increasingly nostalgic about the trousers and now sometimes wore them herself to bed for old times' sake.

'To be frank, Sabanack, you're a disappointment to us. A scholar! Why not go the whole way and become a lens grinder in Walthamstow or an accountant anywhere?' Fortunately Hayden was saved from responding to this by the return of the steward carrying their curried quails. Hayden took the opportunity offered by the interruption to turn up the heat on his underalls. Unlike the General, he was definitely feeling the chill. But altering the setting proved a mistake. Almost immediately there was a smell of smouldering cloth which was noticed by his host and the steward alike. Soon, small flames began to lick around Hayden's left kneecap. The scholar stood up abruptly and began to beat out the flames with his hands. The General was watching this performance with something approaching awe as he marvelled at a man whose trousers could spontaneously combust. The steward, seeing Hayden's mounting discomfiture, moved smartly to a side-table and snatched up a soda syphon.

'May I be of assistance, sir?' he said, training a stream of carbonated water on to the flames, which went out with a hiss.

'Thank you . . . eh . . .'

'Wilkins, sir. Thought I recognized you. My grandfather served under your father in North Africa . . .'

'By George!' interrupted the General, 'you *are* your father's son. 'pon my soul! Would you be interested in leading our tercentenary expedition to the Great Himalaya next year?'

'I'll have to check my diary,' replied Hayden with difficulty, as his underalls had begun delivering a series of small electric shocks to his lower extremities.

14

The Yacht Party

Hayden spent a tranquil afternoon at home. First, he wrote a note to the milkman, being careful to preserve his blotting-pad for posterity should it be required by archivists and cultural historians, then he finished Schubert's *Unfinished Symphony* again, as well as Bach's *Art of Fugue*. After penning two articles for the *New Yorker*, he arranged for the disposal of his mother's collection of Victorian industrial postmarks to the Smithsonian Institution. Then he made some marmalade.

Sophie sat at the new drawing-board, working up the design for the Mark II Existometer which her boss had sketched on a beer mat the previous day while lunching at the Warbler. She was ignoring her computer, which threw on to its screen the words 'Use me!' followed by exotic graphic display after exotic graphic display. 'I'll be good,' it declared. 'Honest!' But paper and pencil – that was Sophie's preferred medium on this kind of project.

She shook her head in awe. The Mark II Existometer was going to be a device of astonishing beauty and complexity!

Like the Astrolabe of Inner Being, which it was superseding, the Armillary Sphere of Destiny was modelled on an astronomical instrument. The armillary sphere is a device which represents the known universe in microcosm. Most were fabricated in the seventeenth and eighteenth centuries, not least to illustrate the difference between the Ptolemaic theory of a central earth and the Copernican theory of a central sun. They were cage-like celestial globes consisting of narrow metal rings representing the equator, the ecliptic, the tropics and so on, all revolving on an axis. The positions of the sun, planets and stars were indicated.

The Armillary Sphere of Destiny was a scaled-up version of the originals, big enough to enclose a seated man or woman comfortably in a private universe of circles within circles, elegant traceries and teasingly filigreed embellishments. Elements of the Contralila-scope were incorporated into the design, though new features were the Points of Illumination, corresponding to Sex, Death, Biology, Physics, Philosophy and Humour, from which light would pulse and stream along 'stellar axes'.

The subject would be suspended and massaged by an air-jet vibro-lift facility within a space bounded by a heavenly drama of pan-holographic movement and change. The orb would be bathed in sounds tuned to the brain's transcendent-pleasure frequencies. Here was a mesmeric sensorium, a tangible metaphor for atomic substance and nothingness, the setting for a liberating destabilization of the subject's critical faculties, permitting a self-elevating act of personal evolutionary development involving the supraconscious mind.

As a self-assembly kit available from all good hardware stores, the Armillary Sphere of Destiny promised to be quite a hit!

Sophie would deliver the design to Sid that day, while retaining a duplicate drawing herself, though not in the office, given recent burglarious goings-on.

* * *

In the early evening, Hayden commenced his preparations for the yacht party. After shaving, washing and sprucing his being, he went down to the kitchen where his robot had recently completed the laundry. Connected to the waste hose of the washing machine was an affinity chromatography column designed to extract from the water the more potent of his bodily secretions. Hayden reasoned that if he smeared a concentrated sample of these on to himself he might drive Babette wild with physical desire. Certainly, if there was no chemistry between them, there would be no biology.

When Hayden reached Babette's hotel, it was to learn that the actress was behind schedule. She had a bad parachutist's mentality when it came to punctuality. She was always downwind of the dropping zone, how far being anybody's guess. After twenty minutes, the parachutist duly floated into sight, her 'canopy' turning out to be a sensational yellow creation in silk, slashed deeply, front and back. Hayden's senses were ravished by the dress and its contents.

The marina was a short cab drive away, but the journey was long enough for Babette to register disapproval of her consort's evening attire, a formal suit in nautical maroon. On principle, he never dressed in undertaker's black as was the norm.

The scholar and the actress sailed into the main cabin of the *Marbella Hood* to find the party well under way. The gathering fell silent for a gratifying moment at the sight of the new arrivals, and Sid Whitney advanced on the couple, bearing greetings and bubblesome refreshments. He was joined by his wife who was wearing a ruched dress in flamboyant pink.

'This is my beautiful wife, Bella,' Sid was saying a few moments later during the introductions. Love walks with a white stick, of course, but for Sid to describe his wife as beautiful was pushing it a bit far. Twinkling eyes and a mirthful expression, however, she did have.

'I'm looking forward to hearing the latest developments on the Existometer front, Hayden,' she said with a smile.

'A crocodile-jaw calendar in plastic is the latest thing actually,' he replied. 'As you probably know, crocodiles are supposed to have three hundred and sixty-five teeth.' Bella chuckled, and she and her husband cruised off to circulate among their guests.

Sophie and Giles were visible through wide open doors leading on to the stern deck. Hayden steered his companion towards them through the milling crowd of business types, politicos, academics, literati and unclassifiables of both sexes. Out on the deck, the air was freshening, and across the marina the storm cones had been hoisted.

'Giles, Sophie, meet Babette Macawley, celebrated thespian.' Amidst the greetings, Giles indicated to Hayden a group of villainous-looking men standing nearby, floozied up and talking softly to one another, presumably of felonious acts. Hayden was appalled to see Granville Markham among them. Why on earth had Sid invited him? As he pondered this, the hoodlum looked up and caught Babette's eye with a look of suave appreciation. Hayden suppressed a feeling of queasy outrage and moved towards the drinks table to replenish everyone's glasses. In so doing he encountered Simeon Urstpoint, looking dolefully about.

'As busy as ever, Hayden?'

'It's the New Renaissance, Simeon. I'm attempting a forceps delivery.'

'Your mother still talks of your managing the estate.' There was a pause while the solicitor wrinkled his nose and sniffed questioningly. 'Have you been rolling in something, Hayden?'

'What do you do for a living?' Babette was asking Giles.

'I drive a taxi.'

'Is that all?' she said, causing Giles some discomposure.

'I believe in reincarnation. I'm letting this life lie fallow.'

'And planting turnips in the next, I suppose?'

'That's it.'

Hayden, meanwhile, had been waylaid by Sid's daughter Gail. The girl was pretending to be grown up and had doffed her pebble spectacles and wore her hair out of pigtails. But she still looked very young.

'I hope you'll like it,' she said diffidently.

'Like what?'

'The picture. We're having a public unveiling in a while, before the buffet.'

'I'm sure I'll love it. I haven't been connoisseured out of my senses, as William Blake put it,' he said pompously, then added, 'What's the picture of?'

'You.'

'Oh, Lord, you're joking! Can't we have a private showing? The subject hasn't, alas, got universal appeal, you know.'

'It has the way I've done it,' she said mysteriously, moving off. As Hayden returned to his group, he noticed Dr Fikansky in the company of Professor Wilfred Shaps, philosophy's answer to rapid retailing. Hayden wondered whether to warn Wilfred of Dr Fikansky's disreputable credentials, but thought better of it. The two academics were in the company of a comely young woman who, though perhaps not possessing the sharpest of faculties, was well enough endowed for both men to be applying for a fellowship. Hayden shook his head complacently at such gaucheries, secure in the companionship of the best-looking woman at the party. The Persians have a word for it, *najud*, a woman of intelligence and good shape.

'Your charming lady friend will be back in a minute,' Sophie said in reply to his question. 'I think Giles has gone to throw himself over the side.'

'Didn't they get on, then?'

'You could put it like that, yes.' There was a pause while Sophie wrinkled her nose and sniffed questioningly. 'You smell fantastic. Is that a new aftershave?'

Some way off, Granville Markham was deep in thought. He had not failed to notice during a tour of the boat how many burly crewmen Sid had at his disposal. A war with the Londoner might not go Markham's way.

The boat, big as it was, had begun to move in the mounting swell. The guests were ushered inboard as the window-doors of the main cabin were closed against the wind which was bringing more than a hint of rain. The time of the unveiling had arrived.

Hayden stood with Babette and their host and hostess in the centre of the cabin as Gail supervised two sailors manhandling the shrouded picture into position. It was surprisingly large at more than two metres square. An expectant hush descended on the company as Sid started to speak.

'Ladies and gentlemen – friends. Bella and I are delighted to see you all on board the *Marbella Hood*. Thank you for coming along tonight. Sorry about the storm. Never mind, we've got plenty of life-jackets! Tonight's party is to introduce us to Brighton society and to establish our new commitment to the world's Number One city state.

'But beyond that, I have a double honour: to thank a man who has done me a great service, and to invite a glamorous and talented actress to unveil a picture by my daughter, Gail. The man is Hayden Sabanack. He

160

will be known to many of you as a renowned scholar, but less well known as a business consultant. Yes, Hayden has been helping me with an industrial start-up venture near the Culture Park. Phase One is now complete, and Hayden is bowing out with all credit. I hope he doesn't think he's been ill rewarded!'

Hayden demurred with a smile and a shake of the head, leaving no doubt of his host's munificence. So that's his game, thought Hayden. That's why the villains are quaffing and scoffing with us tonight. Good old Sid! Sophie and I should be safe now.

'I want to thank you, Hayden, for your invaluable assistance. It's been a pleasure working with you. Best of luck in the future.' There was polite applause and one or two thoughtful looks.

'Turning to the picture, which neither Bella nor I have seen, I call on Babette Macawley, our gifted actress friend, to unveil the picture, Gail's first life-size portrait.'

The star of *Adam's Navel* moved towards the picture. She wore a look of mild interest as she pulled the sheet aside. The sight which greeted her caused her to freeze in amazement and sent a shocked gasp through the cabin. Hayden gaped. Gail, sweet, innocent child, had painted two full-frontal nudes representing Adam and Eve. Hayden was Adam, Babette, Eve. Adam's navel, and only his navel, was covered by a fig leaf. There was no foliage on Eve. Excited chattering broke out all around the room and there was nervous laughter and even a full-throated guffaw from over by the drinks table. The painting was exquisitely sexy.

Babette had remained cold-quiet with tightened lips, but she now looked as if she was going to suffer explosive decompression. Suddenly she gave a half-shriek, approached Hayden and slapped him hard on the cheek. Caught off balance, the scholar fell to the floor for the second time in two days. Before he could clamber to his feet, his assailant launched a drink into his face and then stormed towards the door.

'Babette!' he shouted after her above the commotion that had greeted her actions. 'Babette, I didn't know!' But it was too late. The crowd had parted at Babette's approach and she was leaving as Hayden leaped to his feet. 'Babette!'

Outside, the rain had begun to lash down and Babette, now on the quay, looked around uncertainly. Granville Markham, who had disembarked via the after gangway, loomed towards her.

'I have a car,' he said putting his jacket round her shoulders and taking her arm. She permitted herself to be marshalled to a nearby limousine, but before climbing inside turned to Hayden who had appeared on the gangway.

'Destroy it!' she shouted. 'Destroy it!' Hayden stumbled at this and might have fallen but for Sid's intercession.

'Forget it, Hayden. Let her go.' They watched as Markham's car drove off down the quay and into the night. 'Come on,' he said, leading the crestfallen scholar back on to the boat. 'She wasn't for you anyway. Fine actress; lousy sense of humour. Don't worry about the painting. I'll get Gail to chop it in half and only preserve your bit – with a few more fig leaves. What a daughter!' he said with admiration.

It was well past midnight and Hayden walked home along the rain-wet promenade, listening to the somnolent surf snoring softly on the shingle below. He felt emotionally disordered over Babette, knotted up inside with jealousy of Markham, and hungry. If he was not careful, he would go to bed with a clenched stomach! He had not tucked into the smoked oysters, lobster and other food available on the boat, though he had punished the Chablis cruelly. His continued presence at the party had been greeted variously with sympathy, admiration, amusement and sarcastic derision.

Hunger drove the New Renaissance man on a short detour to the twenty-four hour banana dispensary on Melcham Avenue. Someone had scrawled a message on the machine: 'These bananas don't write.' Hayden didn't put his to the test.

At home once more, and still famished, he foraged a spring onion, a piece of cheese and a glisteningly aged piece of salami from the refrigerator before polishing off the dregs of a bottle of Somalian red wine and downing a cup of strong black coffee. He then retired to bed and sank instantly into a deep and dreamless sleep.

15

F.

Romantic loss is like childbirth in reverse: the spasms of pain come less and less frequently. Fortunately for Hayden, the amatory miscarriage of the previous night was proving less painful than expected, such that he was now feeling surprisingly sound in heart, wind and sinew as he strode east towards darkest Brighton, otherwise known as Kemp Town West. He may have lost his blonde lady friend, but he had his work and his freedom. Down these side streets a man must go who is not himself on anyone's side, neither cross with the world nor double-crossing.

In any case, there were other women in this world besides curvaceous, blonde actresses of stunning . . . no, he must be strong! One of those other women had contacted him that very morning via a typed note: 'Be kind enough to meet me at noon at the above address on a matter of mutual interest. F.'

'Mutual interest' indeed! How fickle were women! And how blessed were men in consequence! He would visit F. before going to L., the library. Sophie was amassing an enormous amount of useful research materials in the office, and he must make his contribution. Day Twelve of the competition was upon them, and there was much to do in the remaining nine days.

He paused for breath at the end of North Street and gazed at the furniture store which occupies the corner. This had once been an electrical shop. High above street level there had been an illuminated sign saying 'Electricity' in a facsimile of the handwriting of Michael Faraday, the Victorian pioneer of electro-magnetism, and perhaps the greatest scientific experimentalist there has ever been. Faraday, who was a man with no formal qualifications, turned down the presidency of the Royal Society.

So far that morning, Hayden had not been offered the presidency of the Royal Society but he had been commissioned over the telephone to write a new leaflet for the campaign to decimalize Brighton's nine-hole putting greens on the seafront. He had produced this quickly enough, then, before embarking on his travels, he had set his robot to do some ironing. It was proving troublesome again and had programmed the washing-machine to sing the kind of wailing lament beloved of launderers worldwide from the dhobi wallahs on the washing-ghats of the Ganges to the Launderama on the Limpopo. Hayden suspected that the robot had become friendly with the televideo and had been watching travel documentaries, but this was hard to prove.

Beyond the Old Steine, Hayden sauntered in the sunshine through the neat gridiron of narrow, seedy streets in an area whose design was said to have been inspired by the capital of Sir Thomas More's island republic of Utopia, Amaurote, Brighton's twin city. The streets were narrow, with the terraced houses along each side abutting directly on to the pavement. As in Amaurote, the local citizens 'kepe the winde oute of their windowes with glasse, for it is ther much used', to quote the first English translation of More's Latin. But this being Brighton, the houses were in private ownership and dwellings were not changed every ten years by lot.

Several begrimed urchins were sploshing noisily in the fetid water of a horse trough nearby. Hayden felt a psychosomatic twinge on his left arm at the site of a recent cholera jab. Further on, a woman was berating a man for his drinking. She was doing the shouting, he was providing a mime-show of baleful facial expressions. Hayden walked on. Life was a pilgrimage in a strange country, as Marcus Aurelius had put it. How is a man to fulfil the great twin ambitions: the uncancellable achievement and the unassailably large cashwad? asked Hayden Sabanack. Perhaps both goals would be served when he had completed the work on the Existometer, crooks and conspirators notwithstanding.

In the window of a pawnbroker's shop, Hayden was surprised to see a display of travel posters and brochures, yellowing with age. Presumably potential punters were being encouraged to hock their possessions in order to trade clammy slums for sunny climes, bankruptcies and bailiffs for expensive beaches and outstretched palms. As Mecca is to Muslims, the Black Hills to the Sioux, so Brighton is to the feckless.

The house he was looking for proved to be somewhat inland of Kemp Town West in a graceful crescented terrace overlooking the north-west side of Queens Park. Hayden spoke his name into an entryphone and a moment later the door swung open in front of him. Presumably he was to wait in an anteroom – Francesca had not deigned to inform him.

When he went inside, the scholar was immediately impressed with the carpet. It was in lush reds and blues against a cream background and, to the mathematician's eye, was a fractal display of remarkable complexity. Hayden fell to his knees, the more easily to inspect the whorls within whorls within whorls, and was discovered in this posture by its owner.

'Ah, Mr Sabanack. Have you lost a contact lens?'

'Good lord! Dr Fikansky! I was expecting . . . that is

to say – inspecting your admirable carpet. Exquisite.'

'Thank you. Please come this way.' Dr Fikansky led him into a back room and invited his guest to sit on a comfortable leather sofa, side-lit by sunshine spilling through an oriel window. The walls were book-lined, the furniture antique. There were several original paintings on display, none featuring Adam and Eve. Dr Fikansky must have read Hayden's thoughts.

'The picture last night was delightful. I can't think what Miss Macawley had against it.'

'It was certainly very saucy, and by no means the low-water mark of Western civilization.' There was a pause, then Hayden added, 'This is a fine room you have here, Dr Fikansky, very fine.' It did not take a man of learning to identify the warm tones and unmistakable aroma of affluence and culture. Was Dr Fikansky on his way to an unassailably large cash-wad, perhaps?

'Thank you again. Well then, shall we get down to business?'

The carriage clock on the mantelpiece sombrely ticked away the minutes as Dr Fikansky elaborated his vision of a future dominated by scholars in a world in which knowledge was the key resource. The right men could make a killing! Why didn't Hayden and he throw in their lot together to beat everybody else out of sight? Hayden was free, and Dr Fikansky could disentangle himself from his existing – unspecified – commitments. Combined, they could offer a wide range of products as 'consulting scholars', and they could name their price!

Hayden was disappointed to learn that his interlocutor was merely another money-orientated megalomaniac like Professor Wilfred Shaps and the rest of them at the Institute of Philosophy, but he was gratified to learn that while they needed him, he didn't need them.

It was intriguing to hear that Dr Fikansky was willing to contemplate deserting the Markham camp. He obviously hadn't thought through the implications of such a move for his health! And what did this say of the rival project? Hayden could hardly restrain his amusement. They must have found the flaw in the Mark I Existometer design by now. What a team! The leader a notorious crook; the expert advisor wanting out; their participation in the bequest competition made possible only through the presumed intercession of a corrupt government official.

During the course of the conversation, Hayden's eye had alighted on a letter rack on a small bureau by the door. In it was an envelope bearing an official crest and, if Hayden's eyes could be trusted, the words 'Planning Department'. Proof of corruption would be of great use to Sid. I wonder if I can get my hands on that letter, he asked himself. Of course, it went against the grain to pilfer a chap's mail, but . . . At that moment, the telephone rang, and Dr Fikansky got up to answer it. Hayden got up, too, in a casual manner, and began to appraise a painting near the bureau. Dr Fikansky was listening rather than talking into the telephone, and had gone rather pale.

'No, really,' he said at one point, desperation thickening his slight accent. 'There is no need for such measures, really. We have enough time, I assure you.'

Was this Markham jollying along his team? If the good doctor's contract had in it a penalty clause for late delivery, then it would doubtless cite concrete shoes or a wooden overcoat. Hayden felt pity for the distraught Dr Fikansky, even as he slipped the letter into an inside pocket and returned to the sofa. He watched as Dr Fikansky replaced the receiver then used a handkerchief to mop his glistening brow.

'Mr Sabanack, I fear that I have other business to

attend to. Perhaps we can pursue our discussion some other time. Forgive me. Can you let yourself out? Forgive me.'

Hayden could see that all was not well in the Fikansky household so he made his farewells and left without more ado. He could not quit the premises, however, without another leisurely perusal of the carpet in the anteroom. It really was extraordinary! Whorls without end, Amen. It was during this inspection that he heard the telephone being snatched up in the sitting room and the beginning of what at a distance sounded like an urgent conversation. Poor Dr Fikansky! More trouble.

Hayden emerged into the sunshine in high good humour. The opposition were clearly rattled, and the filched epistle would probably seal their fate. He withdrew it from his pocket and leaned against a railing to read it. 'Dear Emile,' it began, and was signed 'Vincent Thorne'. The intervening text was innocuous enough save for two sentences: 'The paperwork is in order and will permit your participation in the prototype trial. Only time will tell whether the rival entry forms have been prepared with similar attention to detail.'

Sid could not have slipped up, surely? Thorne's remarks could only mean one thing: the rival application forms had been tampered with to ensure a no-contest. The unscrupulous blackguard! First an antedated entry form, now this! So engrossing was the letter's content that when a car pulled up nearby, it went unheeded. Hayden felt a sudden shiver run up his spine, then down it, and then stop when it was neither up nor down. He was being watched.

'Wotcha, Mr Sabanack.' Hayden snapped out of his reverie and was aghast to bring the Slab into focus, standing in front of him. 'A certain person tells us you've been a naughty scholar. Now, that won't do, will it? Hand over the letter.' Without a moment's hesitation, Hayden turned and fled towards an alleyway he had passed earlier. Reaching it, he looked back to see the Slab loping after him.

'We're not going to be difficult are we?'

But Hayden was by now deaf to anything but the beat of his own cowardly shoes on the grimy flagstones. He emerged on to the next street ten metres ahead of his pursuer, and he made off left towards the city centre. Hayden broke into a sweat when he realized the Slab had scarcely broken into a trot.

Ragged urchins and gossiping women alike were silenced by the sight of Hayden speeding past them pursued by an immense figure loping menacingly behind. Years of watching film chases had taught Hayden the value of crowds and of fast-departing buses and trains. But where were the throngs and the public transport? How do you shake off a man who would soon be close enough to read the lines on the back of your neck?

Hayden had an inspiration. A short distance away was the fruit and vegetable market. If he could reach that with a few seconds to spare he might yet win through to safety. He dug deep into his reserves and spurted across a road in a diagonal run over a traffic island. He was gratified to hear that the Slab was now having to run fast to keep up and was breathing hard. Being a professional bully was obviously no more bilitating than being a professional polymath.

There in front of them was the market entrance, crowded with customers and traders. Hayden ducked into the cavernous hall and performed a running crouch behind a mango and kumquat stall before coming to rest astern a pile of broken boxes. He stopped and, careless of curious glances, tried to suppress his wretched panting. Cautiously, he peeped from behind the boxes. The Slab was nowhere in sight. Moving gingerly, Hayden crawled towards a rear door,

170

only pausing to age ten years when a bunch of bananas fell hand-like on to his shoulder. He was nearly safe. Only a courtyard, seven lorries and a stream of overburdened market porters stood between him and safety. Hayden lost no time in shouldering a crate of melons – and in putting them down again with a painful moan. Instead, he selected a small box of grapes. He then walked nonchalantly to the nearest lorry and slid between it and the next vehicle. At the cab he got rid of his load and then, after scoping out the courtyard, scurried into Grand Parade and across Victoria Gardens to Marlborough Place. He had done it! The man they called the Slab had missed the man who would, if this story came out, be called the Poltroon. Hayden turned into Church Street to seek refuge among bibliophiles.

A particularly satisfying suicide can be contemplated in Brighton Library because it is possible to cast yourself from the philosophy section on the balcony into the psychiatry section below. The elevated section was ideal for the high browse, and Hayden had so far collected himself as to be lost in thought on the balcony when a hand, like a bunch of bananas, alighted firmly on his shoulder. Hayden yelped squeakily in a manner worthy of a diver on helium, and turned to take in the monumentally awful presence of the Slab. As his assailant's free hand closed round Hayden's neck, the scholar perceived the imminence of a severe throat problem; at any moment he might be croaking. From being a humble culture trafficker, Hayden had definitely become the Man Whose Luck Had Run Out, particularly since, at the sight of the Slab's activities, librarians and borrowers alike had recollected urgent commitments elsewhere.

'Been for a little run, have we?' Hayden, who could think of no reply that would get past the constriction in his throat, confined himself to a nod. 'You don't seem

171

to be getting the message, do you?' This provoked another nod, more vigorous than the first, followed by a shake of the head, the scholar vacillating between trying to convey 'Yes, I am getting the message' and 'No really, I am getting the message.' Hayden felt his feet leave the ground as the Slab lifted him effortlessly into the air by his lapels. His throat was now resuming normal service, but did this levitation presage an out-of-balcony experience? It did. Dangling at arm's length several metres above a stone floor, Hayden at last conceded to himself that his mail theft might have been a mistake. The Slab seemed to think so, too, as he repossessed the missive in question.

'If I meet you again, it will be for the last time,' the Slab said, playfully tapping Hayden on the nose with a spare fist. 'Understand? This time I'm going to let you go without a fuss.' Hayden so far misconstrued this last comment as to be commencing a sigh of relief at exactly the same moment as he commenced a journey to the floor. 'Argh!' was the *beau parleur*'s parting comment.

16

Sophie

When Hayden was half an hour older, he sat at his desk with one foot in a small bath of steaming water. It had been injured in his fall. On his nose was a cold compress.

'Why don't you let me ring the police?' Sophie pleaded for the third time.

'What! And deprive myself of the pleasure of watching from beyond the grave as my foe is brought to justice? Never! Anyway, a charge of assault and battery is hardly likely to deter a big man with brooding fists. No, we'll have to try a different tack. Do we have any body armour and guns in the office?' His flippancy fooled no-one. He was becoming a frightened scholar. The only man who should make an attempt on your life in a library is a biographer; local hit-men were definitely out.

'Our hero, who art endeavouring, hallowed be thy name,' Sophie recited sacrilegiously, then somewhat spoiled the effect by adding, 'You're an idiot. But I like you. A lot.'

'You've done superbly with the new design. Well done. Our end of the project is going well. The question is, how is Sid going to crack the conspiracy without documentary evidence?' For the first time as he spoke, Hayden became aware of a large potted plant near Sophie's desk. 'What's that?'

'It's a large potted plant.' There was a pause while Hayden sighed tolerantly.

'I mean, how did it get here? Have you checked it for explosives?'

'It's a present – from an admirer.' She spoke with slow emphasis, adding, 'It's not unusual, you know, for girls to get this kind of thing – from thoughtful men.' Hayden knew a despatch delivered by hobby-horse when he heard one and maintained a careful silence which was broken a few seconds later by the telephone. Sophie answered it, and Hayden wiggled his toes appreciatively in the warm, briny water. After salutations and preliminaries, Sophie asked three questions, the answers to which were to seal Hayden's immediate fate.

'Fran, it's lovely to hear from you, but why do you want to speak to Hayden? Where are you? And what's that banging noise?' There was a pause while Francesca explained that she had forgiven Hayden to the extent of shinning up the drainpipe into his spare bedroom to surprise him later, when the robot had gone berserk at an imagined breach of security, and had attacked her. Barricaded in the scholar's boudoir, and daunted by the downward journey by the external route, she was speaking on the extension, and would someone send some help, please! Oblivious of the tempest that was about to engulf him, Hayden chose that moment to glance up and catch a look of dawning comprehension on Sophie's pretty face.

'You mean . . . you and Hayden! YOU AND HAYDEN!!' Sophie had dropped the instrument and was evidently searching the top of her desk for a length of lead piping. At last Hayden sensed danger. He, too, rose to his feet, painfully, and gestured with his hands and face in a way which could only mean no, please, Sophie, you don't understand!

'No, please, Sophie, you don't understand!' he said

in alarm, but Sophie's face was going from red to purple alert, and only violence would do.

'You rat!' she shrieked, ripping the telephone from its socket and hurling it at him with jealous velocity. This was quickly followed by a telephone directory, a stationery holder, two notepads, an encyclopedia-dictionary and a bag of tuna-mayonnaise sandwiches.

By this time Hayden was over by the back window, wrestling desperately with the catch. He wrenched up the sash as a fusillade of books hit the wall next to him.

'You beast! You revolting fink!' Hayden stepped smartly out on to the fire escape and, seeing Sophie advance with the plant in its pot, he slammed down the window and stepped aside with relief. A moment later, the plant smashed noisily through the window and plummeted to earth to crash in the twitten below. Hayden caught a brief glimpse of Sophie gaping in floricidal horror at the enormity of her action before he scampered down to street level via the metal staircase. At the site of the floral tribute, he bent down to read the label attached to the stem. It said: 'This is my omni-present to you – yes, it's for everything and always. Giles.'

Hayden felt a surge of remorse at being the cause of this romantic despoliation. As he retreated miserably down the alley, his nose began to bleed for the second time that day.

Harmony in a room, according to Japanese philos-ophy, is essential for spiritual calm. Hayden would have to remember to tell Sophie this if she ever calmed down. Why had Francesca rung up and bared her soul? And why had Sophie got so worked up? What was wrong with good honest concupiscence, even if it found expression with your assistant's best friend? He reflected on sins of omission, commission and intromission as he limped with one bare foot towards the Warbler and refuge.

A good pub has a lot in common with a marsupium: plenty of liquid refreshment combined with warmth and a snug intimacy – though, as far as was known, marsupial joeys don't go in for playing shove ha'penny. With a brown ale in front of him, the monster of depravity was able to look across his sea of troubles and see no ships, only relationships and hardships in close convoy. In under two days he had fallen victim to a footpad, or *pied à terre* as the French say, and been traumatized by three women. Life was sublimely unpredictable: that is some of its charm and a lot of its horror.

Suddenly, Sophie was standing in front of him wearing her coat and clutching the potted plant, newly wrapped in a plastic bag. Hayden reared up in alarm, but his assistant had come only to deliver a forlorn valedictory.

'I'm leaving, Hayden,' she said in a quavering voice, her big blue eyes brimming with tears. 'I'm taking that job I was offered. I'm sorry I missed you . . . I mean, I'm sorry I'll miss you. Your robot is giving our mutual friend a hard time. You had better go to her. Goodbye.' With that she fled, leaving Hayden to reach deep into his larynx for a reply.

'Sophie! Sophie! Don't go! Sophie!' But it was too late, his companion had gone for good, and Hayden slumped down in lonely dejection. But only for a moment. Francesca! He suddenly remembered Sylvia Crolien's mediumistic prophecy about a woman in aristocratic distress. It must be Francesca! Wasn't her second name Earle? It was! He must rescue her at once.

Try sleeping with an injured foot and a clot-clogged nose. The foetal position is out if you have a bleeding diathesis; as is the straight, supine position if your foot

won't bear the weight of the bedclothes. That leaves
the semi-corkscrew, and a consultation with an osteo-
path later. All this lay ahead of Hayden as he called
off his robot and made to release Francesca from
captivity. But if he sought consolation there, it was not
to be. She had summoned up the courage to use the
drainpipe after all, and was now long gone. So much
for spirit messages! This left the Master of Thought
with what he felt to be a useful task: the massive re-
programming of the robot to accept, nay, encourage,
female intrusion into his bedroom, howsoever that
intrusion might be effected.

17

Out of Town

All deviations from perfect health are an illusion –
essentially the product of an inadequate mental or
spiritual outlook. Faith in the fact of the illusory nature
of illness is sufficient in itself to ensure total restoration
to health. This was the view of Mary Baker Eddy, the
founder of Christian Science and one exception,
incidentally, to the rule that men found religions and
women prepare the lunch.

None of this was any consolation to the peripatetic
scholar as he uncomfortably mounted the stairs to the
crowded upper deck of the open-top bus in Churchill
Square. His foot had swollen overnight, prompting
him to wear a well-padded walking boot as the 'pair' to
the ordinary shoe on his other foot. He sank with relief
into an empty seat next to a careworn woman in her
forties carrying a handbag on her lap. The bus lurched
into motion and they started their journey towards the
country.

Given the events of the last few days, Hayden was
feeling increasingly like the universe itself, at least in
one cosmological model: a hot past and a cold future.
With this thought, he lapsed into a reverie which lasted
until townscape turned to countryside at the old City
Wall which since the thirteenth century had oft-times
saved Brighton from war and pestilence alike.

Several miles of neatly hedged field were soon
superseded by acres of tunnel greenhousing thronged

with oversized tomato plants heavily trussed with fruit. Beyond this was the primitive, sedgy pastureland which runs up first to the his 'n hers villages of Codpiece and Middlewitch, then onwards to Much Wedlock. By a stream, women washed clothes on exposed rocks. Further on, a man was making money from selling old rope by the roadside. Some people have the knack.

As they jolted by the small shrine to the Reclining Madonna, to which hundreds of pilgrims struggled each year to reap plenary indulgences, Hayden became aware that the woman next to him was gazing questioningly at a man in the seat in front. She seemed to be weighing him up. Was there anything to compare with the curiosity of women? Just then the bus drew sharply to a halt by a village green and the man turned and addressed the woman.

'Ready, dear? This is our stop.'

At the foot of a long, low hill, Hayden alighted from the bus and stood watching as it nosed off noisily to the east. Choosing a woodland path rather than the road, he began his painful ascent to a cottage just visible in the distance through the trees.

The path was dry and took him through the vestige of an ancient forest, a mixture of oak, beech, sweet chestnut, birch, ash and field maple. Its floor was frosted with small blue flowers on long stems. These must be bluebells, thought Hayden. The fern-like vegetation strewn in patches on either side and round the roots of trees must be ferns. And this sunlit clearing could only be a glade, such as one has read about in books. Mother Earth, you have a beautiful Nature – and how do you manage to look so good year after year? His smile was transmuted into a grimace of discomfort as the less-than-hardy backwoodsman limped on to a sharp stone.

The cottage was now some two hundred metres

distant. He was approaching it from an angle. A curtain moved – he had been seen! A few seconds later a woman scurried out of the back door into the garden with some sort of container under her arm and carrying a spade.

The cottage was constructed on the anthropomorphic principle of two eyes, a porch-roof nose, and a door. Vines, tortuous and varicose, clothed the house, giving it the overall appearance of a man peering through a hedge. Hayden made his way round to the garden which was an enchanted pleasance of flowers and bowers. Under a fruit tree the woman had started digging determinedly. It takes at least 3000 years for Nature to dig herself a spade's depth of topsoil. The woman was removing the product of this toil in a matter of seconds. At close quarters the container was revealed to be a metal casket. Hayden came up and, as he drew close, he could see that the woman, though getting on in years, was still attractive and well turned out. She is the kind of woman who must have at least one appealing and talented child, Hayden concluded.

'Hello, Mother.'

'Oh, Hayden!' she said, eyebrows raised in feigned surprise. 'You gave me a start.'

'Is it worth my asking you what you're doing?'

'This is a duplicate of my will, Hayden, in case the one in the cottage is destroyed by fire and Simeon is abducted.'

'And his office is also destroyed by fire.'

'Exactly.' Without offering to help, Hayden waited patiently while his mother completed the interment.

'How's that young lady of yours?' Mrs Sabanack asked, rather breathlessly.

'Oh, she's well enough,' Hayden replied, not knowing to whom his mother was referring.

'Actually, I heard that she had flounced out of your

life.' Hayden was treated to a shrewd inspection. Flounce? That seemed to rule out Sophie. Francesca could flounce with the best of them, but had in fact disappeared down a drainpipe, so to speak. Babette could flounce too, but hadn't. Had Simeon been gossiping? Hayden decided to change the subject.

'Doesn't this lawn need hoeing?'

'Mowing, Hayden. One *mows* the lawn.'

'And what about this Old Swain's Ardour,' he said, indicating a bomb-blast of yellow flowers. 'Shouldn't this be pruned?'

'Forsythia, Hayden. And no.'

'Good, I'm glad to see everything's under control. Had any problems with flying spiders this year?' Mrs Sabanack exhaled in disbelief, not least at the sudden sight of Hayden's hybrid footwear.

'Hayden . . . ?'

'Yes, Mother?'

'Oh, never mind,' she said, completing her task by patting down the soil. Hayden hobbled over to a hammock slung between two trees, and prepared for a well-earned rest. The hammock swung gently in the breeze as its human contents daydreamed of being asleep dreaming of being awake, daydreaming. The question occurred to the scholar as to whether women knew something – or, rather, Knew Something. Some spoke of the 'numinous female'. Hayden had long suspected women to be the keepers of life's mysteries, but in a way which could only be unlocked by the male. Misogynists were deeply suspect.

The big house at the other end of the sweeping drive was to be converted into a conference centre – or something. A discussion on this was the purpose of his visit, but the topic did not interest Hayden much in truth, though he was pleased that his mother had managed the transition from great house to gatehouse with such apparent ease, even pleasure. The move had awakened her sleeping repertoire of gardening skills and sharpened her ability to deter intruders. She had dealt with the problem of maintaining a flower garden next to her own deer park by adopting the simple expedient of eating any interlopers. Thus it was to be roast loin of venison for lunch.

Back in the house, Mrs Sabanack disappeared into the kitchen to prepare the meal, carrying a glass of Madeira. This was Hayden's opportunity to found a new religion, but instead he turned on the old wireless on the mantelpiece. The sunset grill glowed yellow as the set warmed up, distant voices entering the room through a crackle of static. Hayden suddenly felt comfortable for the first time in days.

18

A Sluggish Sunday

Comfort was not the keynote of the morrow. The swelling on Hayden's foot had gone down a bit, but the swelling in that part of his brain associated with self-delusion had not permitted him to cancel a Sunday morning squash game with Duffy in spite of a persistent limp. At the club behind the county cricket ground, they replaced two men on a court, and as usual the air was like a block of boar taint. Why is the male of the species so malodorous?

To settle his stomach from the night before, Hayden had had a full English breakfast: eggs, bacon, sausages, mushrooms, kidneys, fried bread and tomatoes, with toast and marmalade to follow. The recording of *Café Society* had not gone particularly well – Max had hogged the microphone. The less charitable in the audience might have been reminded of the Jupiter effect. The solar system's second largest body, Jupiter, is a giant gas planet. Were it only a little larger, it would have high enough central pressure and temperature to initiate nuclear burning, and so become a star.

After the show, Hayden had gone on to the Gehenna Club, which by reputation had taken over where the Hellfire Club had left off. But that was long ago. The last all-night sex and drugs orgy was a distant memory, alas, and the club was now a haven for insomniac card players rather than shameless voluptuaries and rakehells. Hayden liked to take an occasional hand of piquet there before turning in, but on this occasion had stayed till 4 a.m., consuming three bottles of champagne and four dozen oysters. His squash was not benefiting from this preparation, nor from the sweltering conditions on court.

'You won't have heard,' said Duffy, between rallies. 'Brighton Aerospace have pulled out of the competition. The rumour is that they couldn't afford the protection money.'

'What protection money?' gasped a badly fatigued Hayden.

'Or the hire of a fleet of ambulances in the event of non-payment. It's now between Peerless Widgets and Whitney Enterprises.'

By fast-hopping to and fro, Hayden just managed to contain his opponent until Duffy executed a series of just-getable lobs followed by just-getable drop-shots. These eventually caused Hayden to collapse in a heap mid-court, gasping with pain and exhaustion. His groans were only curtailed by the appearance of a head over the viewing balcony and by the sound of a voice from the same location.

'I say! Are you on for a spot of cricket? We're short of a man.' It was the captain of the Sussex team.

'Can't you see I'm injured,' expostulated Hayden irritably.

'I was talking to Duffy actually. We need some crafty bowling.'

Hayden fought to conceal his miffed surprise. 'You carry on, Duffy. I'll knock a ball around here, then I'll come and cheer you on.'

'Are you sure? I don't want to leave you in the lurch, just when you were getting into your stride.'

In the shower, Hayden lathered himself in the usual mixture of sodium salts of long-chain carboxylic acids, which comes in the form of aromatic blocks. The problem with 'soap', as it is called, is that it has no pharmacological activity to prevent secondary perspiration after the shower. One could use an antiperspirant to physically block the pores, of course, but there was always the danger of an internal haemorrhage of moisture, or so it seemed to Hayden whose biology was not always as strong as it might have been. The same could not be said of Nigel Stebbins – as regards biology, that is, not perspiration.

The morning's mail had brought Hayden several items of interest, not least a voluminous tract on evolution from the scientist. Nigel's most arresting point was that while beliefs about creationism were widely diffused among primitive peoples, the same was true of proto-evolutionary ideas. This was especially so for totemic tribes whose members imagined that their ancestors sprang from their totemic animals or plants, and thus believed that man was not created but evolved out of lower forms of life. The ideas of creationism and evolutionism have both existed down untold ages, but in terms of accumulating evidence and hence fitness to survive, the latter appears to have time on its side.

On the basis of life's complexity and interrelatedness, some people infer the existence of a creator, but this is neither verifiable nor falsifiable. Evolutionism and belief in a *compassionate* creator, however, are certainly not reconcilable since evolution operates through the weak going under. Witness Hayden on the squash court!

There is a lot of suffering in the world, the scholar reflected sadly, both in nature and among humans. Those who believe that an all-engendering deity exists, traditionally ascribe to him omniscience, omnipotence and unbounded benevolence. But if he is like this, why all the pain? This is, of course, the famous 'problem of evil'. To put it another way: if God made the world,

185

knows all about how it is continuing to function, and can change it for the better, why doesn't he? One way out of this difficulty is to assume that God, like us, partakes of both good and evil. Another, is to assume that, unlike us, he doesn't exist.

Besides Nigel's epic submission, which ran to about ten pages, the mail also brought the promise of a couple of tickets for the opening performance on Monday night of *Adam's Navel*. A card in Babette's hand concluded with the simple message: 'A parting gift.' So he was going to see her again after all – if only at a distance. He didn't need to think hard to recall that the next week was going to be a quiet one: there was half a hectare of white space in his diary where his social life would normally have been. Whom should he take to the theatre?

Another short note accompanied a photograph of Gail Whitney's infamous portrait which had evidently now been bisected to exclude Babette and enfoliaged to preserve Hayden's modesty. This note was even simpler than the actress's: 'Paxxx', it said in Gothic calligraphy. As mathematicians know, the symbol x can be positive, negative, integral, fractional, irrational, imaginary, complex, zero and infinite. Coming from a mischievous youngster, that might be only half the story!

Hayden made his way to the members' pavilion on the west side of the cricket ground to find that Sussex were in the field and that Duffy had already opened his account with a double wicket maiden first over. Hayden watched as his friend ambled innocuously to the wicket at the start of his second over, eyebrows a herring-bone of concentration. The batsman lunged desperately at the ball to preserve his stumps as Duffy deployed his spin bowler's guile to almost mystical effect to contrive idiosyncrasies of flight, bounce and inertia. Hayden pitied the poor batsman his plight.

Becoming aware of a presence beside him, Hayden turned to find a young somebody by the name of Buster Swiftington.

'Sab, old fossil!'

'Hello, Buster, are you well? Doing anything gainful these days?' Hayden knew perfectly well that his new companion was in his sixth year as a student of the arts.

'Oh, I'm still at Oxford, you know.' Hayden met this statement with a look of such utter blankness as to cause Buster's confidence to stumble momentarily. 'There's a university there.'

'Oh, I see, yes.' Hayden returned his attention to the game, and Buster followed his gaze.

'Who's the bladder of lard with the waddling run? What a sight!' Hayden winced at this description of Duffy while conceding that if he was chaired from the field as man of the match, the entire Sussex team would be requiring deep physiotherapy. But the likes of Master Swiftington could keep their views to themselves.

'Sir Dufryn Cairns; proud old Sussex family; worth millions; has a part-time job with the International Monetary Fund; currently negotiating a multi-billion credit line for a Latin American country, or so I'm told: very hush-hush. I can rely on your discretion.'

'Yes, indeed. My word!'

'Has a young, unmarried sister. Phenomenally beautiful. That, and the money, of course. Oh, and the old baronial estate.'

Buster's interest had stiffened more than somewhat, as Hayden knew it would. The callow youth had once been fond of saying that he couldn't be expected to shoulder his financial commitments alone. 'I shall therefore share them with a woman. I mean, naturally, my mother.' Latterly, his views had developed considerably. Now he was determined to make good by his own hand, even if it meant giving that hand in marriage to an heiress. Buster was said to be the only man in Sussex with a nodding Buddha in the rear window of his sports car.

'The lunch interval is due shortly. Ingratiate yourself with him.'

'How do I get to meet his sister?'

'Lend him your hunting lodge; invite him on to your launch at the regatta – that kind of thing. Don't let on you know what a big cheese he is: modest man. Call him Duffy.'

'Right, yes. I'll do what you say. My word, Sab, you're a good friend.' I am, thought Hayden as he moved off towards the buffet and bar to precede the hardened guzzlers and swillers.

While a waiter organized a drink for him, the friend of Sir Dufryn Cairns inspected with particular interest some noisettes of wild boar laid out on the buffet table before him. He looked up straight into the face of Sophie, a few paces distant, and his heart missed a beat. She was wearing a scowl that would have descaled a kettle. To his restrained eyebrow flash of greeting she responded with a look of determination and a tensing of the body. Hayden sensed he was about to get a plate of vol-au-vents launched at him from close range, but slapstick was averted by the restraining hand of her father who had seen the danger and come up beside her. Hayden retreated from the bar in some disarray, forgetting his drink in the process.

Shortly afterwards, the teams came off the field to polite clapping. Sussex were clearly on top, Duffy having taken a clutch of wickets cheaply. The spin bowler would be dining with his team mates, so Hayden took himself over to an alternative eating-place, the 'Forbidden City on Wheels', a Chinese barrow-stall. Hungry spectators were already tucking into the customary fare of fish stomachs, marinated snakes and ancient eggs, among other things. Hayden settled for a smoked sea-slug dish and a tumbler of rice wine and went over to some deckchairs for peace and rumination.

In China, windmills formerly turned horizontally and white is the colour of mourning; but sea-slugs seem to taste the same everywhere. If we ate like mice we would eat not three meals a day, representing one-fiftieth of our body weight, but seventy-five meals, representing one-half. Given that Chinese food does not satisfy for long, would an oriental mouse . . .

Hayden's thoughts were interrupted by loud snoring from a nearby chair. An old buffer, white maned, with bulbous nose and ample underchin, was respiring reverberantly from the recesses of a rough-woven rug. Spectator sports rather took Hayden the same way.

Can sport ever occupy the highest grades of significance? Not in Hayden's view. This is one difference between sport and art. A second is that artists do not rub liniment into their legs. There is a similarity between the two types of activity, though, when we consider 'degree of paraphernalia'. Motor racing and photography, for example, both have a strong technological component that arguably relegates each to a lower category than, say, athletics and painting, respectively.

The deckchair intellectual finished his slug of food and slug of wine and made for more peaceful surroundings. Faith is a vice unworthy of the reasonable man, but even the reasonable man needed something of the balm to the spirit provided by an old English church on a glorious Sunday in spring. Accordingly, Hayden repaired to the billiard room under the main stand in a mood of contemplation. There lay before him a night reconnaissance.

19

Tunnel Vision

Their eyes soon became adapted to the dark. They could see that there was no light at all in the hole.

'Hayden, do you think that if I whimper pitifully enough someone will come and rescue us?' Giles had dropped his voice in deference to the reverberations. Hayden and he were about three metres below ground level.

'If there's any pitiful whimpering to be done, I'm the one to do it. You think constructively.'

'Tell me something. Why does this factory contain nothing but a pile of packing-cases and a big hole? Are they building a left-luggage depot next to a stupendous latrine?'

'I don't know,' Hayden replied, anxiety in his voice. It felt as though they were trapped in the darkened conning-tower of a submarine. 'Have another go at opening it.'

'It's no good. It's jammed!' Hayden's bad foot had caused him to slip on the ladder, bringing down a heavy hatch-cover in his lunge for safety, and smashing the torch. If he could have seen better, he would have kicked himself for his stupidity and for succumbing to temptation. So as not to alert Peerless Widgets to Hayden's continuing role in the Whitney Enterprises effort, Sid had urged the scholar not to visit the factory. But Hayden had been consumed by curiosity to see the prototype of the Armillary Sphere of Destiny – and perhaps even try it out! A clandestine visit at the dead of night had seemed the best bet. They had eluded the nightwatchmen, with difficulty, but the factory had proved a crushing disappointment: no machinery in sight. With seven clear days to go, Whitney Enterprises seemed to be well behind schedule.

'I'm truly sorry, Giles. It looks as though things are going to get worse before they get better. Or to put it another way, I think we're going to have to go down before we go up.' So saying, Hayden dropped to a crouch and felt for the edge of the metal platform on which they stood. There was another ladder. Within a few minutes the two men were standing in a large brick-lined tunnel, listening to the sound of running sewage and dripping water.

'Well, at least we're not going to drown,' Giles whispered, his back pressed firmly to the damp brickwork. 'But we might be asphyxiated.'

They were evidently beside what must have been a central channel containing a trickle of sewage. Heavy organic smells hung in the dank air. A scurrying noise caused both men to freeze.

'It's all right. It's probably only a rat,' said Hayden, wondering whether his friend would find acceptable this use of 'all right'. He did.

'That's a relief. I thought someone was following us.' This caused Hayden to peer into the blackness behind them with anxious intensity.

At that moment, Duffy was further above ground than his two friends were below it, and in even greater danger. He stood, a wide man on a narrow ledge, *en route* to the Planning Committee's office window on the fourth-floor at City Hall. He was clutching a thin file of papers. It had been the only way. The night security man, though dubious about his intentions, had let him in, but Duffy could not very well ask him for the keys to the inner office. That left brute force on the door, or a perilous ledge-walk. Duffy had opted for the latter.

With his back to the wall, he edged towards the target window. Even though it was well past midnight, occasional vehicles and pedestrians moved on the street below. If he were spotted, he would feign suicidal intentions, but for the moment, all was quiet. He had the horror and the darkness to himself.

The rat, or whatever it was, had seemingly retired out of earshot. Hayden and Giles had the horror and darkness to themselves, though the stench of sewage offered company of a sort. The tunnel was rounding a long bend and there was a faint improvement in visibility. They could now see clearly where total darkness ended and deep shadows began.

'In terms of usage,' said part of the total darkness, 'there's probably a morning rush-hour effect in this sewer.'

'Thank you for that comforting thought. But never mind, if we can't walk to freedom, we can always swim to it.'

'I can't swim,' said Giles after a pause, then he nearly passed out as a bearded tree root hanging from the sewer roof trailed unnervingly across his face.

By now, Duffy had released the window catch with a screwdriver and was climbing into the office in shattered relief. He was in a muck-sweat at the thought of the return journey but, quelling his fear, he turned his mind to the task in hand. Replacements for Sid Whitney's entry forms had to be lodged covertly on file if disqualification on the day of the play-off was to be avoided. That wouldn't take a moment if the lock on the chairman's filing cabinet was small enough to

192

yield to one of Hayden's more useful inventions, a sonic skeleton key. It was! Now only some fast work with the files and a funk-filled foray along the ledge lay between Duffy and the rest of his life.

'Ouch!' Hayden cried after butting his nose against a metal bar. 'It feels like a ladder!' He swung up on to it and commenced an awkward ascent into what must have been a storm drain. His foot complained intolerantly. Eventually he reached a dead-end represented by what felt like the underside of a manhole cover. He strained to open it. There was a scraping noise as of rusted metal against rusted metal, and then the cover rose free and Hayden was able, with difficulty, to push it aside. He hoisted himself up to look out of the hole at what proved to be a hard standing, lamplit, between darkened buildings. Giles was on the ladder below him. Wasn't this the Culture Park? And wasn't that . . . ? Yes! It was Giles's taxi.

If Hayden had rung Granville Markham beforehand, he might have spared himself a tour of Brighton's sewers. Some hours previously the racketeer had received a report in his office which confirmed his suspicions.

'There's still a lot of activity on the boat, boss,' said Stair-rods Wilson. 'That must have been some party you went to.'

'That was three days ago, you idiot. Clearing up doesn't take that long. Whitney's up to something.'

No activity at the factory; bustle on the boat. What was Markham to make of that? Whitney must be constructing the prototype on board ship, for safety's sake. But he needn't have bothered. Markham had already concluded that an assault on Whitney's factory might invite unanswerable reprisals.

Fikansky and the other boffins had run into

difficulties, so Markham had been dismayed to learn, yet Whitney appeared to be pressing forwards. The rumour Fikansky had picked up days ago must have been right after all. The opposition *were* working on a new design – a design by Sabanack!

20

The Green Liquor

Hayden's lower mandible, never short of work, found
an unusual use the next morning when he of whom it
was a part stopped in drop-jawed amazement on the
threshold of his office. A noise at his side summoned
him back from stupefaction and signalled the arrival
up the stairs of Sophie's father.

'You didn't need to do it, you know, Hayden,' said
James. 'I know you two have quarrelled, but you didn't
need to get out because of it.' They stood together
inspecting Hayden's office, which had been almost
completely gutted. 'And then there were the books.
They were mine, you know. Quite valuable really.'

'I didn't do this. Someone's stolen my office. And
your books.' Desks, chairs, even the carpet and curtains
had disappeared along with some of the wallpaper.
Only Hayden's telephone remained, sitting on the bare
boards.

'I think someone's trying to tell you something,
Hayden. Perhaps I can tell you something: I'll make
you a cup of tea.' With that, the bookseller retreated
and Hayden was left alone with a sense of loss and
impending denouement. His notes, files, discs, reprint
collection, books – everything had gone. Fortunately,
though, the duplicate drawing of the Existometer was
with his ex-assistant. The time for serious measures
had arrived. He resolved to make some telephone calls,
starting with one to Mrs Grim. He lifted the receiver of

195

the telephone to be immediately assailed by a recorded message.

'You were warned. The next thing to go will be you.' Click. The voice was unrecognizable. The speaker had evidently lodged a sock in his vocal chords before taping the message. The return of the dialling tone allowed Hayden to make his calls before leaving the office an hour later. James had volunteered to call the police, and had promised to tell his daughter when next he saw her to send the duplicate drawing to Hayden. It was unsafe for Sophie to store it.

The gutted office presumably meant that the opposition knew of the deficiencies of the Mark I device and that they had guessed at Hayden's continuing involvement in the Whitney Enterprises project. In that case he could count himself fortunate not to have fallen victim to the Slab's homicidal tendencies. The time for desperate measures had arrived. A council of war had been called.

It was the right of anyone in Brighton to insist that an official inquiry be set up into matters of urgent importance. All that was required was a petition bearing the signatures of twelve citizens. For Hayden, a police investigation alone had not seemed enough. Conspiracy, corruption and intimidation warranted more. His idea was that Mayor Yalton, using the wide-ranging powers at his disposal, would look into the affairs of Peerless Widgets, preferably with the result that Markham and his evil henchmen would be sent into perpetual exile from the city as a threat to public safety.

Hayden had reported the burglary to Sid, and pointed out that something drastic needed doing. The Londoner had accepted the need to meet, but grudgingly. He had sounded oddly evasive. Hayden's other would-be petitioners had agreed to rally round with rather more enthusiasm.

When the partially dispossessed and fully intimidated scholar got home, he went straight to the cupboard under the stairs and struggled to pull out a substantial trunk. Men of goodwill had been summoned to stand shoulder-to-shoulder in the fight for right, and to sign the petition. But even men of goodwill would need some refreshment. In the trunk were two large earthenware jugs, heavily bunged and wrapped around with thick metal strips. Hayden pulled back a hinged lid to reveal the jugs, which he scrutinized suspiciously. No obvious signs of menace.

Two months ago Hayden had run off the first distillate from the linoleum-still into these receptacles. According to his computer simulation, the liquor must be drunk soon or it would turn into rocket propellant.

'Hey, robot, where are you?' Noiselessly, the robot joined him. 'Take these jugs into the courtyard, please, and await my instructions.' The robot hesitated a moment and seemed troubled; it, too, knew the results of the computer simulation. 'Come on! It's only a drop of hooch.' Before the robot picked up the first jug, the distiller stepped smartly into the cupboard, for safety. The robot moved off. Meanwhile, Mrs Grim could be heard arriving through the side door, doubtless with provisions for the lunch-party. Hayden shouted for her to stay clear of the courtyard.

Out in the sunshine, Hayden asked the robot to move the jugs nearer the small, central fountain and away from his miniature orange bushes in their terracotta pots. There were three of these at each end of the courtyard, Hayden having observed, in a modest manner, the Buddha's injunction to plant and see to the establishment of one tree at least every five years.

Down the length of one side of the courtyard, Mrs Grim had set up a long trestle table over which was draped a white tablecloth. From behind this, Hayden peered at the proceedings as his robot worked loose the first bung. When it finally came out, a cloud of greenish vapour emerged with it, causing the robot to sway momentarily before hanging motionless in the air. The lights on its sensor array panel flickered out.

As the miasma dissipated, the robot revived sufficiently to tackle the second bung. This time, it was only halfway out when, with a mighty whoosh! the stopper shot skywards out of sight.

The robot was clearly shaken by these events, so it was sent off to help Mrs Grim prepare the food. Hayden sat on while the liquor settled, and reflected that this courtyard was perhaps not dissimilar to the orangery in Tunisia where in 1942 his father had twice been offered the position of Caliphate of Carthage, once during the heroic retreat of the 8th Army, once during its glorious advance. Although a largely honorific position, being Caliphate did entail the upkeep of a forty-woman harem – well beyond an infantry captain's means – and ten eunuchs. Hayden's father had settled instead for receiving the Order of the Eversharp Scimitar.

The fluid was about ready for testing. Should he invite Mrs Grim to join him? Perhaps not. During a pharmacological experiment recently, he had inadvertently given her a cup of coffee containing a few granules of a Haitian zombie poison. He'd been amazed at the results. Only on reading the small print did he see that the chemical had an anaesthetic potency five orders of magnitude greater than cocaine. For three weeks in February Mrs Grim had been unable to do the housework. While zombified she had stood immobile in the laundry cupboard with empty, staring eyes.

The tasting could be left until the guests arrived. In

the meantime, Hayden would dig out his straw hat, which was in a rakish 'flattened pith helmet' style, then locate his other important accessory.

When he returned to the courtyard towards midday, it was to find the table loaded with enigmatic comestibles. The game pie was recognizable enough, as was the coronation chicken, but less identifiable were some escalopes of goat in onion sauce, sundry unfamiliar cruciferous vegetables, and a fruit bowl containing pomelos, jaffarines and ortaniques. A silver salver of battered pheasants reminded Hayden that his former 'bird in the hand', Francesca, had groused more than somewhat when invited to the theatre, but had finally swallowed her outrage and accepted. The 'Forgive my robot' card received at her embassy office desk that morning had done nothing to damage his cause.

Mrs Grim had gone home by now, leaving the robot with the final task of bringing glasses into the courtyard. Knowing that the electromechanical contraption would fret if left unoccupied, its master sent it back into the kitchen to spend a few hours boiling up old paper handkerchieves.

Sitting alone and mindful of recent losses, Hayden felt like an emotional amputee groping for the missing limb. He decided to pour himself a stiff, green drink, but before he could get the glass to his lips, Giles bowled in through the high wrought-iron gate with Linden close behind. They were talking animatedly, but at the sight of Hayden's black armband, fell silent. The bereaved handed them drinks and spoke in hushed tones. He felt an ache in his soul and had been surprised to conclude that there must have been a place in it where once had dwelt Sophie.

'I am in deep mourning, friends. Honour me by raising your glass in memory of that which was dear to me and is now lost. My office.' The three men drank reverently. Hayden shut his eyes in shock; Giles stamped a foot and coughed hastily; Linden clutched his throat. 'What do you think?' Hayden wheezed when the initial pyrexial reaction had passed.

'It's fantastic!' replied Linden. 'But then I'm biased because I like it.' Hayden pondered this casual destruction of the basis for critical evaluation while Giles struggled to bring the left and right sides of his body back into some sort of co-ordination.

'It's amazing,' the taxi driver averred throatily. '*Vin Chlorophyll de Château Sabanack*?' Hayden nodded modestly. 'What about this office thing? Have you been booted out?'

'Stolen. Every stick of furniture, every sheet of paper gone.'

'That's remarkable. I was just saying to Linden that I've had my taxi stolen. One moment it was there, the next – an empty road!'

'It's a crime wave, and no mistake,' said Linden, as his host refilled the glasses from a decanter. The three agreed that Granville Markham was undoubtedly behind the office burglary, and that he and his gang had to be stopped. As they talked, the other guests arrived in ones and twos. Uncle George turned up looking cool in a linen suit, bow-tie and panama hat. Simeon and Nigel came next, followed by the wraith-like figure of Didier from the cafe. He was accompanied by Max, walking with a cane, who was happy to consume a free meal even if the table talk was not to be broadcast. Duffy rolled in next with Ted, who had left someone in charge of the Warbler. A few minutes later, Sophie's father James arrived just in front of two representatives of the Explorers' Club, General Roscius and a small, brown, weathered individual billed as 'Naipur Chettan Sherpa, Himalayan guide'. This character wore ethnic garb consisting of a russet-coloured wrap-around coat and trousers, and a dark, squarish cap with earflaps.

The liquid refreshment proved an immediate triumph. Men who were unknown to one another vowed friendship; men who were friends vowed brotherhood; and Naipur permitted the trace of a smile to play on his otherwise impassive countenance.

Linden, who for religious reasons had long subsisted on a diet of beans, lentils, leeks and turnips, was first to move in on the rich victuals laid out before them. Soon, they were all sitting at table, ranged on one side looking into the courtyard, with Hayden at their centre.

'It's a funny thing,' Duffy was saying with difficulty, his forkful of downland lamb and mint sauce halted in mid-air. 'You know Buster Swiftington? You do? I bumped into him at the cricket ground. Well, my motor was going in for repairs, so he lent me his sports car as a favour. Insisted on it! I hardly know the man. And you know what happened? The car was pinched from the City Hall car park this morning! Would you believe it?' Duffy's incredulity spilled into a guilty snigger, then he began to shudder as he tried to suppress the seismic tremors of an impending mirthquake. The nectareous beverage had got to him.

'Same thing happened to Giles,' said Linden, causing the company to turn to the news vendor then to the proprietor of Battledress Taxis. But Giles's mind seemed to have gone into receivership, so Linden carried on unaided. 'He said he only had his car key left. So I said, "Your khaki what?" Get it? The key for his khaki car!' There was a pause for immoderate hilarity. 'Can't trust anyone these days,' added Linden. 'Did you read that bit in the paper about the carpenter being trowelled to death by a plasterer for putting a door in crooked? What's the world coming to when a carpenter can't even put a door in straight?'

During this news bulletin, Simeon, at the end of the table, had begun discoursing learnedly on some legal nicety to one of the orange bushes. He was distracted by Giles staggering to his feet.

'I should never have let Jane go!' he declaimed wretchedly, staggering off into the honeysuckle-clad wall behind them, then subsiding to the ground. At this, Hayden and Naipur caught each other's eye and exchanged a look in cross-cultural assessment. Neither disliked what he saw. Between them, Didier began to sing the 'Brighton Boating Song' to the tune of the 'Marseillaise'. Nigel hummed along for a moment then slid peacefully under the table, as though reeled in from below.

Six glasses of the green stuff had called into question Max's ability to function as a gastronome. He tried to spear a stuffed olive on his plate, but ended by scooping it up clumsily instead.

'A spoon is just a bent knife without a fork's pretensions,' he said thickly after a few moments' thought. 'Make a note of that, Boswell, will you?' If James, next to him, had heard any of this, he showed no sign of it. Indeed, he showed little sign of anything much: he had passed out ten minutes before.

Meanwhile, Uncle George was prodding a pickled gherkin into a bowl of what looked like activated sludge, but which may well have been a caviar-based dip. Hayden turned to him and spoke with raised voice for all to hear.

'Why don't you give us one of your celebrated toasts, esteemed relation?' There was a scattering of applause from the conscious guests and one or two cheers. George, on autopilot, had no problem in complying. Taking a last swig of elixir, he pulled himself to his feet, a generous napkin trailing from his collar.

'Gentlemen,' he said, rapping the table and silencing the General who for the third time had been

202

complaining to Ted that Upper Volta should never have changed its name to Burkina Faso. ('More like an anagram than a country, begad!')

'Gentlemen, when the sap has climbed the stem, the buds have broken into blossom, and the air is heavy with pollen, should a man try to repress the irrepressible, stop the unstoppable? No, I think not. There is a desire which must find physical expression. If I omit description of a certain protrusion, an uncontrollable muscular spasm, and a satisfying outrush – you will doubtless appreciate my sensitivity. Let us drink to a very natural process. I refer of course to the summer sneeze. Gentlemen, hayfever!'

Amidst the guffawing and applause which followed this speech, there entered into the courtyard a slight figure squinting in the sunshine and laden with artist's paraphernalia. It was Sid Whitney's daughter Gail in T-shirt, shorts and sandals. At the sight of Hayden and his dozen guests, her nerve almost failed. But Hayden saw the new arrival and beckoned her forward, eyeing her gear with distrust.

'My father sends his apologies. He can't attend. He asked me to, er, convey . . . I was painting the pier . . . if you see what I mean.' She broke off in confusion, indicating the long canvas she had dropped with relief on to the floor.

'Sit down and have a drink. Or at least, no. Have something to eat. Please help yourself.' With Naipur turning up unexpectedly and taking the unfilled seat, Hayden had quite forgotten that Sid had been on the guest list. He had particularly wanted to ask him something about the factory, but he could no longer remember what. Was it to do with the riddle of something or other? And why had he got everybody together in the first place? The liquor had dissolved the contents of his memory. His thoughts were disturbed by the sound of oxen trundling a litter-cart along the seafront, yoke-bells clanging. Visitors to the city invariably commented on how Brighton was prepared to try out any idea, at any level of technology, from anywhere in the world. Flexibility was the key to success.

When the oxen had passed, the party host listened to the conversations around him, punctuated as they were by occasional eruptions of laughter. Nigel was snoring under the table, and Didier had also sunk into oblivion. Simeon was getting on with his orange bush sufficiently well to offer it a buttered roll, perhaps aware that 'companion' literally means 'sharer of bread'.

'Linden, can I pour you a drop more?'

'Well, perhaps just a sip, Hayden. But you know how I feel about alcohol – the devil's embrocation.' As Hayden reached across to pour the drink, he regretted inviting further indulgence. Linden was looking pretty loaded – eyes unfocused, cheeks sallow no more. His usual tipple was rainwater from a butt. There might later be the stool of repentance.

'You know, Duffy,' said Uncle George, turning to Sid's daughter, 'you've lost a lot of weight, yes, indeed.' This proved to be his valedictory as he too slid into placid unconsciousness. Even Ted, to whom alcohol was no stranger, felt a delicious languor invade his limbs.

'Hayden, this is a fine . . .' But Ted could not finish his sentence as he keeled over against the huge, well-stuffed cushion that was Duffy, to pass into a more restful realm.

'Have at you!' said Hayden to no-one in particular, using the medieval jouster's cry in what proved to be the last toast of the session.

So it was that Naipur alone saw the young girl move to the other end of the courtyard beyond the splashing fountain, set up her canvas on a tripod, and begin to paint. He watched quizzically through narrowed eyes as she worked quickly and confidently, all self-doubt behind her. There was no way that the Sherpa, or anyone else for that matter, could foresee that this young girl would be the indirect cause of a tragic death – that of a geranium.

21

A Box at the Theatre

The recently inebriated scholar arrived at his destination that evening after a rinse, a scrape, a change of livery and a brisk walk. He was in magnificent fettle, and felt taller, stronger and more handsome than usual. Even his foot felt better. There were evidently no adverse effects associated with the green liquor. At any rate, his guests had failed to show any. Perhaps it should be marketed as a panacea.

As he entered the Theatre Royal, his mind was not on *Adam's Navel* but on the Existometer, which was now synonymous with the Armillary Sphere of Destiny. Today, Monday, was Day Fifteen, so there were just six clear days till the test run. The loss of research materials would probably not badly affect immediate progress but would certainly set back the post-prototype development stage. It was in Hayden's mind to ring Sid again and tell him this, while also taking the opportunity to quiz him about the absence of activity at the factory. There was also the news that the police had raided Markham's office in connection with the burglary, with predictably fruitless results.

If that telephone call had yet to be made, so had another. He had still not contacted the mayor to set up an official investigation into Peerless Widgets. Forgetting to raise the petition over lunch had been an act of inexpressible folly. He would have to try to stir up something without one, in the morning, first thing.

Hayden's dual failure of dynamism he attributed to the relaxing effect of his home-brew. Remarkable stuff! To think earlier in the day he had even contemplated going into hiding, against all the traditions of the Sabanacks. He would not be outfaced by villains! If he had an engagement at the theatre, then he would keep it.

The crowd in the foyer was a-twitter with anticipation. Hayden stooged around to find Francesca, but she had yet to arrive. This gave him time to pick up the tickets – which turned out to be for a box – and order some drinks for the interval. By now he, too, was beginning to feel the first-night flutter and nerves which had transmitted themselves to the audience from backstage. Here was a prospect indeed! The ravishing Babette in a revamped . . . His thoughts were interrupted by the arrival of Francesca wearing an elegant outfit in blue. Her greeting was both haughty and brusque.

'Ah, there you are Mr Sabanack. Pray conduct me to my seat.'

Hayden masked his surprise and extended an arm upon which his companion rested a delicate hand. Together they ascended the wide, thickly carpeted stairs to the upper tier. Francesca appeared mollified to find that they had a box to themselves, and began to peruse the programme Hayden had acquired for her. After a while she frowned and spoke: 'Listen to this piffle. "Tragedy, transduced comedy, purges the mind of meanness and self-preoccupation; comedy, subverted tragedy, purifies us of our pretensions and vanity."'

'Yes, a load of rot, isn't it?' he replied, recognizing one of his own contributions to the wretched publication. He was spared the trial of hearing more when the house lights dimmed and the curtain rolled back. He felt a sudden pang of apprehension on Francesca's behalf: *Adam's Navel* was scarcely the stuff of unforgettable theatrical experiences.

The curtains opened on the bustling courtyard of a coaching inn. The stage was athrong with scurrying ostlers, saucy serving wenches, flagon-swilling gallants and pipe-smoking elders. Since Hayden had read the play, it had been time-shifted into the seventeenth century to become some sort of rumbustious Restoration comedy. A few minutes of scene-setting dialogue between minor characters were followed by a cry heralding the arrival of the midday coach, stage left. An expectant hush fell on players and audience alike. Hayden craned forward in anticipation. Yes! It was none other than Babette, hair piled high and ringleted, her delectable form clothed in a luxuriously cascading dress of astonishing *décolletage*. A sharp intake of breath greeted her appearance on stage. Strong men mewed; weak men mewed; Hayden mewed. Here was the woman who had occupied his recent dreams.

'She's wearing a wig,' hissed Francesca. Babette was no more wearing false hair than she was wearing false . . . Well, never mind, Hayden could not sit by and let their benefactress be defamed in this way.

'You're right,' he said cravenly, opting for peace.

The play proceeded swiftly, the plot turning on the activities of a handsome highwayman, evil Nick Nubbins, and on the guileless progress of the Adam character himself, who, though of noble bearing, has been orphaned young and knows nothing of his origins. They both conceive an early interest in the lately arrived, and far from unsophisticated, Miss Evesham (Babette). There were sub-plots a-plenty involving the unrequited love of a maidservant for Adam, buried loot, a cuckolded magistrate and lost travellers. But there was no cloaking a lack of inner substance, for which inadequate compensation was provided by the surface attractions – none more alluring than the lead actress herself, at one point seen in scanty chemise. The first half culminated in a duel between Nick and Adam over Miss Evesham's honour, an event comically interrupted by the arrival of the magistrate with a warrant for the highwayman's arrest. As the curtain fell, the applause was muted as though the audience wore oven gloves.

When the house lights went up, Hayden nearly suffered a cardiac arrest. Granville Markham was sitting in the front row of the stalls! The gangster was rising to his feet. As though sensing the gaze from above he glanced up, causing the scholar to bound from his seat into the back of the box.

'What's up?' Francesca asked in surprise.

'Oh, nothing. I just think we should hurry along to the bar to avoid the crowds.' Hayden had repressed a desire to hurl himself towards the nearest emergency exit, and was reasoning that if Markham wanted an interval snifter, he would not traipse upstairs in search of one. He would use the crush bar at the rear of the stalls. That left Hayden safe, as long as he wasn't seen. What it was to be a marked man! Summoning up suavity, he ushered his guest towards the quintuple gin and tonic awaiting her in the circle bar.

'Well, it's not as bad as all that,' Francesca said after sampling her drink. 'The sets and costumes were fantastic. Where do you think they got the gibbet from? Mmm, this drink is just what I needed.'

'The one-liners were good, didn't you think?' Hayden ventured, self-servingly, composure mostly restored.

'Meretricious. Like the leading lady: over-made-up.'

'Adam lived to nine hundred and thirty, you know.'

'I bet you got that from that beastly programme.' She paused, then added, 'They could do with more rehearsal. Every time your lady friend speaks her lines, the rest of the cast look as if they can't contain their surprise. Haven't they read the script?'

They were forced close together in the crush of the bar and Francesca's proximity and perfume sounded a croon of muted trumpets in the scholar's soul. He kissed her lightly on the cheek, causing her to draw away in indignation but without haste.

'Now you know that I said last time was the last time. Well, it was.'

He placed his arm around her waist and drew her towards him for another kiss.

'Now stop that,' she murmured as their lips brushed. 'Stop that . . .'

Just then the second half bell rang out, and, disengaging, they returned ruefully to their box. Hayden was careful not to let himself be seen by Granville Markham, though he had become calmer on that score. Gangsters don't expunge people at first nights, now do they?

The second half proved even busier than the first but scarcely less dire. The hero was mistaken for the gentleman of the road and there followed a hectic chase involving the irate magistrate and a platoon of hastily recruited militiamen. Adam was caught, and only the intervention of the love-struck serving girl saved him from summary justice. Witnesses were summoned for a trial which Hayden could not recollect in the original. Obvious padding. His attention wandered to Francesca next to him. Her attitude to him had softened appreciably during the evening and the ambivalence was deliciously provoking. After discreetly unhitching the tie-back on the curtain next to him in the interests of privacy, Hayden returned his attention to Francesca. He put his arm around her shoulders and was pleased to note no resistance. He then began to rain gentle kisses on her neck while moving his free hand south of her shoulders.

'No, no,' she moaned yieldingly. Now they were kissing each other eagerly, without restraint. Mercifully, the box opposite was empty, but the same could not be said of the one below it. Unbeknown to them, an elderly gentleman had chanced to see these events through opera glasses, and his eyes all but erupted from their sockets when the two people suddenly disappeared from view towards the floor of the box. His wife next to him had seen nothing; she was intent on the play. He looked at her tremblingly with a wild surmise. No, perhaps not. He shook his head regretfully.

'What are you doing?' Francesca gasped, pliant with desire and all too aware that she had been skilfully divested of her knickers.

'I'm planning a theatrical event,' Hayden whispered into her ear. 'Sexual Act One. Obscene One. Enter woman stage right.'

'Not here, surely . . . I said never again . . . Oh!'

'Perhaps I can interest you in a small part.' There was a pause for decision-making.

'Not too small, I hope . . . Oh! Oh!'

Meanwhile, on stage, things were also moving to a climax. Adam's sentence had been commuted to a severe flogging, sure to prove fatal, for which purpose he had been divested of his shirt. Thus was revealed the birthmark on his navel which signalled to the lost travellers his noble origins and his right to a vast fortune held in trust. Miss Evesham sensibly repents of her previous infatuation for the knavish Nubbins, and there burgeons in her bosom a maidenly passion for Adam, leading her to enter a plea for clemency on the hero's behalf. Adam is visibly moved by this shift of allegiance, but other ears are deaf to her entreaties. The magistrate is bent on revenging himself on the man who has supposedly cuckolded him. Once again only the loyal serving maid can save Adam – this time by

211

unmasking the true villain. This she does, but only at the cost of her life as she is run through by a vengeful blade wielded by the highwayman himself. In Adam's arms, the girl draws her dying breath, vowing eternal love. A pitched battle ensues between Nubbins and his accomplices on one side and the forces of justice on the other. Wicked Nick meets his end at the hero's hand, and the Happy Couple fall into a satisfying embrace.

'What?!?!' exclaimed Hayden at the recumbent Francesca as he lurched to his feet, dragging on his trousers in alarm. 'You did what!' He was oblivious of the stares of hundreds of theatre-goers and of a troupe of players, including that of an actress who until recently had held a special place in his regard. The elderly fellow across the auditorium shook his head in disbelief as the unknown man in the darkened box wrestled with his zip.

Francesca witnessed these events from closer quarters. All she had said, as they lay quietly in each other's arms, was that it was a joy to make love without the noise of that awful linoleum-still. Anyway, she had fixed the still on her last visit to Hayden's place before being cornered by the robot. She had turned the thing off.

The impact of this news had caused Hayden to leave the box in instalments. First to flee was his imagination which had flown in horror to the spare bedroom and its menacing occupant. Then followed his body, as soon as it could, leaving only the sounds of his footfalls on the carpeted stairway to bring up the rear.

Outside the theatre, Hayden searched desperately for a taxi. There were none in sight. He would have to run all the way, and give it the full hoof. As he made off, he calculated frantically. It was now Monday. Francesca had done the deed on Friday. That made about seventy-eight hours in all. Am I already too late?

The linoleum-still could not be turned off. That was

the point! Hayden had previously given his attention to the decommissioning process but had yet to tackle the details, such as how it was to be achieved. Deep-sea dumping was one alternative, another was emigration – for Hayden.

The device might already have entered final melt-down mode, he admitted to himself, as he swung round the corner into North Street and bolted towards the Clock Tower, scattering the few pedestrians he encountered before him. Suddenly his injured foot gave way, however, and he pulled up in pain. He would have to take it a bit easier and trust to luck. After all, the still was in part fabricated from a fibre composite material containing tantalum carbide. It might hold.

As he lumbered on, he passed a pack of pariah dogs picking at some rubbish strewn outside a trattoria. The dogs turned to yelp at him. It used to be said, he thought, observing the litter and avoiding the dogs, that the English were not good at towns: too slovenly, too irresponsible. We were reckoned to be better at villages and country houses. Until Brighton emerged as a separate entity, that is. Good God, why am I bothering about litter and stray dogs, when the fate of mankind might be in the balance?!

This caused Hayden to break into a shambling trot as he turned into Churchill Square before descending the concrete steps towards Russell Square. He was able to maintain a fairly good lick to his front door, where he arrived a few minutes later, very nearly spent. It was 10 p.m. exactly.

Inside the house, Hayden went to the cupboard under the stairs where resided the main switch for the electricity. On the assumption that Francesca had not touched the still's subsidiary controllers, he would turn off the power then quit the premises for a day or so, just in case. He had rejected the alternative course

213

of action which was to go up to the spare bedroom, switch the principal controller back on, then quit the premises for a day or so, just in case.

As it happened, shutting off the power was precisely the wrong thing to do. While Hayden was leaning against the cupboard wall, gasping with relief, the linoleum-still went critical and, after a single, small explosion that neatly punctured the roof, the house was engulfed by a mighty detonation which levelled both dwelling and dweller alike. The noise was heard throughout Brighton, even, distantly, in a certain theatre still abuzz with the events of earlier that evening. A spout of flames flared high into the air, giving off a blinding light which was monitored by Brighton's own UN reconnaissance satellite, remote in the earth's atmosphere. The entire Fédération Française went on to a war footing that same evening. It was 10.01 p.m.

22

Throbbing

At Le Throb, the morning shift of the infamous and anagrammatically named establishment was attending to the last of the night shift's customers. Granville Markham was reclining contentedly in the hot, soapy water of a sunken tub when the morning paper arrived. He glanced at the front-page story and let out a cry of surprise, causing the two women next to him to stir in alarm. He reached for the phone.

'Of course it's me, Stair-rods, who do you think it is? I know it's early, for God's sake. Have you seen the paper? No, not the racing results, the front page! You heard the explosion last night? That was Sabanack's house going up. The Slab's gone berserk! And he didn't even manage to knock him off! Tell the maniac to go into hiding, as of now. You get over to the hospital. I want to know the moment Sabanack throws a seven. Not now, darling, please. No, I'm not talking to you! Get on with it!'

That was all Markham needed, the Slab out of control! He reached for a plastic duck distractedly.

'You're a ruthless swine, Wilfred,' said the Institute's director of operations, entwining herself around the professor as they stood at the office window looking out across the rooftops in the direction of Hayden's house. Wilfred had heard the news of the explosion on his car radio and had had plenty of time to adjust to the idea that an intellectual rival was now out of the way. He had yet to adjust to Miranda's unexpected display of intense physical arousal.

'A man's got to deal with his enemies,' the professor said hoarsely, his glasses askew as a result of his colleague's attentions.

'God, I like a hard man,' Miranda purred as she dragged him towards the office couch.

Some times are good, some are bad. This was 10 a.m. And it was bad. For some hours Hayden had lain in an oxygen tent with one foot in the grave and the other in a plaster cast. Beside him sat his mother and Sophie. Suddenly, the patient shuddered like an old refrigerator and opened his eyes. He felt terrible. That's what twelve hours inspecting the inside of your eyelids does for you – that and being blown about in a lumber cupboard. He saw where he was and was relieved. It might have been a funeral parlour.

'How are you, Hayden?' his mother asked, craning over him. He groaned but could not speak. He tried again to move his lips but no sound came. Unbidden, Sophie placed a pen in his hand and held a notebook to which he was to commit his thoughts. 'Existo,' was all he could write.

'Existo?' asked Mrs Sabanack. 'What does that mean?'

'No need to send it down to Pathology. It's a substitution code. He means that he loves us both dearly – the one filially, the other with passion. His brain unfortunately has emerged from the explosion unscathed.'

'Oh, I see.' They looked at the poor man sympathetically. His eyes had closed. 'Why do you bother with him, Sophie?'

'I don't know. Why do you?'

'A green son has a certain novelty value.' They

216

managed a laugh, for it was true. The two square metres of skin wrapped round Hayden's lithe frame had turned green in the cataclysm. Doubtless this was due to some hideous vapour released by the linoleum-still, but nobody had guessed that yet.

The fumes from the explosion had incapacitated fourteen firemen, two policemen and an ambulance crew, and it was only with difficulty that Hayden had been extracted from the rubble at all. The injured men had been rushed to the accident department of the City General Hospital, there to take their place in the queue behind the victims of a blood feud which had broken out again in the Balkan quarter that same night. There had been no bed for Hayden. At one time it looked as though he would have to stay in the car park overnight in the ambulance, then the Brighton Lying-In Hospital had offered a bed in the Near-Term Unit. So it was that a green man had come to share a ward with five heavily pregnant women and two new mothers complete with shrieking infants.

To be dead in dreams announces freedom from anxiety. To be dead in reality signifies the same thing. To be half-dead is to be alive with fears for the future. Hayden's brain was in tortured disorder. Would he be able to walk again? And be able to drink mead from an ox-horn, and call for wenches? And what about this noise in his ears of crying babies? Was this a concussive effect or some ghastly clairaudience?

He drifted in and out of consciousness. On one occasion he fancied he was under the lights in an operating theatre, listening to a male voice.

'This woman isn't very pregnant,' it said. 'Obviously a pseudopregnancy. Do a pseudodelivery, nurse, and report back to me later. I'll be in the bar.' This was followed by the sound of retreating footsteps and swinging doors.

Then he was travelling fast, and there was star-

217

stippled blackness on all sides. He realized suddenly that he was inside the Armillary Sphere of Destiny and that the fabled machine was careering at fantastic speed around the Milky Way. Weirdly, there was a near-collision with a small flying saucer – which turned out to be his kitchen robot, now green in colour.

A soft landing in Brighton, in a gigantic snowdrift, then he was tunnelling, tunnelling. He must claw his way out! There was daylight – then he was clear. It was a city centre street, snowbound. A battalion of old women was clearing the snow, bundled against the cold and bearing long-handled brooms stoically. He woke to find a plump, shabbily overalled woman sweeping the floor round his bed. She smiled waspishly, showing yellow and black teeth.

Two miles out to sea, on the *Marbella Hood,* Sid Whitney stood on the bridge, telephone in hand. He was determined to find out what had happened to the only scholar on his payroll. They had heard the explosion, of course, and debris had even landed near them, but the news on the radio that morning had been scanty.

To have Hayden subtracted from the Whitney head-count was bad enough, but for his daughter to go into romantic bereavement was worse. The black taffeta dress had been the last straw.

The news he learned surprised and cheered him. Green, indeed – there was a thing! The news caused Gail to come out of mourning and to reconsider the events of the previous evening. For if there was a man suffering greenness in this town, there was also a girl. And both, coincidentally, had been in the theatre the previous night, the one recognizing the other's voice.

23

The Distiller

'There is a pile of rubble where your house used to be,' said Sophie to Hayden when he had finally cleared customs and re-entered the land of the living the next day. 'You've done well. You've made the front page two days running.' Hayden was breakfasting on a kind of gruel made from oats called porridge. It was proving surprisingly palatable. He neglected it to inspect the morning paper, which Sophie had brought with her. The *Spume*'s headline ran thus: 'GREEN MAN IN PREGNANCY BOMBSHELL!'

'I have to say that I prefer you flesh coloured. And not pregnant.'

'You say that you dropped off the duplicate drawing on the night of the disaster?'

'Yes, that's right.'

'What time?'

'About eight thirty in the evening.'

'So why didn't I see it on the doormat?'

'Is your memory reliable in this instance?'

'And you couldn't find it near the wreckage of the front door?'

'No. I'll have to make a more thorough search, though, before I can be sure.'

'So we're down one drawing of the Mark II Existo-meter, and according to this paper I'm carrying another man's child. Where did they get this tripe?'

'No idea. Perhaps they have an informant in the

hospital. Changing the subject, the police have found Giles's taxi in a quarry near Lewes, and that sports car Duffy was borrowing was there, too.'

'Why were they stolen?'

'No idea. It's left both Duffy and Giles a bit rattled, particularly Giles. When he thought you'd been bombed into hospital, he was close to buying an air ticket to Rio. Not that he could afford it. That's all the news. I must be getting off to work now.' Hayden felt distinctly piqued at the thought of Sophie working for someone else, but managed to conceal the fact.

'Will you be coming this evening?'

'Only if you want me to.'

'I do.'

'Then I'll come.'

When Sophie had gone, Hayden put down the newspaper and pushed aside his breakfast things. This was an odd turn of events. To find himself pregnant and in hospital! He who believed so strongly in home deliveries! It was the unexpectedness of life that was so predictable.

Overnight the score as between pregnant women and mums had narrowed from 5:2 to 4:3. The noise of truculent neonates had thus increased by a half. Hayden marvelled at the evidence of fecundity all around him. The Roman Emperor Augustus had legislated against celibacy. Such a law would be superfluous in present-day Brighton.

The doctors' rounds were due shortly. The nurses and auxiliaries were scurrying to and fro in preparation for this momentous event. The three other patients on Hayden's side had been tidied up, and now it was the turn of the four opposite, two either side of the double doors. A booming voice from across the ward greeted Hayden's glance.

''ow yer doin', 'ayden?'

'Fine thanks, er . . .'

'Molly.'
'Molly.'
'You've got some lovely colour on your cheeks. Lift yer sheets and let's see if it goes all over.' There was a ripple of laughter round the ward and one or two disdainfully shaking heads. In truth he *was* green all over, though palpably lighter where his clothes had been. Rather than engage in further *risqué* conversation with Molly, he smiled at the woman to his left, the end bed to his right being vacant. She was black, and flashed him a pleasant smile. Her name was Carola ('not Carol'), and her husband was unable to visit because an office colleague had contracted measles. Unimmunized, Carola's husband would appear below their window to wave a greeting, as he had done that very morning.

Hayden leaned over to peer at the view from their second-floor vantage point. Beyond the lawns and shrubberies around the hospital lay several acres of neat allotments, including Duffy's own flood-prone rectangle. Beyond these, on rising ground, was the Brighton Necropolis, last resting place of the city's great and good, famed for its exotic mausoleums and monuments, giant urns and obelisks. Hayden was pleased not to have become one of its more colourful occupants.

The ward doors swung open and in strode a chevron of white-coated doctors with a self-important air. They separated in ones and twos like planes in an air display. The moment of truth was arriving. Would Hayden admit to distilling liquor in his spare bedroom? And admit to causing an explosion which had crippled eighteen people beside himself? No, he would not. Going straight from crater to hospital to gaol was not to be contemplated. He would lie low.

'Ah, the man who not only hospitalized himself but eighteen others as well. Mr Sabanack, the distiller.' He was being addressed by a middle-aged woman with straggly grey hair who stood, clipboard in hand, at his side. An old floral frock was visible beneath her unbuttoned white coat. She wore a name badge which said 'Dr Tyler'. Hers was an air of world-weary geniality. 'Fortunately, the other eighteen have been discharged, and your only physical damage except extensive bruising is a small fracture of the heel bone. Hence the plaster cast. You're a lucky man, Mr Sabanack.'

'I am, Doctor.'

'There was some confusion when you came in. Nobody bothered to tell us the circumstances in which your injuries were sustained. There was talk of gangrene, gall bladder disease – you can imagine. There are thousands of diseases in the database. Quite a few cause discoloration. Then, when we plastered your foot, we took a skin biopsy sample and analysed it. The green stuff was some sort of polymeric substance not unlike that used in flooring materials, according to our chemist: absorbed percutaneously under pressure. Which, I suppose, is why the other eighteen were spared the pigmentation – too late on to the scene. It all tied in with the accident report which eventually arrived. Of course, it would have saved us a lot of trouble if someone hadn't disposed of your clothes. I suppose they were green, too?'

'I couldn't say.'

'No, quite. Blast effect such as I might have expected in a chemical plant really,' the doctor continued, her eyes defocusing as if, even now, she was searching amidst a tangle of pipework, pressure vessels and gauges for corpses of unusual hue. 'First interesting case we've had in here for years actually. Pity to lose you.'

'You mean . . . ?' Hayden asked in alarm.

'No, no. You'll fade – but you won't die. We'll keep

222

you here on a care and maintenance basis for a few days. You'll have to sit it out. I can banish warts and pimples with a pass of the hand, but with greenness I am powerless. As for your foot, I've prescribed a drug that will accelerate the knitting-together of the bone.'

'Thank you, Doctor.'

'Oh, and Mr Sabanack. I've told the police that they can't arrest you until you're discharged. I won't have my patients disturbed.'

'Thank you,' Hayden mumbled, with a vacant feeling where his innards used to be.

'Cheer up. I have some good news for you. We've checked: you're not pregnant.'

While Dr Tyler had done nothing for Hayden's morale, he had to concede that medicine overall was an *enabling* profession. By making people well, and at least in principle encouraging self-reliance, doctors liquidate the need for their services. This has to be the highest professional ethic. Teaching is even more enabling because those given knowledge are made more self-reliant than those who enjoy good health: knowledge is cumulative in a way that personal health is not. A relapse into ignorance is less likely than a bout of illness. Since teaching promotes maximum self-reliance, this has to be regarded as the highest profession.

Medicine, the croak-and-dagger business, had never appealed much to Hayden as a career, but education was a different matter. He occasionally did a turn as guest lecturer at one or other of the local schools. This ensured that he skirted the perils of pedagogic routine while sampling the pleasures of the avuncular state: pa without responsibility.

If teaching is at one end of the professional scale there are activities at the other end whose practitioners seldom foster self-reliance. One of these *disabling*

223

professions is the law. Consider an analogy with house-painting. If a painter decorates your walls in such a way that you need to re-employ him every few months, he's a 'lawyer'; every few years, and he's a 'doctor'; only once, and he's a 'teacher'. Hayden would have to get in touch with Simeon before he left hospital. He groaned at the thought of the expense.

Disablement was very much on Hayden's mind as he swung his legs over the side of the bed as an experiment in mobility. The plastered foot clonked noisily on the floor. He overcame a bout of dizziness to reach painfully for the clipboard which Dr Tyler had returned to the bed-end. Against 'Diagnosis' was the acronym 'GOK'. Hayden recognized this as meaning 'God only knows'. He hoped that Dr Tyler would maintain this line in discussions with the police. Following the diagnosis, and looking like an ECG trace, was the doctor's signature.

'Now, Mr Sabanack, you mustn't be getting up. Back in bed with you. Shoo!' A nurse was gesticulating at him from a desk in the centre of the ward. Forgetting for a moment what a pigmented fellow he had become, he gave her a debonair and flirtatious stare. She was having none of it. 'Bed!' she ordered with simple finality, wagging a stern finger.

'Well, now we know what that raised thing under the covers was,' said Molly in a super-penetrating stage whisper. There followed a shriek of laughter which set the babies crying, Carola chuckling merrily, and Hayden's brain jangling. A headache had begun to drum at his temple like a high priest.

'I can't find him, boss. He's nowhere in the hospital.'

'Of course you can't find him, idiot. He's over in the maternity unit.' Granville Markham stared round his insalubrious office in exasperation, then returned his attention to Stair-rods Wilson. 'Go and find him,' he said, drawing some counterfeit banknotes towards him in dismissal.

'Right, boss.'

Now more than ever Markham needed this philosophy venture to be a commercial success. The role of Babette Macawley's escort was crimping his resources in inverse proportion to the boost to his ego.

'Eh, boss?'

'Yes, what is it?'

'Why is he in the maternity hospital?'

'Good God, it's obvious isn't it?'

'Er, yes boss.'

Markham now knew that the Slab hadn't been responsible for the explosion at Sabanack's house. Who could have caused it? It had to be Whitney! He must be more ruthless than Markham could ever have imagined. With success in sight, he was thinning his workforce! If Whitney was prepared to bomb his own people, Markham had better watch out. This gave the gangster an idea, whose focus was the *Marbella Hood*.

24

Homicide and Suicide

'Your aunt once tried to kill me, you know.'

'Look, Uncle George, no woman tried to kill me . . .'

'Took exception to my interest in one of her female friends. I said to her: "A three-legged stool won't rock." So she tried to beat me to death with one, a rock, I mean. Beware of jealous women, Hayden.'

'It was the linoleum-still, that's all. An accident.'

'But it was caused by a woman.'

'Yes, *accidentally*.'

'So say you.' There was a pause while both men watched a passing nurse. What was it about women in uniform? 'Anyway, how do you feel?'

'Not too bad. Being blown up has at least augmented my experience base.'

'Perhaps a swig of this will augment it further,' said Hayden's mother's sister-in-law's adulterous husband, extracting a flask of something consoling from his hip. 'My new tipple. White port.' While Hayden had a sip, Uncle George looked around curiously as if expecting to see piles of stomach pumps and surgical boots. 'I was in one of these places once with a lung infection, though they thought it was something else. I kept telling them I was cyanosed until I was blue in the face!' After a moment he added, 'That was a great lunchtime session on Monday. Unforgettable. Speaking of which, have you booked me in for a bite to eat?'

'I have,' Hayden said, picking up a menu card and reading from it. 'Stilton soup as a starter. Mussels in white wine to follow, with plantain and amaranth among the vegetables. Sussex pond – the eighteenth century recipe, of course – to finish.' As he concluded, the gong sounded din-dins with satisfying onomato-poeia.

When lunch was over and Uncle George had gone, Hayden complied with the ancient maritime tradition and slept. He had decided after all not to contact the mayor about Peerless Widgets – what was the point without a petition or hard evidence? Instead he had meant to give himself over to worrying about the where-abouts of the Existometer drawing or about the possibility of criminal proceedings, but lunch in bed had had a soporific effect. His repose did not last long, however. It was interrupted by a merciless prodding in the ribs close to one of his most sensitive bruises.

'Now you've recovered you can tell me why you tried to commit suicide,' said Mrs Sabanack ac-cusingly, heedless of her son's yelp of pain. 'That is scarcely a Sabanackian thing to do.'

'Nurse! There's a mad woman here. Help!' The nurse strolled over and addressed the woman of unsound mind.

'Hello, Mrs Sabanack. Everything as it should be?'

'Yes, thank you. But could I trouble you for a cup of tea? A sudden weariness has come upon me.' With that she tottered histrionically into a chair and eyed her offspring wistfully. 'I contemplated ending it all once. It was in the early days of marriage. Your father was very demanding. Heaven knows what it would have been like if he'd been younger. I found it difficult to cope. At first, anyway.'

'Mother, I don't have any sexual problems if that's what you're implying!' Carola was listening spell-bound without intending to.

'I have to say that your father, who had many regrettable opinions, would have approved. Being a military man he was very fond of massive explosions.'

'It was an accident with a liquor-still. And before you say it, no, I am not a closet alcoholic – even though I was in a cupboard when the report from the spirit world reached me.'

'An accident? We Sabanacks are not subject to the laws of chance,' she explained with an expansive gesture which almost knocked the tea cup from the hand of the returning nurse. 'Oh, thank you,' she said, turning back to her son. 'I've brought you a couple of nightshirts. Hospital pyjamas are so unappealing. Let me know if there is anything else you want.' Peace and quiet, thought Hayden. Peace and quiet.

At that moment, a young man appeared through the ward doors, carrying several cumbersome leather containers rather like violin cases with straps but shaped like small human beings. He deposited all but one on the floor, and this he held aloft. All were agog.

'Get your child-proof containers here, ladies! Come along now. No more fuss or noise from the children on those long journeys. Pop them in and strap them up. The ultimate child-carrying device. I'm not asking one hundred, I'm not asking fifty . . .' But he didn't finish. A burly commissionaire burst into the ward and came towards him.

'That's enough of that,' the commissionaire said, jerking a thumb towards the exit. 'Out!'

'Have a heart, guv! A man's got to make a living. Now there's no need for force. Here, hold on!' The man was legged smartly to the door with his clobber, to a ragged cheer from the stalls. He was ejected, but not before making a sale to a solitary, eager customer. Hayden gave incredulity a free rein. Private enterprise! His mother seemed unperturbed by the incident.

'Hayden, you mustn't let the physical side of a relationship put you off. If I were you I would . . .'

'Mother, I repeat I have no physical problem other than blast damage. And, furthermore, unsolicited advice is a form of pollution.'

'So your unsolicited advice is not to give it?'

'Precisely.'

'I just wanted to say . . .'

'No.'

'Just . . .'

'Please!'

'Oh, very well. I was only going to say that you could do worse than marry Sophie.'

'Mother!'

'You won't be on the cradle side of thirty for ever you know. Sophie was very loyal. She stayed awake throughout your coma; which is more than you did.'

When his mother had gone, Hayden had another visitor.

'Giles, it's marvellous to see you, but can I ask you to come back another time? I'm totally blown, so to speak. No offence.'

'Of course, Hayden. I've brought you this plant. In return you can get me the names and telephone numbers of all the nurses on the ward.'

'Will do.' Then he added, after a pause, 'Giles?'

'Yes?'

'That tie of yours looks like a multicoloured brick-layer's trowel.'

'Yes, it's rather good, isn't it? It's the only one I own – so far. It's to project my new image as a successful entrepreneur. You are looking at the creator not just of the Battledress Taxi concept, but of the Blunder Bus and the Amphibious Rickshaw. I am now the Novelty Transport Initiative.'

*　　*　　*

229

'Still no sign of the drawing, I'm afraid,' Sophie was saying a few hours later to a revived Hayden. Do you suppose it could have been burned up or something?'

'Possibly. Did you double-check?'

'I scoured the wreckage for an hour.' Then she added with studied carelessness, 'With Giles.'

'With Giles?' The green man felt an uncomfortable twinge at this news. What were these able-bodied people getting up to? 'So you didn't find it?' There was a pause. 'Are you and Giles . . . ?'

'I couldn't find your robot, either,' Sophie said, ignoring his question. 'It seems to have totally disappeared. But your desk was more or less in one piece. At least you'll get the insurance money for the house.'

'What? Oh that. I haven't got any insurance. They wouldn't touch me. Not with a particle accelerator in the basement.'

'Good heavens! I didn't know that.' Carola, too, looked surprised. Perhaps she wanted to ask if it was a cyclotron or a synchrotron.

'Now would be a good time to realize a few assets, I suppose.'

'Have you got any?'

'Only you, Sophie. Only you.' There was mutual surprise at this utterance. 'I'm really very grateful to you, Sophie.' There was a silence while Sophie and Carola waited for more.

'Yes?' said Sophie at last.

'Well, that's what I wanted to say really,' he ended lamely. He might be imagining things, but her eyes seemed to be becoming brighter – almost cornflower blue against cornflour white. Was she receiving attention from someone special? A woman found attractive by an attractive man becomes more attractive, so attracting more attention from attractive men. Such is the jizziness of these things. Surely the man wasn't Giles? Perhaps it was someone at her new workplace?

Hayden was alive with unaccustomed feelings.

Sophie reported that a box of papers from the house had been found floating in the sea. In it was the manuscript for a book entitled *A Remembrance of Light Repasts*, a gastronomic parody of Proust's twelve-volume masterwork. Hayden had completed this during a school holiday when he was fifteen. The book opens with a recipe for psychotropic madeleine cakes and ends with a diatribe against cucumber sandwiches. Juvenilia.

More important was the draft report of an archaeological dig which Hayden and others had recently completed at a coastal site twelve miles away. This had shown conclusively that George of Cappadocia, patron saint of England, had landed in the third century at Seaford to open the Michaelmas fête there.

'The postman left some mail on your desk this morning,' said Sophie. 'I don't know when he thought you were going to pick it up. There were several pieces of junk mail including one advertising chest-wigs and muscle-suits. I didn't send off for details. Did I do right?'

'As always.'

'The only significant letter was from the Civil Aviation Authority. Your private pilot's licence has been reinstated. That means you can fly under the pier again and kill yourself like a reckless buffoon.' This was a reference to the occasion when Hayden had taken an aerobatic biplane under one of the piers, flying upside down. Devil-may-care aviators were forever flying through hangars, under bridges, and the like, but this stunt had struck him as particularly amusing. The Civil Aviation Authority might have taken a similar view had not the intrepid birdman incompletely fastened his safety harness. He had duly fallen out into the sea under the Palace Pier, the aircraft continuing in flight until it clipped the West Pier, which caused it to cartwheel spectacularly into the surf, fragmenting as it went. Hayden's pilot's licence had thus been revoked as a result of this, his first, fully fledged solo flight.

25

Ungovernable Urges

Over twelve hours later, after an uneventful night's gestation, Carola sucked in her breath in surprise as Sophie appeared at the foot of Hayden's bed, brandishing a tabloid newspaper and wearing a menacing expression on her face.

'You loathsome rat!' she shouted. 'You unspeakable skunk!' This outburst gained the attention of the whole ward, but only Carola and Hayden could read the headline on the front page of the *Spume* which had prompted it: 'GREEN MAN IN SEX DRAMA!' This meant nothing to the pregnant girl, but the pregnant man immediately transpierced its meaning. The story of his theatrical evening with Francesca had suppurated into the press. His heart fled. How he abhorred violence! Especially Sophie's. He prepared his cringing menagerie of cowed, quailing and sheepish expressions.

'There's been a mistake, Sophie. I can explain.'

'I know there's been a mistake,' Sophie replied, trembling with emotion. 'That's why Francesca left town on Tuesday for an indefinite holiday, isn't it? You cesspit! You wretch!' Sophie knew she was succumbing again to an ungovernable urge – and Hayden knew it, too.

'Help, nurse!' was all he managed to say as Sophie seized a box of chocolate truffles and hurled them at him. A bag of fruit and a pile of magazines followed. Then she took hold of Giles's potted plant, a geranium, and launched it at the patient with all her might. It missed completely and sailed crashing through the window to the accompaniment of a scream from Carola and a whimper from Hayden.

'Go on, love, you give it him!' Molly shouted in encouragement. 'He deserves it!' In Molly's book all men were guilty until proven very guilty. The doors swung open next to her bed and in ran the commissionaire once again.

'Now then, miss. Murder is an ugly crime,' he chortled, gathering in Sophie's flailing arms and steering her towards the exit. At the sight of this, some of the women patients took exception. ('Can't a girl have her say?' 'Isn't this a free city?')

A thirty-pack of disposable nappies hit the commissionaire on the head as he and his captive reached the door. More packs followed, and as Sophie was steered into the corridor, a plastic specimen bottle bounced off the floor beside them.

'You shouldn't treat your wife like that,' boomed Molly. 'Playing around with other women. Disgusting!'

'She's not my wife. She's . . . Oh, God, I don't know what she is,' Hayden said, taking refuge under the covers. He was beginning to feel that he might previously have underestimated the force of Sophie's emotional response to him.

In England, for bachelors, there is something of a bestial gradation, or de-gradation, in the matter of description: with increasing public revelation of sexual mischief a dark horse becomes a black sheep becomes a beast of the field. Hayden's reputation was doubtless ruined. He partook not at all of the Judaeo-Christian association of sex and guilt, which he deemed pathological, but he was a little surprised not to be more embarrassed by the affair. He began to chuckle, then to laugh outright. Before long, Carola

234

echoed his laughter in sympathetic merriment. Unknown to either of them, Carola's husband lay lengthways on the lawn outside, unconscious. He had been felled by a defenestrated geranium.

'In the theatre, Hayden! I mean, how could you! Wasn't it a bit cramped?'

'Giles, don't believe everything you read in the papers.'

'You mean it wasn't true?'

'Well, it was true, but the box was quite spacious really. The contortions were much exaggerated.'

'Were they, by God!' gasped Giles, breathing heavily. His involuntary renunciation of the flesh was having its effect. The Emperor Augustus would not have approved. 'You beast of the field,' he said with envy. 'Who was she?'

'Giles, that is an indecorous question. I've had a demanding morning. Please spare me the interrogation.'

It was true. He *had* had a demanding morning. Even ignoring Sophie's assault – and who could do that? – and the three bed baths the nurses had insisted on giving him, there had been the hammering and cursing of the glazier as he restored the deflowered window. It was the glazier who had noticed a prostrate black man lying outside. Carola had created much commotion over this, quite reasonably. But when she learned that she had not been widowed, she took it all with commendable fortitude. ('I would have worried more if it hadn't been his head.')

The mail had brought a note beginning '*Caro* Hayden', and ending 'Farewell, F.'. His pains from the explosion were going to be compounded by a throb for Francesca. Ah, sad departure! With Babette just a memory and Sophie alienated again, it seemed he might have to settle for little Gail, who had sent him a bunch of blue roses.

It had been then that Hayden had noticed the postmark 'Marina' on one of his unopened envelopes. A note from the *Marbella Hood*? Yes! 'Sorry to hear of your mishap. Progress excellent at this end. You concentrate on recovery. Sid.'

'Progress excellent at this end.' It could only mean that Hayden had guessed correctly: Sid was assembling the Armillary Sphere of Destiny on the boat. The crafty so-and-so! But did he know of his daughter's apparent sentimental attachment to the scholar? Unlikely. Fathers seldom notice these things.

Get well cards had arrived from Mrs Grim and Linden, and Buster Swiftington had sent an invitation to the first abseiling party of the year. The card bore a watercolour representation of the five holy mountains of China, swathed in ethereal clouds, but Hayden could detect no descending figures. Perhaps they didn't abseil over there.

Particularly interesting had been a note from the General on the tercentenary expedition. Although Hayden had been non-committal, the tone of the note suggested that all was decided. Naipur had returned home to organize things at local level. The General had enclosed a slim paperback published by the Explorers' Club itself, entitled *Gadding About, A Guide for Travellers Abroad*. This proved to be a trove of extraordinary information. To stop a tiger, shout 'Hut! Hut! Hut!' loudly and stare at it. To stop an elephant, use the filthiest language and loudest voice. You can tell when a polar bear is going to charge because the whites of its eyes turn red. Flee from grizzly bears and other animals larger than yourself by running uphill. Stick to the flat with smaller pursuers. Nothing about jealous women, Hayden noted ruefully, but there was some stuff on how to commission a performance from a Rajasthan desert folk singer, and some more on how to haggle with an offal-hanger in Turkestan. All in all, an excellent read.

A stream of interview requests from press, radio and television had been turned down. No, he would not pose in the nude for pictures. For how much money?! Even so, the answer was no. One enterprising individual had tried to gain access to Hayden disguised as a snuff-merchant. He was only exposed when the absence was noted from his vending tray of a government health warning. More work for the commissionaire.

Hayden had several meetings with people from diverse backgrounds. There was a cardinal, whom he remembered to call 'Your Eminence' and who had autographed his plaster cast; a French ambassador, who was pleased to be addressed as 'Your Puissancy' and who had been persuaded to secure a promotion for Francesca; and a taxi driver, who settled for 'Giles'.

'What's for lunch?' said the man called Giles.

'Have you been talking to my Uncle George?'

'Well, I did bump into him. He said the grub was good here.'

They inspected the menu card together. A small inscription at the foot of it in old English presented formidable problems for the scholar, but it eventually yielded this message: 'Roughly twenty amino acids, a handful of fatty acids, glycerol, glucose and phosphates dominate the molecular basis of life.'

'Hayden?'

'Yes, Giles?'

'Didn't I give you a geranium?'

In Granville Markham's office, a strained silence was about to end.

'Snuff! I ask you. In a maternity unit. Didn't you think that might attract attention, clot!'

'I got confused, boss. The place is swarming with

237

reporters. But I did get a glimpse of him. He's definitely green, and he ain't dying.'

'You'll have to go in there, then, and knock him off.'

'In a ward full of pregnant women! Can't it wait till he comes out?'

'No, we don't want him fouling things up. Get him out of the way, Stair-rods. Make it look like an accident: a fall from a window or something like that will do.'

'Er, yes boss.'

Markham's new plan called for the elimination of both Whitney *and* Sabanack. In the light of new developments it was the best way.

The good news, reflected Markham, was that the publicity surrounding Sabanack's 'sex drama' exploits had already caused queues to form at the theatre box office. *Adam's Navel* was now certain to transfer to London, and with it would go the play's desirable, but oh-so-expensive, leading lady. Even scholars have their uses!

26

A Seneschal

After Giles had left, Hayden basked in the quiet that had descended on the ward. The babies, now four in number, were for the moment at peace. Taking one thing with another, he felt much better. A ride in a wheelchair earlier was but a memory. Action was needed. When the going gets easy, the easy-going get up. Hayden positioned himself near the edge of the bed – and promptly fell off heavily on to the floor. As a nurse hurried over, he passed out.

He awoke to find his mother at the bedside. His feeble smile triggered a neuromuscular response in her which culminated in the movement of a jaw.

'Well, it's not the done thing at the theatre, of course, but at least it shows you've got over your earlier problems. I suppose if you go on the straight and narrow for the rest of your life we will find it in our hearts to forgive you.' There was no doubt who the 'we' referred to here were. Mrs Sabanack was taking her son's exploits surprisingly well. Indeed, his hospitalization, now he was out of danger, was acting as a tonic on her. No more talk of imminent death; she felt on top of the world! After all, at such a time a mother was *needed*, wasn't she? Crises she could handle; it was the times in-between that were so very trying.

'Not being caught at it is the thing, Hayden. Mind you, your father and I once tried it in a . . . Well, anyway. I have some good news for you. I have had a word with the police and they are not going to pursue a case against you in connection with the explosion. The chief constable was an old friend of your father's. He rather enjoyed evacuating half of Brighton.'

'Mother! You're an absolute gem! No son was ever luckier.'

'That's true. Anyway, the police are preoccupied with these thefts. Appalling, aren't they? I've made sure our pictures and books are safe, not to mention the archives.' She paused, then added, 'The police are baffled. But then that's normal, isn't it?'

Hayden had learned from Carola that museums and libraries throughout the city had been robbed, including the Exquisitorium and the Inventery at the Culture Park, and literary and artistic collections at the university and polytechnic. His own office robbery remained unsolved. This was acceptable to Sophie, he knew, at least in one respect. She was far from anxious to have her computer restored to her.

'Is Duffy around?' asked Hayden, ending a silence. 'I have a distinct recollection of hearing his voice.'

'Yes. He was here when I arrived. Since you were sleeping he went off to play with those children over there. Very noble, I thought. Ah, he's seen us talking. He's coming back.'

As his friend with the double chin and the double waist ambled over, Hayden pulled himself up into a sitting position and poured a glass of water. This action surprised him almost as much as it did Mrs Sabanack, who put the consumption of an odourless, colourless, tasteless liquid down to the after-effects of his attempted suicide.

Hayden looked outside. It was dark. What day was it? Thursday, that was it. Day Eighteen. The deadline was next Monday. He looked round, and Carola caught his eye.

'Back in the land of the living, then, Hayden?' she asked smilingly.

'Yes, fine thanks. How's your . . . um.'

'Not long now. I'll need some close moral support soon.'

'Happy to oblige. Hello, Duffy. Got no overtime tonight?'

'Don't remind me of work, please. I thought you'd be greener than this.'

'The doctor says I'm fading fast.'

'Shall I notify your next of skin?'

After several minutes of pleasantries, Mrs Sabanack intervened and turned the conversation to a more serious matter.

'You won't know this, Dufryn, but I am going to convert my house into a conference centre – the big house, that is. And I shall need a seneschal, which was what the stewards of the great medieval houses were called: a general manager in modern parlance. Well, Dufryn, what do you say?'

'You want *me* to do it?' he said with surprise as a thrill ran through his body. For the first time in his life he was being head-hunted. He sat straighter in his chair with amazement and pride.

'Yes, Dufryn, I do. My son tells me you are the ideal man for the job, and in everything save matters of the heart I respect his judgement. Naturally, we shall be able to o'ertop your current level of remuneration comfortably.'

As she finished speaking, a boy of about eight bounded up to them and rested his chin on the bed-rail. Mrs Sabanack had seldom seen a childish visage so untroubled by intellect. There is no point in being precocious, of course, unless you anticipate dying early. But one can take a slow start too far. The boy was joined by a girl about one year younger. She, too, had what, with charity, might be called the hidden intelligence trait.

'Whose are these wretched offspring?' demanded Mrs Sabanack imperiously.

Duffy, alarmed to see his new credibility in such immediate jeopardy, could only mumble: 'Mine.'

'Well, of course, you don't need to live on the premises,' Mrs Sabanack said hastily. Her love of children was strongest when she didn't encounter them. This did not stop her wanting more for the species. The potential usurpation by Sophie of her own primacy in Hayden's life was tolerable as a trade-off only if it brought a brace of grandchildren.

'We've got moving headlice,' exclaimed the boy to a shocked silence. Mrs Sabanack managed to stifle the desire to say that she didn't doubt it for a second. Comprehension dawned first on Duffy.

'Jack means moving *headlights*, retractable ones, on Buster's sports car. Which we have the use of at the moment,' he added, for Mrs Sabanack's benefit. Hayden took pity on his friend, who was beginning to look burdened with inexpiable sin.

'That's agreed, then. The job's yours Duffy. Start date to be settled later. All right, Mother?'

'Yes, it's agreed.'

Mrs Sabanack left shortly afterwards. Before Duffy went, he presented his friend with a small envelope.

'Buster sent a couple of opera tickets for me and my sister. Since you invented her, they're yours. Thanks for the job, Hayden. You've saved my life.'

It must have been hammering the nail into the wall next to it that had roused the old pendulum clock from its reverie. After some years of slow running, it was keeping good time again to the surprise of its owner, the café's proprietor.

Danielle broke off from wiping a table-top to look once more at the portrait of Hayden in the nude.

Where had the little girl got it from in the first place?

It had certainly caused a stir, *zut alors*! Danielle could see why: Hayden looked to be in the rippling prime of manhood – and would have looked even better without the fig leaves!

The Slab was reconnoitring the *Marbella Hood* when a young girl stole down the after gangway, carrying a single, flat, square piece of wood, several long, thin pieces of wood joined together in a triangular arrangement, and a wooden box.

What's she up to? he thought. Is this Sid Whitney's daughter? It has to be!

The girl hid momentarily behind some coiled ropes on the quay, then peeped back surreptitiously at the boat as if fearing pursuit. From his own vantage point behind a pile of timber further off, the Slab could see that the girl had come ashore undetected.

Gail crept off towards the ship's chandler at the end of the quay, and the Slab did likewise.

In the run-up to the prototype proving day, Sid had confined his daughter to the boat. Going ashore would be too dangerous. But Gail was feeling so hemmed-in! On a blustery, exuberant kind of day, doesn't an artist deserve open spaces and broad vistas? Gail thought so.

The Slab suddenly saw a plan less drastic than Markham's: not a sinking, but a snatch – then blackmail! He seized a black plastic bin liner which lay among some rubbish behind the ship's chandler, and followed the girl on her journey out of the marina to freedom.

It wasn't really a case of disobeying her father, after all. She wouldn't visit the town, she would head east towards Rottingdean on the Under Cliff Walk. That should be safe enough, particularly if she didn't stray far. A short scramble would take her on to one of those low cliffs which afford such an interesting view inland. The sea was wonderfully rough, but she had the urge to paint a landscape.

Thus it was that the crumbling chalk cliffs saw enacted a scene from that age-old drama in which the frail figure of Art is menaced by brute Philistinism. But who could have foreseen the outcome? Only Nature perhaps, for cliffs, sea and wind conspired to protect the little girl, while she remained unaware of her peril.

As the Slab advanced to 'bag' his quarry, the ground subsided alarmingly beneath his feet and he fell in an avalanche of grassy sods and chalky scree across the promenade path down to the shingle beach below. Trapped there by a thrashing high tide, the would-be kidnapper was in no position to hinder Gail's eventual departure.

27

ERC

'Any problems?' asked Dr Tyler the next morning, looking first at her clipboard then inspecting with disapproval the evidence of Hayden's champagne breakfast. 'Good. Well, keep up the progress.'

'Why am I getting all these bed baths?' Hayden asked indignantly. 'It won't wash off, you know.'

Dr Tyler was aware that fighting had twice broken out among the student nurses as to who should bathe Hayden. They had all agreed to have a go, in turn. Dr Tyler had put a stop to that.

'A precautionary measure, that's all. I think we've caught it in time. Keep up the good work. Cheerio.'

Caught what in time? thought Hayden as his medical advisor receded from view. He felt quite relieved to be anxious, though; at least it would give him something to think about till Sophie arrived with the office mail – if she came at all, which seemed doubtful. The spectre of under-utilization loomed before him. While he counted the minutes, he took out a pad and doodled a thumbnail sketch of the toenail which protruded from his plaster cast. As a footnote, he scribbled down the Equation of the Cosmos: $| \text{Cosmos} > = \sum a_i \ | \ \Psi_i > | \ \Phi_i >$ He could have another crack at solving it, but he felt no relish at that moment for abstruse mathematics. Please come, Sophie. Even without the mail!

The hospital post earlier had brought some more get

well cards, including one from Ted and the regulars at the Warbler, and another from Wilfred Shaps at the Institute of Philosophy. There were also twenty-four offers of marriage from single women – presumably as a result of the previous day's news of his activities at the Theatre Royal – and eleven offers of something less regular from married women. But there was little of substance.

Overnight, the number of babies had risen to five. In this batch of mothers, only two had yet to produce: Carola and a woman at the other end of the ward who was so uneventfully with-child that she looked as though she was going for a twelve-month pregnancy.

The new baby was taking on some wet merchandise, as Damon Runyon might have put it. In about thirty or so species, including the black widow spider, desert scorpion and praying mantis, the male is eaten by the female after mating. Presumably this is a sound strategy in evolutionary terms, so why don't the young consume the surviving female, and so start their lives with a good, square meal? Nigel was due to visit that evening. Maybe he could supply an answer. Then again, perhaps Hayden wouldn't bother asking. A two-hour lecture might retard his recuperation.

Just then, a cheerful-looking fellow came up to his bed, carrying a bag. It was James Stevens.

'I thought I'd drop in and see how you were. You're hardly green at all, are you?'

'I wear it well.' There was a pause. 'How is . . . Sophie?'

'Well, the state of mind of women is one of nature's best-kept secrets, of course, but I would say she's jealous.'

'You would?'

'Does that sound plausible?'

'We could certainly entertain it as a working hypothesis.'

246

'It was the theatre thing, really. Remarkable. Was the play any good? No, well, I suppose you didn't see much of it.'

'You haven't by any chance brought in my mail, have you?' Hayden asked, eager for a change of topic.

'No, I'm afraid not. My daughter would have rendered herself fatherless if I had done that. You know how she's been lately.' Hayden did. The two men exchanged haunted looks. 'If you can't stand the heat of the kitchen, get out of the frying pan into the fire. And let he who is without sin call the kettle black, et cetera. Please keep quiet about my visit, will you? I've brought along the scandal-sheet for you.' So saying, he produced from his bag the newspaper that Hayden was learning to loathe, the *Spume*. 'You've done it again – you're the lead story!'

With a queasy feeling, Hayden assimilated the headline: 'GREEN MAN'S BLAST SUPPER!' Beneath it was a picture of what looked like a painting in oils. It was captioned '*The Ultimate Luncheon*, courtesy of the Whitney Collection', and depicted a Hogarthian scene of drunken revelry. Gail! What a mischief-maker little G. was proving! Had she also alerted the press to the theatre story, or at least, established the Green Man's involvement therein?

Alongside the main story, as the second lead, was a piece headlined: 'BLACK "POTTED" AT HOSPITAL BY GREEN'. Hayden laughed delightedly, then became thoughtful. Looking along the line of men in the picture, his eye alighted on Nigel. Suddenly he knew that here was the man who had given away information on the progress of the Existometer. Nigel was pictured sprawled on the floor against a table leg, mouth agape. Although these were unappealing traits, Nigel was by no means an unappealing traitor – a shade loquacious perhaps, that was all.

'You're looking very distinguished,' observed

247

Hayden, indicating the picture. If Gail was an ill wind, at least she had blown somebody some good.

'I thought so, too,' agreed James, contentedly patting his midriff bulge, nature's cummerbund for the middle-aged man. 'Sophie said I was treating with the enemy. She called me a turnpike. She wanted to know why you were shown wearing a halo. I couldn't work it out.'

'It was a hat, that's all.'

'Oh, yes, that's right. I feel honoured really to have been at an event that has passed so quickly into the legends of immortal feasts.'

'Well, we made the paper anyway.'

'I've got to get over to the mayor's parlour soon, for more salt-bearing. It beats working! Before I go, though, let me give you a present.' He handed over a book which Hayden removed from its slip-case. It was handsomely bound in what looked like goatskin, with marbled end-papers. Hayden prepared to look pleased even if it was only a novel. His appetite for made-up stories had been sated during childhood. 'I wanted to give you something with a strong local content,' continued James. 'There was a lot to choose from, of course. Lots.' He was right. Brighton was a very literary town in spite of a relative dearth of guilt-ridden Catholics, neurotic Jews, emotionally traumatized divorcées, Americans either exploring adolescent sexuality or trying to find themselves over one thousand pages, academics writing campus novels, or female romantic fantasists. 'It's an anthology of verse by local authors. There are a couple of yours in it, from the early period, before you became derivative.'

Later, Hayden took an uncomfortable tour on crutches, then sat with Carola, who was showing signs of approaching parturition. It was while he was engaged in the undemanding pastime of hand-holding that he received a hamper from Danielle. The food was on a Russian theme and included beef Stroganoff, *blinis* and caviar, sturgeon in jelly, chicken Kiev and other delicacies. A nurse arranged for the chef to complete the preparations, then Carola and Hayden consumed it. 'Compliments to Madame.'

The peaceful consumption of a post-prandial coffee was disturbed when the woman at the end of the ward went unexpectedly into labour and was delivered within five minutes.

'What's the meaning of life, Carola?'

'We're here to find out why we're here, aren't we?'

'Have you found out why we're here yet?' asked Hayden.

'For this, I suppose,' she replied, patting the protuberant evidence of pregnancy. In spite of intermittent labour pains, Carola shone with fulfilment. Impending motherhood imparts to many women a charming aura of self-importance, of jizz, indeed.

The way people look at themselves, Hayden ruminated, has an important bearing on the kind of lives they are able to lead and on their ability to enjoy fully developed human relationships. It affects the goals they set themselves and the grade of significance they strive to occupy. That is why, when we treat of matters relating to self-esteem, we are not referring merely to vanity and egotism.

Hayden's esteem train of thought was at that moment derailed by a gnat. It was circling a bunch of blackberries in Carola's fruit bowl, reminding the scholar of atomic nuclei and electrons. Maybe the reason that rather nothingy atoms come across as substantial is that they feel good about themselves. In other words, the appearance of solidity might be jizz in one of its forms!

If a high sense of self-esteem is facilitating individually, an analogous effect can be seen at the level of societies. Since independence, Brighton had acquired palpable jizz. Anything seemed possible here! Well, almost. Hayden had to admit a difficulty in this regard, and it was this: he had a sense of destiny, the secular equivalent of a religious vocation. Why he, a rationalist, had this he could not say. The naming of the Armillary Sphere of Destiny had not been arbitrary. Since he was a youngster he had had an overwhelming conviction that he was going to change the universe. Not surprisingly, he had been loath to share this insight with his confrères. Changing the world was clearly within his compass, but Hayden saw himself operating on a more cosmological scale.

Plato posited an autonomous and timeless world of perfect ideas, mathematical and otherwise, which he contrasted with the real world of imperfection. It was accessible to the intellect alone. Perhaps those with a sense of destiny have a supraconscious awareness of a realm in which our lives are being led ideally, though Hayden hardly knew what to make of this notion, given that he had always regarded Plato's theory of forms, so called, as nonsense. He reminded himself that the idea of destiny – like the concept of an afterlife, indeed – did not entail a theistic view of things as a logical necessity, but what, if anything, it did entail was far from clear to him. Maybe he should just try to fulfil his destiny, and worry about what it all meant afterwards. But how? The prodigy of learning was baffled, though not lacking in self-belief.

He was an intelligent, carbonaceous, gas-breathing, bipedal scholar without an overdraft, and he was, above all, *free* – not least because he was neither constrained by the absence of talent, nor constrained by the presence of but a single talent. His planet, though watery, was hospitable enough. But the local star – there was a problem!

When its hydrogen nuclear fuel is exhausted in a few billion years' time, the sun's energy output will increase as it burns helium instead. The outer atmosphere of the sun will expand enormously to engulf the earth, boiling away the oceans and incinerating the biosphere in the process.

If we stick around on our home planet we humans will render ourselves liable to extinction – unless the earth can be saved, that is. What if the sun's expansive problem is due to ego overcompensation brought on by a poor sense of personal worth? The salvation of our planet might then be quite straightforward: reinstitution of sun worship.

This led Hayden to consider a larger question. What is it all for? The universe, he meant. Is it just a convenient way of storing lots of clumpy bits of matter in a very large space? In globular clusters, galaxies, galaxy clusters, superclusters and supercluster complexes, there are about 10^{22} stars, i.e. 10,000,000,000,000,000,000,000. Why so many? Why any at all?

Suppose that the universe were underachieving until it produced intelligent, self-conscious life, and that we were the only such life in the universe. Suppose then that we humans experienced an access of self-belief such that we could take our most important evolutionary step, courtesy of the Existometer – a species-wide expansion of our supraconscious powers of insight and imagination. In this view, which sees the cosmos as an organism rather than a machine, we would be projecting not only ourselves but the entire universe on to a higher level of meaning-awareness.

Intelligence, self-affirmation, supraconscious development. The first two stages could be summed up by an Ancient Egyptian text, suitably augmented.

In the beginning, the world has nothing at all
heaven was, nor earth, nor space
Because it was not, it bethought itself:
I will be. It emitted heat.

Time passed. It bethought itself again:
I will be great. It radiated jizz.

Was this to be the fulfilment of Hayden's destiny?

'How should I make my mark on the cosmos, Carola?'

'Marry Sophie.'

Women! Did they think of nothing else? Since she mentioned it though, he had been feeling a strange and restless hankering for his sometime assistant. Was this l---? Had he at last become a true *philosopher*? (Greek: *phile,* love; *sophia*, wisdom.) Remarkably, he had.

The whole of Brighton wanted him to make an honest woman of Sophie, but that was no reason not to do so. He was a free man, or so he told himself again, at least for the moment. Wilful contrariness was a sign of insecurity. Anyway, there was no denying she had become deuced attractive to him of late.

All this meant that he would have to build into the Armillary Sphere of Destiny an additional point of illumination. To Sex, Death, Biology, Physics, Philosophy and Humour, must now be added Love. There, he had brought himself to say it.

''ere, what's going on?!' Molly exclaimed, removing her headset and banging it repeatedly on the bedside table. 'What's happened to my music programme?'

Hayden reached lazily for his own headphones, which hung above the bed, and selected the station to which his fellow patient had presumably been listening. His look of sceptical amusement was erased by what he heard. A message in morse code. No, not morse! It was surely Hayden's own subtle and super-fast shorthand variant of morse – the code he used, indeed, to radio-control his domestic robot!

The scholar was now sitting upright in bed, hands clapped to headphones, eyes shut. The message was quite short and was being transmitted over and over again. Signal strength was varying. Suddenly, the transmission began to fade, and in a moment, was gone.

'I should think so too!' said Molly indignantly. 'Bloomin' cheek. I bet it's them blessed students again!' She hadn't forgotten what turned out to be a rag prank the other day when she had been sold a child-proof container for one of her offspring. Yes, it was for charity – but it hadn't fitted!

Hayden was left alone with the mystery of the radio interference. There could be only one source – his robot. The signal strength was varying regularly, so it must be moving in some way. But where was it if the message could be picked up by the hospital's radio receiver, which was presumably on the roof?

Suddenly an explanation occurred to him. Perhaps the robot was above them, far above them, tumbling in space even! That would explain much, including the variation in signal strength! Was it possible that the explosion had hurled Hayden's domestic robot, like a discus, into the heavens? Yes, if a massive, ultra-short release of energy from the robot's own levitation system had contributed to its thrust. If it's true, he thought, I ought to be able to determine the robot's approximate position and plot its course – making a few assumptions, of course. And so it proved.

The celestial computation upon which the scholar embarked was not quite as daunting as it sounds: a nurse was kind enough to obtain an abacus for him from among a pile of toys at the end of the ward. At one point he broke off from calculating to scrutinize the sky in wonderment, but a mist disobligingly wreathed the hospital, obscuring all.

It really was extraordinary! The robot was on a double swing-by trajectory which would take it round both Jupiter and the sun, and so out of the solar system altogether.

Then the full story dawned on him. The robot was not alone. The rooftop radio telescope's massive array of wires must be entangled with it, enabling the robot to transmit and receive messages over vast distances.

Hayden could scarcely suppress his excitement. He had inadvertently launched an unmanned spacecraft, and now all that remained was for him to send instructions to it on what to do next. He would have to stop the thing tumbling crazily, but that should be easy enough. The robot could hardly be badly damaged if it was ringing home! Fortunately, it had a massive reserve capability, technologically speaking, which had been rather redundant in a household gadget but which would come in handy for an interstellar probe.

There was also a comprehensive self-repair facility . . . Of course! The self-repair facility! Wasn't that akin to a *self-reproductive* facility? The robot could be programmed to produce replicas of itself whenever it encountered a new star system, using asteroids, meteors, comets, interstellar dust and other raw materials. Each replica could search for habitable planets. A rapid calculation on the abacus showed that the robot and its clones could explore and colonize our entire galaxy, the Milky Way, in less than three hundred million years. And after that? Why, the rest of the universe!

But the robot would need a power source. As soon as it had a spare moment, it would have to fashion for itself some sort of ion propulsion system, or perhaps a solar sail from the radio telescope. Hayden would have to give the matter some thought.

The scholar would reprogram the robot after he left hospital, which shouldn't be long now. It was already programmed to display perpetual loyalty to its inventor, and Hayden would ensure that it always responded benignly to any alien life-form encountered *en route*, even hostile ones. Without being able to comply with it himself, he had always been impressed by the Christian injunction to love thine enemy.·

After the robot had got itself sorted out, Hayden would have it fabricate a name-plate from such materials as came to gripper. It would say this:

Earth Robot Colonizer 1
Launched by
Hayden Lovett Sabanack,
Brighton

It would be known as ERC 1 for short. He couldn't wait to tell Sophie!

One small enigma remained. When the explosion occurred, why had the robot been in such close proximity to the linoleum-still, as it surely must have been?

All this was proving too much for the potential master of the universe. He sank back under the covers, closed his eyes, and began an exploration of inner space.

The big man was going to leave it till later, but the sea-fret that had clung to the coastline since late afternoon offered perfect concealment. The surprise was that vessels – some pretty big – were still moving about in the foggy murk. He would have to be careful not to get run down, particularly with a limpet mine clamped to his harness.

The outsized frogman swam silently through the

255

cold waters of the crowded marina. If the Slab was sure of one thing it was that he had enough explosives to complete the job in hand. So heavy was the charge, indeed, that even before detonation he was in danger himself of going to the bottom. He was like a shark: if he didn't swim, he sank.

The white craft was identifiable enough even after a quick glance through steamed-up goggles in the shadowy gloom. The name could just be discerned: *Marbella Hood*.

As a foghorn sounded funereally in the distance, the Slab submerged once more and swam smoothly down to the keel, taking care not to strike it accidentally with his aqualung, lest the crew be alerted. An explosion below the water line would undoubtedly seal the boat's fate.

After securing the mine to the hull, and activating the time fuse, the saboteur changed his plan. He had been intending to swim the long distance round to the other side of the quay, but why bother? If he climbed out on this side, no-one stood a chance of seeing him as he let go the mooring ropes fore and aft.

It sank without loss of life in fifteen fathoms of water – to subsequent universal bafflement as to motive. The *Martyr to Food*, which had replaced the *Marbella Hood* at her berth not half an hour previously, was a refurbished tramp steamer converted to a fish res- taurant. As the *Martyr* found an aqueous resting-place, the intended victim stood offshore, biding her time.

28

Dr F. and the Question of Faith

That same Friday evening, while Carola slept, Hayden was talking to Nigel when Dr Fikansky approached them diffidently.

'What on earth are you doing here?' Hayden challenged indignantly.

'Look, I know how you must feel but I didn't realize Markham was going to try to blow you to bits. You have my word on it. I'm sorry.'

Nigel was about to say that he thought it was an accident, when he was quelled by a look from Hayden, who said, 'You'd better tell us what you know.'

'I'm running a big risk even being here.'

'Tell us your side of it, otherwise you're wasting our time.'

'Perhaps I owe you that. Yes, perhaps I do.'

'Sit down, we're listening.'

'Very well then, though I expect you've already worked out most of it for yourself. I'd better go right back to the beginning, hadn't I? When was that, though? I suppose it was when I told Wilfred Shaps about the DeWit Bequest while at the Institute on other business. Sad day! He liked what he heard and resolved to set up a rival consortium to be headed by Granville Markham on the grounds that since the closing date for applications had passed, there might need to be some dirty work before we were accepted into the contest. So it proved.' The information that

257

Shaps was the real leader of the opposition came as a deep shock to the freelance scholar. The mallets encounter had been even more one-sided than Hayden had imagined. And Wilfred had deliberately tried to confuse him. So much for honour and integrity!

Markham had suborned Vincent Thorne in the Planning Department without much difficulty, Dr Fikansky reported, and the Shaps consortium was in business.

Dr Fikansky as expert advisor had come up with a design for a device which had found favour with the head of the Institute of Philosophy. A team of forty philosophers and engineers had been assembled, generously funded and sworn to secrecy. They had moved into the factory Markham had been given. Dr Fikansky himself had been given a staff of ten drawn from the university and polytechnic. Hopes were high of winning the prototype trial and with it the DeWit fortune.

Markham had worked only with Fikansky, and knew nothing of Shaps's involvement. The boss of Peerless Widgets had been single-minded, but Shaps had wanted to conquer the market for philosophical scholarship. Markham's expert advisor, it had to be said, became fired with the same vision. It had induced a crippling loss of clarity. According to Shaps, the new device had to be appropriate for sale throughout the chain of retail outlets to be established shortly by the Institute worldwide. Fikansky had not demurred.

'Markham had a pretty rough way with the opposition,' Dr Fikansky continued. 'He was behind the burning-down of the Yelland factory, as you must have guessed. He also scared off Brighton Aerospace by demanding money with menaces – more, indeed, than they stood to gain if they won the competition! But Whitney Enterprises was going to be a tougher nut to crack. You don't intimidate men like Sid Whitney and expect to survive the experience.'

'But he's only a businessman, isn't he?' interrupted Hayden.

'If you say so. Well anyway, we had far greater resources than you – one office! – but there was always a chance you might win. By coincidence you and I had met previously over the chessboard. I knew you weren't going to be a pushover. We developed a two-pronged strategy. We would plunder the information bases before you got to them, and Markham's men would put the frighteners on you. As regards the information, we would have succeeded, but for the diligence of your research assistant. On the second point, the campaign started modestly with a visit by the Slab and Stair-rods Wilson to the bookshop, then I know you encountered the Slab at a swimming pool.' He paused, covering his face with his hands in desperate disbelief. Misery was exaggerating his mid-European enunciation. 'I know what you're thinking: how could I stoop to this? I don't know. But you want to try working with someone like Markham. The Slab used to attend some of our meetings. I tried to pull out, but I was told that the only way I was going to leave the team was feet first. The irony is that I started it all. I only acted as Shaps's front-man for the money. I had massively overreached myself; I had piles of debt. If only I'd known where it was going to lead!

'Soon after the Slab had his word with you, it dawned on us that our device wasn't going to work. That was when you lost your design to burglary. We stole the drawings because they didn't photograph well. I have discovered that after I'd taken a look round your office myself, the previous week. Please, don't look at me like that. I'm feeling bad enough as it is. I've come in to see you, haven't I? We found we couldn't achieve remote penetration of your electronic systems because your level of technology was too low. I was amazed to find only one computer, and that an old one.

You were still using pencils and paper! Even so, what you had achieved was impressive. We reckoned that even if we couldn't stop Whitney Enterprises building the same thing we could eliminate you from the prototype line-up by getting Thorne to tamper with the entry forms on file at City Hall. We constructed your Astrolabe of Inner Being but we were dismayed to learn, when we tried it out, that the secret of life was that there was no secret.

'We weren't sure we had something that qualified as a device to further human understanding. It would always be possible for the judges to argue that there was a secret and that we had missed it. We might be the only competitor – though that wasn't certain given the efforts of your friend in the Planning Department to thwart Vincent Thorne – but we might be disqualified in any case! That would leave the mayor to pocket the money for Brighton. We needed something that wouldn't fail. A massive programme of modifications was put in hand, involving fundamental research and round-the-clock work. Two libraries, four laboratories and a wind tunnel were pressed into service for the purpose. Still the modified device would not perform as desired. It was then that we learned that you had abandoned that design entirely and were working on something far more revolutionary, though Markham took some convincing of that fact.'

'How did you learn that?' asked Hayden.

'A rumour at the university.'

At this point, Nigel bowed his head and groaned repentantly. 'I'm sorry, Hayden, I really am. That could only have been me. I can't keep my mouth shut. I'm sorry.'

'Think nothing of it, Nigel, really. Go on Doctor Fikansky.'

'Things were going pretty badly. Most of our team

were working on a modified version of your first design. Some had been detailed to cannibalize our own first effort, while a small group including myself were working on something dreamed up by Shaps himself, though it scarcely looked promising. Time was running out. We needed your second design – and fast. With our way of doing things we knew that we would need all the time we could get to construct a working model. I blench even to think of the bureaucracy. You'd almost ruined the whole thing by stealing Thorne's letter from me. There was just enough in it to spur some questioning in high places. It had to be retrieved. You were a fool to take it. The Slab got it back in the library, didn't he? I knew it was relatively safe to call in reinforcements because Markham wasn't prepared to wipe you off the map. He feared an investigation. It was some time later when we got our hands on your second design. That came about after the Slab burgled your house.'

'My house?'

'Yes. Markham reckoned that you wouldn't leave anything unattended in your office again. So the Slab went in on Saturday night and ransacked the place while you were at the theatre – as we learned later! He found nothing, but while he was there something was pushed through the letter-box. It was the drawing! The Slab hadn't relished the prospect of meeting your robot. You had apparently put it through its paces once in security mode for Markham. So we gave him a jamming device, which in the event didn't work and wasn't needed! All your robot did was try to usher the Slab into your bedroom! In the end, the Slab locked it in your spare room.' Hayden managed a wan smile. Sophie had evidently delivered the drawing at precisely the wrong moment. And it was now clear to him why the robot was next to the linoleum-still at the time of the explosion, facilitating the launch. But why

261

couldn't the house have blown up when one of the villains was in it, rather than me? Is there no justice?

'You also emptied my office to be on the safe side,' asked Hayden, 'and stole my friends' cars to put the wind up them?'

'The cars, yes; office, no. I don't know anything about that.' Dr Fikansky broke off and took a deep breath before continuing. 'So we got the design right enough, but why Markham made an attempt on your life when he did, I don't know. He couldn't have known whether the new version was any good. I suppose if your first design had been fully successful you would have suffered this fate earlier. I have been declared off the project now, which is why I have risked coming here today. There's lots going on in the final phase which I wasn't supposed to know about. The construction of your second device was going well when last I heard. The Armillary Sphere of Destiny is an incredible invention!' Dr Fikansky paused before delivering the Bad News. 'It is important you realize how highly expendable you've become. You must watch your step. That's what I came here to tell you. Markham will want you out of the way before they go into full production. He won't want any disputes about intellectual property rights.'

'What went wrong with your own approach?' asked Hayden, reflecting with satisfaction on the massive resources Shaps and company committed to so little avail.

'There was an unaccountable religious bug in the initial design and we never got rid of it. Faith was the flaw. Well, you know what the position is. In the medieval Christian world it was believed that the existence of God could be proved; so taught Thomas Aquinas and others. Well, of course, it is a characteristic of the modern world that belief in God can only be supported by faith. And faith is inimical to reason and

262

truth.' As Hayden and Nigel nodded in agreement, Dr Fikansky went on, 'It also gives rise to dogma, which breeds intolerance – and that's absolutely useless in a device to further human understanding. Faith is truly corrosive. I've mentioned Thomas Aquinas. Do you know what the "angelic doctor" thought should be done with heretics who revert to the true doctrine and then relapse again? He said they should be received into penitence, then killed. That, from a man who was later canonized.'

'Aquinas was expressing an opinion,' Hayden said. 'Actions are worse. The Grand Inquisitor of the Spanish Empire had forty thousand people burned at the stake. He was also canonized – as recently as 1860.'

'Well, with a bug like that in the design, we were doomed,' added Dr Fikansky. 'We found ourselves having to strengthen the structure in all sorts of places, which inevitably led to over-engineering. The project had gained a momentum of its own. We had sub-committees and working parties on everything. Once we had spent money on something, it was hard not to justify using it. This led to overloading – and disaster!'

Dr Fikansky looked crushed, defeated, bereft of jizz. Both Hayden and Nigel pitied him in spite of his behaviour and his odious confederates. It was time to move the conversation on.

'What's the Christian position on scholarship?' Nigel asked. 'I know that Augustine tried to quell his interest in lizards and spiders when he became a convert.'

'He also said that a man should serve the understanding of things,' commented Hayden. Since the conversation was turning into a symposium or Greek-speak, the chairman rang for ouzo-based cocktails and stuffed vine leaves.

'Scholarship's Christian charter,' said Dr Fikansky, 'is provided in the psalms: "Great are the works of the

263

Lord, studied by all who have pleasure in them". But in Ecclesiastes we read that "much wisdom is much grief: and he that increaseth knowledge increaseth sorrow".'

After his two visitors had gone, Hayden reflected upon the moral turpitude of Dr Fikansky and Professor Shaps. What a pair! In league with hoodlums. It was strange to think that by despatching him to the relative safety of a hospital, Francesca had, by nearly killing him, probably kept him alive.

This being Friday, there was just a weekend before the play-off on Monday. Duffy had substituted fresh entry forms, so that side of things was in order. Sid's efforts on the prototype would be nearing completion. Should the scholar contact the mayor about Dr Fikansky's revelations? Would the miscreant testify against his former accomplices? It seemed doubtful. There was still a need of documentary proof of illegality.

The question of faith raised by Dr Fikansky was interesting. A man of sovereign consciousness has to respect truth, which means founding his understanding on defensible statements, not on 'because it's so' beliefs. Evidence can be adduced in favour of rational ideas, or against them, but how do we select between competing irrationalisms, except on the basis of personal whim? Submission to an irrationalist creed is unfitting because the sacrifice of intellect involved amounts to self-betrayal, or so Hayden held.

He reached for his headphones and turned on the radio. It was the news – and more thefts: a film library and the Old Observatory this time. What's more, the earlier thefts had been found to be even more serious than first thought – a veritable plundering of the choicest items. Were there no depths to which people wouldn't sink? Apparently not. As Hayden was digesting this news, the first report was broadcast of the culinary disaster at the marina.

Nigel and Dr Fikansky quit the ward together. As they were about to leave the hospital, Dr Fikansky suddenly tugged at Nigel's arm.

'Don't look now, but that man coming towards us is one of Markham's men. I think his name is Wilson. And that,' he added, indicating a length of metal in Wilson's hand, 'is a stair-rod. He's after your friend.'

'Good God, what shall we do?'

'Let's follow him. Come on.' After a while it became clear that Stair-rods Wilson was indeed heading for Hayden's ward rather than the Seafood Clinic next door. For once, the commissionaire was nowhere to be seen.

The two men followed Wilson up several flights of stairs, then the interloper stopped at a laundry trolley, looking round furtively. Seeing no-one, he picked up a white coat from the basket and started to pull it on. It was difficult to imagine what species of medical staff he hoped to imitate – a Lobstetrician perhaps – but Dr Fikansky wasted no time in speculation. Seeing their chance, he led Nigel in a charge on the temporarily disadvantaged Wilson and the two men succeeded in bundling him into an adjacent chute marked 'Disgustingly Contaminated Swabs'. His stair-rod dropped to the floor with a clang, and Wilson never saw his assailants as he disappeared into the bowels of the building.

'Right,' said Nigel in a voice filled with redemption and triumph, 'let's get on to Security and make sure Hayden's ward is sealed against intruders.'

It was just as well that Stair-rods Wilson never made it to the ward because Hayden would not have been in a state to defend himself. Just when he was thinking of cracking some nuts before turning out the light, a series of tight contractions gripped his abdomen. The male couvade, or sympathetic birth pangs, affects a number of men. In Hayden's bed, the number was one. Carola marvelled as both she and the green-tinged, prenaissance man went simultaneously into full labour.

29

Endgame

By next morning, Carola and Hayden had between them produced two charming girls. Besides Carola's twins, the evening had seen the birth of a Sabanack suspicion. This had emerged during the course of a thought-experiment conducted under the operating theatre lights and related to the Mark II design and the decision to add Love to the points of illumination. If Dr Fikansky's design had had a religious bug he was beginning to wonder whether his own was less than perfect. The Armillary Sphere of Destiny wasn't flawed exactly, particularly since it explained the force of Sophie's ungovernable urges. But there might be scope for a refinement of concept.

As much as it would do for its user, the Existometer was not going to yield up a neat solution to the riddle of existence. Post-partum, this was becoming clear to Hayden. The reason was fundamental: there is no such neat solution. Sid was going to be disappointed.

To find the meaning of something – the action of a person in pursuit of a goal, for example, or of a word – we have to refer to something else. But what else is there to refer to when we ask if the universe serves any purpose and whether our lives enter into this purpose? Nothing, unless we invoke a superior being, for whose existence there is no evidence.

The question 'What is the meaning of life?' translates for most of us into 'Why do we go through all this hardship and misery?' and 'What's it all for?' We seek not only a statement of our position in the scheme of things, which a scientific world-view can provide to an extent, but also a justification for the painful fact of existence. Life could perhaps be said to have a meaning, Hayden mused, if events were moving towards some specifiable end, but there is no reason for thinking that this is so. Even if there were such an ineluctable end, and it was discoverable, it would be entirely arbitrary, seen from the point of view of the individual, and not open to influence, by definition. These facts would be unlikely to reconcile us to our earthly woes. In any case, logic tells us that we would not get any answer to the question 'Why?' only 'How?' at a higher level. The explanation of our role would in effect merely be a more general description of how things are. No reason for living would be forthcoming which was more profound than the mere facts of existence.

Does belief in a superior being offer a route to meaning? To an extent, yes, Hayden conceded, but only illegitimately. Take the hypothesis of a creator. This is vacuous – and thus of minimal interest – because it fails to specify the end for which the world was designed and the way its various features promote that end. To the creationist, all things are as God willed them. Let's assume, though, that there is a supreme agent and that he constructed the universe for some definite purpose, rather than on a whim. Where does that leave us? As hapless puppets, presumably, in a preordained play, or as laboratory animals in an experiment whose outcome is unknown. If the latter, then it must be granted that the experimenter-cum-deity has limited knowledge. This opens the way for the existence of an even more superior being with his own purpose – a purpose, however, which is no less arbitrary, seen from our viewpoint, and outside our influence, and no less subject to the foregoing puppet/laboratory animal analysis.

Invoking God does not help to reveal the meaning of life. It merely complicates the answer to the question by introducing an untenable assumption – that He exists – and by pushing the level of explanation to a further stage. Religions provide a superstitious cosmological framework of a more or less comforting kind. They do not reveal the purpose of life.

The meaning question is not a crossword clue waiting to be cracked, Hayden concluded sadly. Then he chided himself quickly. That a question goes unanswered because it is logically unanswerable should not be an occasion for sadness or any other emotion. Life cannot have the kind of meta-level meaning conventionally sought.

The Existometer would not, then, reveal the meaning of life, but it could make life more meaningful. It would do this by activating the punter's supraconscious faculty. The poor functioning of the latter leads to a sense of purposelessness and an inner life of low intensity. Adequate supraconscious expression would provide the necessary condition for establishing harmony between the unconscious, conscious and supraconscious parts of the mind. This integration is the precondition for the full achievement of selfhood and the establishment of a life-enhancing self-image, externally manifested as jizz. The Existometer could thus be seen as an indirect jizz generator!

Hayden found his mind turning to Sophie. In that department, the day had already seen a development.

Giles had arrived to cadge an early breakfast – Brighton roc cooked in a clay oven according to a fabulous old Eastern recipe for fowl – but had left walking on air. A nurse had come to attend to Carola. Hayden had not seen her before – he would have remembered if he had! But if she made a strong appeal to Hayden's senses, there would plainly soon be a smoking crater where once resided Giles's head. Hayden saw his opportunity to offload a rival – or at least one who was confusing the issue.

'Nurse, I'm sorry to bother you, but my friend here would like a word with you.' Giles goggled in confusion. Hayden inspected him dispassionately. His friend wore a chequered shirt and a pair of light-coloured cotton trousers; a metre and a half of cloth piled shapelessly between shoulder and instep. How Giles expected to attract a woman was beyond Hayden's comprehension. 'He's very shy. What he's trying to say is that he has two tickets for the opera tomorrow night and would be charmed if you would accompany him.'

'Glyndebourne?'

'The very place. That's right isn't it Giles? A box, no less!'

'Yes, yes. Please come.' There was a pause as the nurse deliberated prettily while subjecting Giles to a discreet inspection. Carola, Hayden and Giles awaited the result with anticipation. To Hayden's amazement, she appeared to like what she saw.

'Thank you. I accept. A box sounds wonderful.'

'That's marvellous. May I know your name?' asked Giles with the eagerness of the emotionally self-employed.

'Yes, of course. Jane.' At this, the two men exchanged a look of fascinated horror and then dissolved into laughter. In this life it is worth trying everything once, including making the same mistake twice.

That had sorted out Giles; what about Sophie? Hayden remembered that years ago his father had been fond of saying that a Renaissance man was at home in all realms of knowledge, while a Renaissance woman was at home in all rooms of the house – the study, the drawing room, the galley and the boudoir. In Hayden's view, a man of letters could not be a Renaissance man unless he was also a man of action. As to the fair sex, Hayden knew Sophie to be a woman of action – and how! But was she a Renaissance woman to boot? She was certainly outstanding at the desk, in company and at the stove. But what about . . . ? There was a thought!

When an inordinately gravid female was loaded into the bed to Hayden's right, he knew it was time to go – even with lunch approaching. But what catapulted him from his repose was a visit from the nurse called Jane.

'The toilets are out of commission,' she reported, 'so it's bedpans and commodes from now on. And watch where you walk – the corridors are flooded.' She paused to extract a piece of paper from her pocket, and as she did so Hayden noticed the plastic bags covering her shoes, secured at the ankles by rubber bands. 'Nobody knows what's going on. They're using an inflatable dinghy in the basement. This note is for you.'

It was a telephone message from Sophie. A message from Sophie! Had the hurricane blown itself out? It must have. 'Believe Sid Whitney behind thefts. Will check out *Marbella Hood* immediately.'

Sid Whitney? Thefts? What?

How did she know Sid Whitney was behind the thefts? And how on earth was she proposing to 'check out' the *Marbella Hood*? Hadn't she heard of calling the police?

In any case she had got it the wrong way round, silly girl. Sid would be *unloading* the prototype not *loading* stolen goods.

Wait a minute, though. Could Sophie be right? The boat was certainly big enough to take the goods. Preposterously so. But how would the booty have been

271

moved to the marina with police everywhere and tons of it to be shifted? Suddenly the full import of Jane's news hit him. The sewage system! Had someone shut off the stopcocks in the main sewers? Was that why the hospital plumbing was awry? Sid's abnormal interest in the sewage arrangements at the factory was now explained. And his choice of that particular unit – for direct access to the principal sewer running under the Culture Park, the university and the polytechnic. The devious swine! And those packing-cases at the factory . . . ! Final loading might even now be in progress.

It was all falling into place. A heritage haemorrhage via the *Marbella Hood*! Sid would have reckoned on road-blocks and a sealed airport, which left the sea. Crates and crates of plunder emerging at the marina. Dr Fikansky had been right: Sid Whitney was no mere businessman. No wonder the Londoner hadn't been keen on coming to Hayden's lunch-party to discuss a mayoral inquiry! It made sense of another thing, too: a radio news item that morning, reporting a raid on a bank in North Street. Sid must have stolen back the money he had himself deposited to establish the bequest competition in the first place!

Hayden was struggling with an awful realization which caused him to emit an agonized groan. It had all been a hoax, a cover for Sid to pillage Brighton! And that was where Hayden's office must have gone! The Londoner had never from the start intended to construct a device to further human understanding. Everybody had been hoodwinked: the mayor and everyone at City Hall, Yelland, Brighton Aerospace, Fikansky, Shaps and Markham, and a certain freelance scholar. So much for the bequest! 'Shiny DeWit' indeed! It was just an anagram of 'Sid Whitney'. How could Hayden have misjudged anyone so comprehensively? And how could a man like Sid do something at such a low grade of significance as this? It might be the most notable cultural enormity since the destruction of the Great Library of Alexandria more than sixteen hundred years ago, but it was still only a crime. And Sophie was going to tangle with the arch-villain! Hayden's blood refrigerated. He must get to the marina at once and stop her.

First, though, there was the small matter of discharging himself from a maternity unit without having made adequate provision for post-natal support. The paperwork might take hours. Then there was what remained of the press in the lobby. He was back to his normal colour but they would still hound him. And again, were Markham and his merry men down there, too? No, there had to be a better way out.

After bidding Carola adieu – 'Call them both Sophie!' – and saying farewell to Molly and the others, Hayden slipped out of the window and leaped to an adjacent drainpipe. It was only there, two metres from the window and eight from the ground, that he recalled that he had one bare foot and was only wearing a nightshirt. What a draught! But there was no going back. He shinned down the drainpipe with difficulty, jumping the last two metres or so. The black man with the heavily bandaged head who was felled by this action was very decent about it, even to the extent of lending the escapee some money for the phone.

On reaching the allotments, Hayden turned and hobbled to a nearby road where he knew there to be a telephone box near a pub. His first call was to Giles. Yes, he would drive over to the Cobbler's Last. Yes, he would pick up Duffy. Yes, he would do this now without lunch. Yes, he would be along soon.

Hayden's second call was to the chief constable. After a third, he felt in need of a tincture, so he strolled over to the Cobbler's Last and spent the rest of the

273

telephone money on a glass of Tristram shandy.

While his drink was being poured, the pub's sole customer selected a cheese sandwich with lime pickle from a complimentary food tray on the bar. A folded copy of the day's paper lay next to the tray. Dare he look at it? He dared.

His satisfaction at not being the lead story turned to amazement as he absorbed the headline: 'EXTRATERRESTRIALS MAKE CONTACT'. A message from Out There had apparently been received from a location occupied by no known spacecraft or man-made satellite, and scientists were baffled by its import. A first decoding, obviously erroneous, read thus: 'Mrs Grim rang about tomorrow. She will leave your dinner in the oven. A fresh shirt is in the drawer.'

ERC 1 was already having an effect!

Hayden's drink arrived. He raised his glass in a murmured birthday toast: 'The twins!' There was a stuffed pike in a glass case above the bar. He looked at its cold eyes, shovel jaws and pitiless teeth with disquiet. Sophie, I hope you're all right.

But Sophie was far from all right. She had reached the end of the West Pier, to which the *Marbella Hood* was now moored, to discover a massive loading operation in progress. Hundreds of boxes, some marked 'Royal Pavilion', were being shifted from a landing-stage into the boat's hold by crewmen. Sophie's crouched inspection from behind a stout railing was interrupted by a tap on the shoulder and an instruction to rise.

'Can I help you?' said a beefy matelot flanked by two equally strapping shipmates.

'Do what?' Sophie replied evenly.

'Don't play games with us. You'd better come and see the skipper.'

This was not on Sophie's agenda, so she delivered a smart kick to the sailor's knee-cap, which sent him

274

spinning away in pain. The second sailor received a slap on the cheek, while the third received a shove in the abdomen.

The commotion was attracting attention. Sophie was having difficulty in maintaining the pretence of being a casual visitor as she sent an assailant rolling down some steps. Avoiding another's lunge, she darted towards the pier rail and sprang on to it. The sea foamed ten metres below.

'I'll jump if you come near me!' she threatened. She didn't; they did.

30

The Last Word

Twenty minutes had elapsed. Hayden was now standing on the tavern forecourt, waiting for his transport and his comrades-in-arms. Where were they? He was becoming agitated, not least because he had company. A couple of shire horses hitched to a dray were eying the nightshirted figure with placid curiosity. Beyond them, two dray-men were unloading barrels down a slide into the pub's cellar.

'Oy, mate, got no trousers then?' shouted one, guffawing loudly.

'Bit early for a nightcap, innit?' shouted the other, slapping his thigh in Falstaffian merriment. Hayden adopted a look of detachment, which was more or less in place when his two friends staggered up exhaustedly.

'Where's the car?' demanded Hayden.

'We couldn't get through,' gasped Giles. 'Carnival Rag Day. Students . . . mayor . . . no way through.'

'Great. Sophie might even now be in the hands of some fiendish criminal mastermind and his gang of desperadoes and we're stuck at the Cobbler's Last half a town away.' Hayden sighed. Was he to be thwarted in his mission of rescue by the charity carnival he had himself invented for the mayor? Perhaps not! His eye had been caught by the brewer's dray. Even as he watched, its two human custodians disappeared into the cellar, rolling barrels before them. Seizing a faint hope, Hayden limp-sprinted over to the cellar doors and slammed them shut, shooting the bolt quickly.

'All aboard,' he yelled excitedly. Duffy was beyond anything other than obeying instructions. He boarded docilely. Giles was slower off the mark.

'Are you sure? They don't look very quick.' As if hurt by this remark, the nearside horse, Felicity, turned her head and treated the taxi driver to a look of equine disdain from between blinkers. Norris, beside her, shook his head and all but tut-tutted. 'Well, I didn't mean to be rude,' Giles said apologetically to the horses. 'Sorry.' With that, he climbed up among the barrels on the back of the dray.

Hayden stood in excitement and flicked the reins. 'Tally-ho,' he cried.

With startling alacrity the two mighty steeds reared as one and clattered out of the courtyard. As they turned into the road, metal hooves slithered on stone flagstones and sparks flew. Norris whinnied with joy. All down the years they had wanted to do a flyer through the streets of Brighton, and here was their chance, 'neath cloudless skies! At his shoulder, Felicity accelerated smoothly towards carnival and marina.

Back at the hostelry, a conversation was taking place behind closed doors.

'That's a bleedin' liberty, and no mistake!'

'Not 'arf, mate! Now we'll have to chuck it in for the day and hang around in the bar until we're rescued. It could be hours.'

'If we're lucky.'

The streets were narrow but mercifully traffic-free. The two horses were perfectly in their stride, and Hayden was exultant at this unexpected equestrian event. Even Giles was looking pleased, and had begun to sing a Sussex drinking song with joyful abandon.

'Hayden, why aren't you dressed properly?' enquired Duffy, after regaining his breath. 'You're drawing attention to us. I've got some great news,' he added, brandishing a buff-coloured folder Hayden hadn't noticed he was carrying. But before Duffy could go on, they encountered the rear end of the carnival procession towards the end of Dyke Road. Only the instinct for self-preservation saved the students as the dray sliced down the middle of the road parting the parading multitudes like a wire through cheese. Hayden searched for some controls but could find nothing beyond a large and inefficient-looking wooden brake. Certainly there was no siren.

The dray slewed round the Seven Dials roundabout into Buckingham Place, nudging a truck on to its side and toppling a huge papier-mâché dinosaur with it. Students scattered to right and left, throwing caveman accessories and charity boxes aside in their flight. Ancient Greece flashed by as they crested the rise before plunging into the long right-hander that is Terminus Road; then Rome, whose centurions and senators on a Coliseum float were routed with effort-less ease into the railway station forecourt; Vikings fled and long ships were shortened; monarchs and court-iers lost their heads; empires fell.

It was Giles who first noticed that there was a car closing on them from behind. To his horror he recognized the occupants as Granville Markham, at the wheel, Stair-rods Wilson and the Slab. Giles released the tail-flap and rolled off a barrel to impede their progress then informed the others. They were safe as long as Norris and Felicity didn't stop, as Queens Road was too crowded for overtaking, with fairground booths lining both sides of the procession route.

Unfortunately, at that moment, the horses did stop. A wheel crashed against a traffic bollard, causing the dray to skid sideways to a halt. The car screeched to a stop, too, the Slab and Stair-rods leaping out towards the dray. Norris and Felicity started to move again, but Stair-rods was aboard. A second later, so was the Slab. Hayden threw the reins to Duffy and jumped into the wagon. The horses had regained momentum and the dray was now accelerating rapidly down the hill towards the Clock Tower.

Stair-rods threw himself at Giles, and the two men fell to the wooden floor, grappling desperately. This left Hayden to deal with the Slab who stood at the tail of the vehicle, trying to maintain his balance. Hayden knew that if he put a foot wrong the only thing that this heroic last stand was going to lack was a Disunion Jack, Brighton's flag.

'Hand over the fat man's file, Sabanack,' shouted the Slab. 'Now!' For a moment Hayden was baffled, then he remembered the folder Duffy had waved under his nose earlier. Had his friend obtained documentary proof of the conspiracy – proof that would place Thorne, Markham and the rest behind bars for years? It must be true!

'Never! You'll have to take it from us!' retorted Hayden, eschewing Ghandian non-violence and closing on his 'victim'. When he was near enough, he threw a punch at the Slab's eye, a seriously uphill task. It connected perfectly. Hayden watched in wonderment as nothing happened. The start of his career as a pugilist had been less auspicious than he had hoped. Fear made him desperate. He poked a fist into the Slab's other eye. Still no effect. Then the Slab smiled menacingly and aimed a punch at Hayden. The scholar's plastered foot had robbed him of some of his agility, but as chance would have it he was able to keep his eye on the approaching fist right up to the very moment of impact. It felt as if he had been hit by a very large man, but luckily the jolting of the wagon had robbed the punch of some of its force.

On a Guildhall balcony bedecked with streamers and flags, assorted dignitaries and enrobed members of the assembly evinced varying degrees of astonishment at the events being enacted below. At their head was Mayor Yalton in red robes, gold chain and tricorn hat. He had not failed to recognize his speech-writer and the speech-writer's predicament. But what could he do? Beside the mayor, and in no doubt, was the liveried bearer of the Official Salt. James Stevens stepped forward smartly and hurled the ceremonial cruet at the Slab, missing completely, but smashing Markham's windscreen to fragments in the process. Inaccuracy seemed to be a family trait.

'Go on, Hayden, get him!' James shouted, waving his fist, but the New Renaissance man was now in clear danger of succumbing to the funks. He pulled a barrel on to its side and kicked it towards the Slab. Then he darted forwards and belted the off-balance hoodlum once on each cheek. This caused the big man to lose his sense of humour. His face became a mask of viciousness as he prepared for the kill. He drew himself up to his full height – and was promptly swept off the back of the dray by a carnival banner slung across the street from the Clock Tower. Hayden was not so stunned as to fail to launch a barrel at the stricken hit-man and the erratically pursuing car. It caught the latter smack in the radiator. Revenge! The mayoral party cheered.

Hayden turned to address the Stair-rods issue. Giles had adopted a close in-fighting, smother and neutralize tactic which, with help from Duffy, had worked surprisingly well. Hayden was in no mood for further games. He wrenched the brake handle free from the side of the dray and whacked Stair-rods over the head with it twice. This did the trick, and Giles seemed grateful for the opportunity of ejecting his opponent on to the road.

In the excitement, the North Street turn towards the marina had been missed, so they would have to go east along the promenade instead. It was as they shot left round the corner of West Street on to the seafront that Hayden chanced to look right at the West Pier and see something that caused him to start in surprise. It was the *Marbella Hood,* moored peacefully in the perfect sunshine. Suddenly, into Hayden's mind flashed Sylvia Crolien's prophecy concerning a woman in aristocratic trouble. Of course: a pier of the realm! And the woman was Sophie. He would never be rude about propheteering again. But in the meantime, the police were on their way to the marina!

Surrendering to panic, Hayden hurled himself from the fast-moving dray, rolling on the road to break his fall. In so doing, his plaster cast broke on the tarmac. Pausing only to free himself from his encumbrance, he started a decrepit dash towards the pier.

It was at this unlikely moment that it came to him that he was not only a scholar-scientist and a man of action, but a lover as well. He was a whole man for the first time, though one with a serious heart condition, thanks to Sophie.

The sound of Sophie's name in his mind's ear caused another thought to click into place. Hayden's lady had been displaying jizz of late, and he hadn't fully appreciated the fact. It was the jizz of romance, the 'look of love'.

When Duffy realized that the rescue team had fallen below a quorum, he and his loyal steeds did their best to slow the dray in the absence of conventional braking, but it was no easy task. As the dray turned, Norris and Felicity, though foam-flecked at the muzzle, perspiring hard and breathing heavily, looked magnificent in the clear, noonday air. They had done it! They had made it to the very seafront itself!

Sophie, how could you have got us into this? Hayden

moaned to himself as he ran along the wooden decking of the deserted pier. But even then he heard a roaring sound in front of him which could only be the engines of the *Marbella Hood*. They were making to leave. My God, I hope I'm not too late!

Sophie had been gagged then trussed up like an oven-ready boneless chicken before being secured to the metal ring of a pier support on the landing-stage. It had taken her only a few minutes to work loose the ring from its rotten wood surround, but it had come out too quickly. Still bound, she took three hops forwards and found herself plunging into the cruel sea. A dolphin-kick brought her to the surface, but things were looking grim for the putative New Renaissance woman. Then she glimpsed a man at the pier rail in night attire. It was Hayden! But would he see her in time?

Mrs Sabanack was propagating plants in her conservatory. How grateful she was to Sophie for rescuing the valuable bits and pieces from what remained of Hayden's house. She had had particular fun with the small telescope that used to adorn his desk. What with all these crooks about, it was a wonder it hadn't been stolen! Just that morning she had observed a big white cruise liner embarking passengers at the West Pier. 'What a sensible idea,' she had said on the phone to Sophie. 'How convenient!' At this, the dear girl had sounded agitated, but Mrs Sabanack wouldn't let her go without first giving her a horticultural tip: success with house plants involves minimal interference. In particular, avoid over-watering!

The research riches looted from Hayden's office had at last been evaluated and stacked to one side. The place was shipshape again, but the mind of the dastardly malefactor was in disarray.

I can never use this material, never, anguished Professor Shaps wretchedly in his office at the Institute of Philosophy. The DeWit Bequest has borne unexpected fruit in the Armillary Sphere of Destiny, but what is even that compared with these further insights, insights of such power and profundity! There is only one man capable of transforming these findings into intellectual domination of the world, though, and that man is not me!

Meanwhile, Sophie's computer, which had been stolen along with everything else from Hayden's workplace, was sitting on the floor in a world of its own. 'The moment you put your strong arms around me, Professor, I was lost,' it announced on its screen. 'I was swept off my feet and got carried away, almost before I knew what was happening. I'm yours, all yours! We'll set up home together, here, just the two of us, together. Though, frankly, this carpet will have to go, and so will those curtains . . .'

The *Marbella Hood* was already thirty metres away when Hayden reached the end of the pier. The sea churned in the boat's wake. No-one was visible on board. He stared at the receding vessel in consternation, then looked down at the landing-stage below. Something was thrashing in the water beside it. Was it? It couldn't be! It was! It was Sophie!

From this height, Hayden would normally have opted for a two-and-a-half somersaults piked with two twists dive, using a rip entry, but in the interests of maintaining visual contact he selected a lower tariff forward dive with pike. The water proved comparatively warm. He came up beyond Sophie, and propelled her without difficulty on to the wooden platform. She was safe! He joined her, and helped her upright.

They stood together and watched the departing craft

in silence, then Hayden turned to Sophie, noticing with awakened interest that her wet blouse was plastered to her chest. Why did she have no undergarment? Had the seawater dissolved it?

'Don't worry about the Existometer,' he said to his captive audience, 'there's room for a Mark III version. The Mark II secret of life was that this is the afterlife. Or at least, the life after the previous one. The design has developed some sort of reincarnation bias. It seems to be saying that we have been married before. Arising from which: will you marry me – again?' Sophie's heart was not so full that she could not reply. The same could not be said of her mouth. Through her gag she mumbled something, but Hayden could not make it out.

'No? Oh well, can't win 'em all, I suppose.' Sophie looked exasperated at this, and began to nod with frustrated emphasis.

'What's that? Is that a "yes"? Come, come, Sophie, out with it!' And so saying, he removed her gag, and with it the last impediment to their union.

Hayden and Sophie became aware of a rowing boat bobbing in the water a few hundred metres off to the east. In it were three men: Granville Markham, Stairrods Wilson and the Slab. Where did the crooks think they were going?

The engine note of the *Marbella Hood* deepened as it gathered speed, and the bow rose defiantly in the swell. At the after rail appeared Sid, Bella and their daughter, arm in arm. At a distance, they looked subdued rather than exultant after their sojourn in Brighton.

'They've got away with our treasures,' said Sophie, shaking her head sadly.

'Don't worry, they won't get far. I rang the navy to have them intercepted.' As they watched, Gail half raised a hand in farewell, then followed her parents inboard. 'Our other mariners look to be having a difference of opinion.' Granville Markham was on his feet, gesticulating furiously at the oarsmen. Something must have cracked inside the Slab, for he let fly at Markham and thumped him clean out of the boat. In so doing, the Slab pushed his foot through the hull and the small craft began to founder. The Markham men were going to have a long swim to the shore, where policemen could now be seen pounding the beach. Beyond the forces of law and order were Giles and Duffy. Beside them, nuzzling the light sea breeze, stood a pair of dray-horses.

'Sophie! Sophie! What are you doing!' Splash! Hayden surfaced a few moments later, wiping water from his eyes and face. 'What did you do that for?'

'I'm tied up right now,' she replied, affecting a distracted air. 'Suffice it to say that I feel I deserve the last word.'

THE END

A Smoking Dot In The Distance
by Ivor Gould

Jeffrey Cork, born 1929 (disappeared from the Skegness Hilton 1989), spent one term at prep school (with the boy with an elephant's penis 'which was tied under the bed to prevent the maids from playing with it'), and desires only to be middle class. Doomed to marry Elspeth (Nignog No 504), he is accused, with his father (inventor and patentee of The New Improved Liberty Bodice), of high treason.

In Moscow ('watched by a man eating the Soviet version of a Kunzle cake') he meets the KGB sergeant once responsible for his toilet training, and in Victory Cottage, Swinehurst, home of the Deliuses (no relation), Rosemary, a tram conductress with a Doric portico and a painted drainpipe.

In a smile inked on a thumbnail he recalls the fall of Singapore; the Jews in their steam waggon fleeing the storm; the wartime religious doss houses for servicemen on leave; the Labour Cavalcade of 1945; the widow Pomfret, her knickers in her handbag; and Bernard, Rif chieftain, whose scrotum was impaled on the Corks' front gate. Not to forget (and Cork never does) the mauve court shoes of Doris Allerdyce, and the ubiquitous homburg hat. Finally, the funeral that made 'the man from the string room' cry; the passing of the best, and with it the hope, of an England already then receding, to become a smoking dot in the distance.

Instantly dubbed 'a comic masterpiece', and 'brilliantly original', another, even funnier *Diary of a Nobody*, Ivor Gould has given us a book to giggle at and snigger over, one to make us laugh out loud and wish that it would never end.

'A glorious flowering of that distinctive English flippancy which reached its apotheosis in Wodehouse . . . delicious moments on every page'
Max Davidson, *Daily Telegraph*

0 552 99466 9

BLACK SWAN

Coming From Behind
by Howard Jacobson

'A literary comedy which cuts through and beyond the
Portnoy school of self-absorbed Jewish fiction, the English
University Novel and the best of Tom Sharpe'
The Times

Sefton Goldberg: mid-thirties, English teacher at
Wrottesley Poly in the West Midlands; small, sweaty,
lustful, defiantly unenamoured of beer, nature and
organized games; gnawingly aware of being an urban Jew
islanded in a sea of country-loving Anglo-Saxons.
Obsessed by failure – morbidly, in his own case,
gloatingly, in that of his contemporaries – so much so that
he plans to write a bestseller on the subject. In the
meantime he is uncomfortably aware of advancing years
and atrophying achievement: and no amount of lofty
rationalization can disguise the triumph of friends and
colleagues, not only from Cambridge days but even within
the despised walls of the Poly itself, or sweeten the bitter
pill of another's success . . .

Coming From Behind is a shrewd, articulate and
consistently hilarious successor to *Lucky Jim* and *The
History Man*.

'Very funny, clever and engaging'
Times Literary Supplement

'A sort of Jewish version of *Lucky Jim* updated for the
eighties, witty, observant, clever, a first-rate entertainment
and something more besides'
Robert Nye, *Guardian*

0 552 99063 9

BLACK SWAN

A SELECTION OF FINE NOVELS
AVAILABLE FROM BLACK SWAN

THE PRICES SHOWN BELOW WERE CORRECT AT THE TIME OF GOING TO PRESS. HOWEVER TRANSWORLD PUBLISHERS RESERVE THE RIGHT TO SHOW NEW RETAIL PRICES ON COVERS WHICH MAY DIFFER FROM THOSE PREVIOUSLY ADVERTISED IN THE TEXT OR ELSEWHERE.

☐	99421 9	COMING UP ROSES	*Michael Carson*	£4.99
☐	99380 8	FRIENDS AND INFIDELS	*Michael Carson*	£3.99
☐	99348 4	SUCKING SHERBET LEMONS	*Michael Carson*	£4.99
☐	99465 0	STRIPPING PENGUINS BARE	*Michael Carson*	£5.99
☐	99455 3	KINGDOM SWANN	*Miles Gibson*	£4.99
☐	99208 9	THE 158LB MARRIAGE	*John Irving*	£4.99
☐	99204 6	THE CIDER HOUSE RULES	*John Irving*	£6.99
☐	99209 7	THE HOTEL NEW HAMPSHIRE	*John Irving*	£5.99
☐	99369 7	A PRAYER FOR OWEN MEANY	*John Irving*	£6.99
☐	99206 2	SETTING FREE THE BEARS	*John Irving*	£5.99
☐	99207 0	THE WATER-METHOD MAN	*John Irving*	£5.99
☐	99205 4	THE WORLD ACCORDING TO GARP	*John Irving*	£6.99
☐	99141 4	PEEPING TOM	*Howard Jacobson*	£4.99
☐	99063 9	COMING FROM BEHIND	*Howard Jacobson*	£4.99
☐	99252 6	REDBACK	*Howard Jacobson*	£5.99
☐	99399 9	THE MIDNIGHT EXAMINER	*William Kotzwinkle*	£4.99
☐	99440 5	THE HOT JAZZ TRIO	*William Kotzwinkle*	£4.99
☐	99420 0	THE LITTLE BROTHERS OF ST MORTIMER	*John Fergus Ryan*	£4.99
☐	99419 7	THE REDNECK BRIDE	*John Fergus Ryan*	£4.99
☐	99384 0	TALES OF THE CITY	*Armistead Maupin*	£4.99
☐	99086 8	MORE TALES OF THE CITY	*Armistead Maupin*	£4.99
☐	99106 6	FURTHER TALES OF THE CITY	*Armistead Maupin*	£5.99
☐	99383 2	SIGNIFICANT OTHERS	*Armistead Maupin*	£5.99
☐	99239 9	BABYCAKES	*Armistead Maupin*	£5.99
☐	99374 3	SURE OF YOU	*Armistead Maupin*	£4.99
☐	99360 3	UNNATURAL SELECTION	*Daniel Evan Weiss*	£4.99
☐	99437 5	HELL ON WHEELS	*Daniel Evan Weiss*	£4.99

All Corgi/Bantam Books are available at your bookshop or newsagent, or can be ordered from the following address:

Corgi/Bantam Books,
Cash Sales Department
P.O. Box 11, Falmouth, Cornwall TR10 9EN

UK and B.F.P.O. customers please send a cheque or postal order (no currency) and allow £1.00 for postage and packing for the first book plus 50p for the second book and 30p for each additional book to a maximum charge of £3.00 (7 books plus).

Overseas customers, including Eire, please allow £2.00 for postage and packing for the first book plus £1.00 for the second book and 50p for each subsequent title ordered.

NAME (Block Letters) ....

ADDRESS ....

....